UNCHAINED

A REX DALTON THRILLER

BOOK THREE

JC Ryan

ISBN: 9781728842714

COPYRIGHT

This book is copyright material and must not be copied, reproduced, transferred, distributed, leased, licensed or publicly performed or used in any way except as specifically permitted in writing by the author as allowed under the terms and conditions under which it was purchased or as strictly permitted by applicable copyright law. Any unauthorized distribution or use of this text may be a direct infringement of the author's and publisher's rights and those responsible may be liable in law accordingly.

This book is a work of fiction. The characters, incidents, and dialogues are products of the author's imagination and are not to be construed as real. Any resemblance to actual events or persons, living or dead, is entirely coincidental.

Dedication

Dedicated to my good friend Mitch Pender, a military dog trainer, for giving me the idea for this series and guiding me through the intricate and amazing capabilities and psychology of those majestic four-legged soldiers.

Mitch has a lifetime of experience and exceptional depth of knowledge as a military dog handler and trainer.

About Unchained

Rex Dalton and his new friend, the military dog, Digger escaped from Afghanistan and made their way into India where they started a new life.

Within a few weeks, Dalton had a new name, a new passport and no worries about money. He and Digger were on their way to Kapal Mochan, India, where Rex intended to dip his hand into a sacred spring.

But then Digger started shifting around in the front passenger seat and looking at him as if to say, "So, when are you going to stop and give a dog a chance to go to the toilet?"

Contents

Copyright 2
Dedication 3
About Unchained 4
Contents 5
One 7
Two 21
Three 25
Four 38
Five 51
Six 58
Seven 65
Eight 73
Nine 84
Ten 97
Eleven 104
Twelve 116
Thirteen 122
Fourteen 131
Fifteen 143
Sixteen 160

Seventeen	174
Eighteen	182
Nineteen	188
Twenty	193
Twenty-One	198
Twenty-Two	207
Twenty-Three	223
Twenty-Four	231
Twenty-Five	239
Twenty-Six	254
Twenty-Seven	263
Twenty-Eight	273
Twenty-Nine	284
Thirty	289
Rex Dalton's Next Adventure	308
Sideswiped	308
More Rex Dalton	310
Also by JC Ryan	311
The Rossler Foundation Mysteries	311
The Carter Devereux Mystery Thrillers	312
The Exonerated	314
Your Free Gift	316
About JC Ryan	318

ONE

WEEKS LATER, REX Dalton would reflect that the pivot point was when Digger started shifting around in the front passenger seat and looking at him as if to say, "So, when are you going to stop and give a dog a chance to go to the toilet?"

Rex would have enjoyed being a tourist if he had just been able to control his decisions on his own. Instead, he had to cater to his dog, Digger's whims, always insisting on having an opinion of his own, which more often than not was the opposite of what Rex had in mind.

They were on their way to Kapal Mochan, India, where Rex intended to dip his hand into a sacred spring, a symbolic act he'd only half articulated even to himself. They were two or three miles short of the goal when Digger bounded through from the back of the van and sat in the front passenger seat.

Surely, he can wait a couple of minutes.

Digger chose that moment to yawn widely, ending on a whine. That was it. Digger's way of answering his thoughts, which the dog seemed to be able to read at will.

A yawn often means the dog is anxious. He'd looked it up, when he finally had a chance. What did he know about dogs? Virtually nothing. For a guy who'd been trained as an assassin, a one-man army and intelligence agency, it had been a deep, dark secret that he was terrified of dogs. Digger was the exception. He'd inherited the highly trained military dog from a friend who died on a mission under Rex's command. Rex was still learning how to not fear the dog, and how to take care of it, and how to handle it.

If Digger was anxious, it meant he'd driven too long without a rest stop. Fortunately, there was a park in the next block. He pulled over.

"Go on, then," he said.

Digger pressed down on the lever that opened the door and pushed out. He hopped to the ground and ran off, soon disappearing from Rex's sight. Rex wasn't worried. Digger wouldn't run out on him. Rex knew he was marking every tree on the way to wherever he deigned to relieve his discomfort.

Rex took one of the plastic bags he had been collecting for this purpose out of a box, got out of the car and pushed the bag into his pocket. In a while, when Digger was done, he'd slip it over his left hand. Left, because that was the proper way to handle this sort of thing in India. In his opinion, it was futile. There were plenty of feral dogs around. No one was picking up after them, he'd noticed. And that wasn't even the worst of it. Monkeys were overrunning India. They didn't have the politest of bathroom habits, either. But Rex had decided he and Digger were not going to contribute to the existing mess.

Rex looked at his watch. He didn't need to. His stomach was telling him it was lunch time. They might as well take care of that while they were stopped. Digger, who also seemed to always know what time it was too, especially when it came to mealtimes, would probably insist.

"Digger!" Rex shouted.

The big, black Dutch shepherd woofed in response and Rex jerked his head in the direction of the sound. There he was, bounding out from behind a bush yards away. Rex grumbled something along the lines of becoming a dog shit chaser and collector while he wrapped the plastic bag around his left hand. He started in Digger's direction, and the dog lay down, waiting to show him the spot. Rex grinned. Digger messed with him, he'd mess with Digger.

He slowed his pace and ambled toward the dog in a deceptive zigzag pattern. Each time he veered off course even a degree or two, Digger would woof again. It was a game they'd played before, jockeying for alpha position ever since Digger's former handler, the former Australian SAS operator, Trevor Madigan, had died. Digger had made it perfectly clear he didn't think Rex was competent to lead their pack of two. Lately, however, Rex was equally clear that if Digger wanted to eat, he needed to concede who was boss. They'd settled into a pattern of push and pull that was sometimes fun, often annoying, but always a game.

Digger knew Rex was the alpha. However, it seemed as if he just didn't want to let Rex get too big a head about it.

When he finally got to Digger's location, Rex said, "Show me." The dog jumped up in that efficient move that got him up and turned in one twist and ran off behind the bush again. Rex followed but deliberately slowed his pace down even further. Digger returned and gently took Rex's wrist in his mouth. Not too long ago Rex would have been in mortal fear if any dog, no matter its size, would even attempt to do that to him. He would probably not even have allowed a dog to get that close to him in any event and would've drawn his pistol and shot the animal for that. But since he'd made a solemn promise on that fateful night, to the dying Trevor that he would take care of Digger, Rex had learned Digger meant no harm and just wanted to lead him.

Behind the bush was the offending artifact. Rex used his plastic-covered left hand to pick it up, walked over to a nearby rubbish bin, and disposed of it.

"What do you say, boy? Shall we eat?"

Digger turned his head up and gave him that dog-grin that meant happiness, agreement, and a few other things depending on context. In this case, Rex took it to mean, "Hell yes. What are we waiting for?" Digger confirmed his guess by quickening his pace to a trot. It was these trivial things that let Rex know he still wasn't in total control. He lengthened his stride to keep up.

When they got to the van, Rex opened the rear doors, took out one of the plastic bottles with water and washed his hands, then began to prepare the lunch he'd purchased that morning when they'd left the hotel. In a small

Coleman cooler, he had his own lunch of chicken, naan, and an orange. He'd tossed in some bottled water to chill it. Beside the cooler, he'd packed a large bag of dry dog food, the kind the vet in New Delhi had said would be best for a dog of Digger's weight and breed.

He took out Digger's bowls and filled one with cool water and the other with the dog food. Digger drank some of the water and then looked with disinterest at the other bowl. Rex was just wrapping the chunks of cut-up chicken in the Indian flatbread, his favorite garlic naan, when Digger fixed him with an accusatory stare.

"This is my food. You eat yours," Rex said, pointing with his left hand at the bowl of dry food. Digger looked at it, and then swung his head back to stare at Rex's right hand, which was full of delicious-looking naan wrapped around some juicy chicken.

Woof

"No, this is mine."

Woof

Rex proceeded to repeat the argument they'd had every day since he'd bought the dog food. "Just because you like human food better, doesn't mean it's good for you." He went on to explain the difference between canine's and homo sapiens' digestive tracts, which he'd read about over the past few weeks.

Digger just sat there, apparently listening but with his head tilted – that pose Rex had come to understand meant "what are you doing?" Or in this case probably "what are you on about?"

Rex was still busy with this lecture when he was interrupted. Well, not so much interrupted as becoming aware something had changed.

He looked over his shoulder and startled at the sight of a very, very skinny, very, very old man, with a wrinkled face and not a single tooth in his mouth. Which was stretched in what could have been a wide grin. His sparkling, almost black eyes danced with mirth as well. He was dressed in a white *dhoti,* a traditional garment made from a single rectangular length of cloth, wrapped and pleated then belted to form a sort of trouser that could be mistaken for a skirt by a westerner. Over it, a threadbare white shirt billowed around him, suggesting he'd once been more corpulent.

Rex thought he was either hallucinating or he must be slipping. He hadn't heard the man – if that's what the apparition was – arrive.

A yogi?

Rex didn't know what a yogi looked like, or rather what his idea of a yogi was. In fact, what he knew about yogis was very little. As far as he knew, there was a mysticism that surrounded them — flying through the air, levitation, ridiculously long lives, and such. Or were they the guys flying on magic carpets? No, wait those guys on the carpets were from Arabia. Weren't they? The problem was he'd never paid attention to that stuff before. Now he certainly wished he had.

However, this yogi was sitting flat on the lush grass, on his ass, legs crossed, like in a Buddha pose. Just like Rex imagined a yogi would sit. However, this yogi was not hanging in mid-air.

This guy was not there a few moments ago. So, where did he come from?

He could've flown in, like a yogi could have. That was a possibility, or he could've walked in, like a normal human would have.

Rex's next thought was that Digger had given no warning, which could mean either he was aware of the man, didn't see him as a threat and was too invested in winning the argument about what he wanted for lunch to pay this guy any attention.

Or this guy *was* a yogi and could materialize out of nowhere so that not even a dog with Digger's skills and inherent motivation to protect, could sense him, maybe not even see him right now. That was a scary thought.

Rex didn't know which it was but for a moment he was inclined to go with the second notion. Because despite Rex having stopped talking to the dog and started paying all his attention to this strange man, Digger didn't even look at the man — as if he wasn't there.

No, wait I don't believe in that stuff. This man is real. He is right there.

So, what to do now? Follow Digger's example and ignore the man or try to talk to him? Was he even supposed to or allowed to talk to a yogi unless spoken to? He had no idea about yogi protocol.

Once again, he chided himself for not paying more attention to those articles he'd read years ago.

The thing was, this guy said not a word. It looked like he was smiling, but it was impossible to tell, considering he had no teeth in his mouth and all the wrinkles, if he was smiling or not by looking at his face. Which Rex estimated couldn't be a day younger than a hundred and twenty years, maybe even a few hundred years more. Usually he didn't have a problem remembering things, but in this case his near eidetic memory failed him miserably. He couldn't remember how long yogis lived. But he thought it could be hundreds of years. This guy certainly looked like he could have been around in George Washington's time.

In the end he decided the man was not a threat, mostly because he had no weapons, remained seated on the grass, and of course Digger had no worries about him.

Therefore, he thought it was probably best to ask this guy if he was a yogi and what the protocol was when a mere mortal wanted to talk to a yogi. Hopefully the yogi, if he was one, would not get his nose out of joint because someone who couldn't fly without an airplane under his ass would have the audacity to talk to him before being spoken to.

Rex asked. In Hindi.

He got no answer.

Okay so now the yogi is pissed at me.

But hang on he dropped in on me not the other way around. So, if he has something to say, he will probably do so at some point.

If he only wants to sit there and look at me and Digger, well I guess there's nothing I can do to stop him.

It's a free country.

Rex turned back to Digger, who was waiting for him to continue the argument about his lunch. He continued. In English.

Digger seemed to be actively listening because he responded with yawns, growls, short barks, smiles, and a tilted head. After a few more minutes Rex knew he was losing this argument.

He had one more trick up his sleeve — the kong.

It was an oddly-shaped item, part cylinder, part cone, with indentations that made it look like a hard-plastic snowman, with a hole running through it from top to bottom. The only toy ever known that a Dutch shepherd couldn't destroy in a few minutes, according to Trevor.

Rex had gone to a lot of trouble in New Delhi to find a pet shop that had kongs. He'd bought five of them — better to have some spares in a country where they were rare. He'd given Digger one right away.

The only regret he had was that he didn't have his camera handy to make a video clip of Digger's absolute ecstasy when he saw that kong. He'd seen it before, when Trevor was training the dog. The kong was a special treat, reserved for times when Digger had done especially well, and given sparingly. Digger worked for praise, not treats.

So, now Rex was going to try the kong trick. The hole was good for putting food treats in, an even rarer treat.

He retrieved it from the van, palmed a few nuggets of dog food and dropped them in and showed it to Digger, fully believing the dog was going to forget about his lunch and go after the toy. It would give Rex time to quickly finish his lunch.

Rex was sorely mistaken.

Digger sat down and lifted his left front foot. The expression on his face could be interpreted in only one way – in any language including English and Hindi — the canine equivalent of the middle finger.

That's when the yogi started laughing and startled Rex again.

***

REX ASKED HIM why he was laughing, and the man started talking. He said it was the first time in his life that he saw a man talking to a dog as if it was a human, and what amazed and delighted him was that it looked as if the dog understood and was talking back. He wanted to know how that was possible.

But Rex had a few questions of his own first. What's your name? Where did you come from? How did you get here without anyone of us seeing you? Are you a yogi? How old are you? Can you fly and levitate? A barrage of questions.

In America, he wouldn't have been so impolite as to ask such personal questions. In India, however, it was not bad manners. It was expected. Soon it would be his turn to answer.

The man held his hand up and started answering, slowly one by one, all the questions. His name was Gyan which meant knowledge or the one having exalted divine knowledge. As for being a yogi, yes, he was, but being a yogi only meant he was someone who practiced yoga and that those stories about levitating and flying were just that, stories, folklore, not real.

Rex was relieved. He hadn't lost his mind after all.

Gyan told him he was seventy-five.

You could've fooled me.

Now Gyan was waiting expectantly, for Rex to reciprocate. Of course, he couldn't say what he really was, so he went with the tourist story. But the old man stared steadfastly at Digger, clearly more interested in the human-dog connection.

Rex explained that the dog was a service dog and was there to assist him. Gyan looked a bit skeptical about that explanation and asked that Rex demonstrate what the dog could do.

Rex obliged by putting Digger through some of his more commonplace paces. A demonstration of just how intelligent the dog was, and his special skills would have frightened the old man.

After every trick, Gyan clapped his hands in child-like delight.

Rex was charmed.

Soon, with Digger on his belly for a rest, Rex sat facing the old man, hearing about his extended family. He was too old to work, but his sons and their families contributed to his support. He and his wife lived in a humble house not far from the park. She didn't want him underfoot as she did whatever women do. He shrugged. Who knew what women were up to?

Then he asked Rex where he was going.

"To Kapal Mochan," Rex replied.

The old man's wrinkled face took on a concerned expression. "Have you killed a Brahmin?"

Rex raised his eyebrows. *What an odd question.*

Rex answered with a question of his own. "Is it only those who have killed Brahmins who want or need the power of the lake to wash away their sins?"

Gyan didn't answer, but his face cleared. "You must know, then, that there is also an ancient site in this place.

The ashram of Ved Vyasa. Did you not intend to visit it? The *Mahabharata* was written here."

Rex did indeed know of the place where one of the epic tales of Indian history had originated. He'd meant to visit it on the way back from his pilgrimage to Kapal Mochan. He considered how to tell the old man this without offending him, but Gyan became animated. He'd had a thought.

"You must come home with me. I have photographs of my family, and they will want to see your remarkable dog!"

Rex took in the poor garments the man wore, and his heart sank. It would be rude to decline the invitation, but he didn't want to go. Not specifically because Gyan was poor, but because he knew that guests in India were treated almost like visiting deities. The family would impoverish themselves further by providing a feast for him, and to make matters worse, he couldn't do anything to repay them or alleviate their sacrifice. Offering them money would be considered an insult.

He said, "But my dog would not be welcome in your house, surely."

The old man gulped. "My wife may not welcome him, but do not worry. I will tell her she must."

Now Rex felt even more obligated. He'd offered the only excuse he could, and though he'd been uncomfortable, Gyan had swept it away. There was no choice but to accept.

"Thank you," he said. "I will come, but Digger will stay outside."

He knew he'd made the right decision when the old man sighed in relief. Rex had never been married, but he recognized the truth: men only thought they were kings in their own castles. Women made the rules, at least where the household was concerned.

Gyan brightened again. "You must come now! We can play a game of Chaturanga."

Now Rex was happy he'd accepted. He knew of the ancient game some believed was the predecessor of the game of kings – chess. However, he'd never seen it played and didn't know the rules. This visit would be an opportunity to indulge his love of history as much as the visits to the ancient sites would be.

"I'd be honored. But you must teach me," he said.

Two

IN AMERICA, IT had been almost a month since Bruce Carson, the former Director of the CIA, had disappeared under mysterious circumstances after retiring abruptly. The media, in yet another case of nine-day-wonder, had it that he'd absconded to Costa Rica after a scandal of some sort was discovered, but Costa Rica claimed he wasn't there.

Mrs. Carson refused to speak to the reporters. She'd given the investigators plenty, though. Her husband had come home late one night and demanded she move with him to Costa Rica under assumed names. Naturally, she had refused. Her alternative was divorce, and she'd had enough. She knew he was cheating on her. Women know these things, she'd explained when pressed for details. She didn't know who, or the details they wanted. She only knew it was time to cut ties.

Then the bastard had cleaned out their accounts and left her with nothing. She couldn't even sell the house for the money, until the divorce was final. It was in his name, but she hoped the divorce decree would fix that.

Eventually, another hot news story took the place of the missing DCIA. America's hyperactive news cycle had forgotten him, but the CIA hadn't. It was imperative they catch up with him. He had knowledge of secrets that would be very dangerous in the wrong hands, including the number and positioning of every field operative the US had and considerable information about allied operations. The consequences of a defection to an enemy country were too drastic to talk of. He had to be found, and when he was, the order was to terminate with extreme prejudice. Every spook from every allied country was looking for him.

Unfortunately for him, it was assumed he'd gone to a country without an extradition treaty with the US.

John Brandt, CEO of the paramilitary organization, Crisis Response Consultancy or CRC, knew what had happened to Carson. He'd watched him board a plane for a flight to the Marshall Islands. He wouldn't stay there, of course, but it did have the advantage of having no extradition treaty. Brandt had a team searching for where he'd gone, too.

He wished he'd never given the man the option of leaving. His anger at the duplicity that got his best agent, Rex Dalton, reportedly killed in an ambush in Afghanistan had overridden his judgement. He'd stopped himself from killing the man with his own hands after discovering Carson was a pusillanimous sex addict, and a kinky one at that. The assumption was that Carson would be the cause of his own downfall because of it, but Brandt didn't want to get his own hands dirty. He should have thought about Carson's other secrets – those that now threatened national security.

Brandt had learned from Carson that there were others in the chain of betrayal who needed sorting. He set a team in motion to find Carson and then put it out of his mind. He had other fish to fry. The next link in the chain was the only one Carson knew, a Senator who was so ancient that Brandt could hardly believe what Carson had told him about the man's weakness.

He couldn't think of anything quite so obscene as the elderly man with little boys, but that's what Carson had claimed. Brandt's team of Old Timers – retired operatives he'd known when he was in the CIA himself – confirmed the information. Brandt was about to move on the Senator when he suffered a massive stroke. Evidently the strain of Carson's sudden resignation and disappearance and the possibility of his own vices coming to light soon if they had not been already exposed was too much for him.

Before Brandt could get to him to wring the name of the person above him in the chain out of him, he'd reportedly suffered two more strokes and died.

Brandt was disappointed. The link to the next person in the chain was gone, and he'd lost his chance to burn the chain all the way to the drug lord in Afghanistan who'd arranged for Brandt's agent's and his team mates' purported deaths.

Brandt always thought of it in those terms, because he had a sneaking suspicion that Rex wasn't dead. That he hadn't reported in meant that he knew he'd been set up. It was natural for Rex to assume he couldn't trust CRC until he knew who'd done it, but it stung.

Helpless to finish what he'd started with Carson's ouster, Brandt decided to take a long shot. Finding Rex was not going to be easy. He'd been the best agent Brandt had ever trained. He knew all the tricks and was used to working alone. It would be like looking for the proverbial needle in a haystack. But Brandt had to try. As he often told his recruits, the surest way to fail was to not even try.

Three

GYAN EXCUSED HIMSELF, saying he must warn his wife to prepare a feast for their important guest. Rex responded with a nod of his head, his hands pressed palm to palm, and said, "*namaste*". The old man reciprocated, and then broke out in the toothless smile Rex had learned to interpret amidst all those wrinkles. Digger *woofed* softly, and Rex turned to look at him. When he turned back, Gyan had vanished.

"Folklore, my ass," Rex muttered. He looked at Digger. "What shall we do now, boy? We have some time to kill."

Digger apparently had no opinion, mainly because he was busy finishing Rex's lunch, which he'd absentmindedly set down when he started talking to Gyan.

Sighing, Rex peeled his orange and ate it. Gyan had given him directions to his home and told him to come at eight. Rex knew good manners dictated he be at least an hour late. So, dinner would be served around nine that night, he reckoned. By the time it was finished and he and Gyan had played their game of Chaturanga, it would be too late to go on to his next destination afterward.

Since arriving in India a few weeks ago, Rex had to remind himself every day about his new chosen lifestyle, no deadlines to meet, no place he *had* to be, and all the time in the world to get there.

He decided to check into a local hotel, switch his plans to visit Kapal Mochan to tomorrow, and visit the ashram of the famous Indian historian Ved Vyasa rishi before his dinner date.

He also needed to shop for a gift for Gyan's wife.

He found the archaeological site near where the paleochannel river left the Himalayas and entered the plains. Excavation of the paleochannel was just beginning, but there were several sites where ancient sculptures and monuments had been unearthed. Rex spent several hours wandering in the forest, along the dry riverbed, and in admiration of the various ninth-century Hindu ruins and the Buddhist monastery Adi Badri, dated from the tenth to twelfth century.

By the time Digger began to let Rex know of his displeasure at being kept on a short leash and not allowed to enter the buildings, Rex was ready for a snack and a short rest. They returned to the village and found an outdoor coffee shop that had Indian pastries. Rex might have shared with Digger, but he was still miffed about being robbed of his lunch, so he avoided eye contact with the dog, who was probably giving him big, sad, puppy eyes.

He asked the server where he could get an appropriate hostess gift, and was directed to a sweets shop, where he bought a carefully-considered box of candies. Not too big, as it would emphasize the difference in his economic status, and not too small, but like some girl with golden hair in a fairy tale he vaguely remembered from his childhood, he found one that was just right.

As the hour approached, Rex found he was excited about the Chaturanga game. He knew that the game was thought to be the predecessor of chess and was thought to have originated in India in the 6th century AD. Chaturanga meant the 'four divisions' referring to the infantry, cavalry, elephantry, and chariotry of the ancient Indian military forces, which had over centuries evolved into pawn, knight, bishop and rook of the modern chess game. He hadn't played chess since before his family was killed in the Spanish railway bombing. His younger brother had regularly beat him. Rex would have given just about anything to have just one more match with his brother to see if he could have won since all his military training.

The object of Chaturanga, he assumed, was to capture the other player's king, like chess.

He hadn't been formally invited to dinner since the last time he'd been on vacation at an island resort in the Caribbean after a mission. That invitation was from a beautiful Russian girl and that was now more than a year past. Rex had a few moments of angst while he waited to be politely late — a strange concept for him. Promptness was not only a virtue in military and American etiquette – it was required. In fact, during his basic training in the Marines they were taught to set their watches seven minutes ahead and forget that they'd done it, so they could never be late for anything. To relieve the stress, he paced the room, repeating to himself the truth that being prompt in India would mean the opposite.

Digger, comfortably ensconced in the exact middle of the bed, watched him, tracking with his entire head, like someone watching a tennis match, having no idea why his two-legged friend was stressed.

At last, it was time to go. Digger submitted to the leash again in his role as Rex's support dog for the eyes of the hotel staff. As soon as they reached the van, Rex unhooked the leash and let Digger bound into the back seat. He got in on the driver's side to find Digger had taken up a station on the front seat again.

"All right, but just this time," he said. "When we're traveling at speed, you're safer in the back."

Digger, turning his head to look out the window and pointedly ignoring him, told Rex he was losing this battle as well. "In that case, I'll have to find a safety harness for you, as soon as we're back in a city of any size."

Digger woofed. Whether that was in agreement or disagreement Rex didn't know. He was only going to find out when he put the harness on him.

Rex followed Gyan's directions, leaving the city on a dirt track that led past tilled fields, crops he couldn't identify in the dark, and hedgerows of taller trees. Eventually, he came to the outskirts of a nearby village where the houses were jammed together on small lots. Gyan's was in the center of a street on the outskirts of the village. It was a low rectangle, with a shallow peaked roof of curved terra cotta tiles.

A wooden door of rough-hewn planks in the exact center of the wall facing the street and one window, shuttered, were the only features in the mud-plastered wall. However, the roof overhung the house all along the front, supported by crooked wooden posts set in a knee-high wall and forming a veranda of sorts.

Rex commanded Digger to stay and knocked on the door with his left hand. He held the box of candies in his right. Gyan answered the door and loudly welcomed Rex, making a fuss that was almost embarrassing. Rex thrust the box into his hands.

"For your wife."

"Akshara will be delighted," Gyan said. "Come, come. You are welcome in our home." Rex glanced back at Digger, who had settled into his waiting pose, on his belly, front paws crossed, chin resting on his paws. He was on his best behavior. Rex was grateful.

The interior of the little house was immaculate but cramped. Apparently, there were two rooms, the room Rex entered as he stepped through the door, and a separate kitchen, from which delectable aromas emanated. Gyan led him to a cushion placed on the floor beside a low table. Across the room, Rex could see a bed. On the walls were dozens of pictures, of family Rex supposed, along with a colorful calendar and images of several Hindu gods: Vishnu, the Preserver, Brahma, The Creator, and

Saraswathi, the Goddess of Learning prominent among others Rex didn't recognize.

A television older than Rex himself was perched precariously on a shelf at the foot of the bed. Incongruously, a large refrigerator occupied a place of honor beside an opening that Rex assumed was the doorway to the kitchen. In place of a door, it had a beautiful hanging of intricately-woven cotton.

As he sat down, cross-legged, on the cushion Gyan indicated, a tiny, withered old woman stepped through the doorway, brushing the hanging aside with an elbow. With both hands, she carried a bowl of enormous proportions and set it on the table. She nodded at Rex very briefly, and then scurried back through the hanging.

Rex took her to be Gyan's wife, though Gyan didn't introduce her. Female members of the household wouldn't usually be introduced, Rex knew, and would not join the men for dinner when a guest was present. He felt a little uncomfortable to be served by her, though, he found some comfort in the knowledge she was not a servant but his hostess and that this is how they did it in India.

His impression, though fleeting, was that she had been lovely as a young woman. Though age had shrunk her, she was still at least as tall as her husband. Her hair was a rich shade of grey, almost blue in the dim light. She had smiled shyly at him as she put down the bowl, and it seemed she'd taken better care of her teeth, or perhaps she had better genes. In either case, she still had some. Her skin was lighter than Gyan's. Whether that meant she'd married down, perhaps for love, or Gyan's skin had suffered the ravages of the sun as a farmer, Rex couldn't say. In any case, he'd have bet that Gyan had been favored by his deity in his marriage.

Gyan sat and dipped two fingers into the bowl, bringing up a chunk of some kind of meat. He popped it into his mouth, evidently judged it worthy, and dipped his head in Rex's direction.

"Please, eat."

Rex was momentarily nonplussed. There were no plates, no tableware. Suddenly he grasped the practical nature of the left-hand and right-hand protocol. Tentatively, he dipped the fingers of his right hand into the bowl like Gyan had, brought up a chunk of the meat, which he discovered was not meat at all. Eggplant, he guessed. He'd never liked eggplant, but the flavor that burst on his taste buds was so delicious that it instantly became his favorite.

For another hour, Mrs. Gyan brought out dish after dish, each more delicious than the last. Rex began to eat sparingly of each, not knowing when it would end. By the fourth or fifth, he was seriously worried that he'd be unable to eat it all, and that it would insult his host if he couldn't. He began to wonder if he should have looked up Indian food etiquette by the time the seventh dish came out. In Mumbai on his mission there and in New Delhi, customs in the restaurants were closer to Western norms.

Finally, Gyan burped loudly, an indication he was finished eating. Rex suppressed a sigh of relief as his hostess brought two bowls of scented water and placed one in front of her guest, then her husband. Rex watched as Gyan cleaned his eating hand with it and did the same. He'd been eating at the same pace as Gyan, watching carefully for cues to how he should be behaving. He didn't remember another meal so satisfying and delicious, and he said so.

Gyan's black eyes twinkled as he claimed his wife was the best cook in all of India. A clanking from the kitchen led Rex to believe that she had heard and was pleased.

Gyan wasted no time in bringing out his Chaturanga board, an eight-by-eight wooden board that was marked off in squares but not colored. He explained how each of the pieces moved as he arranged them on the board.

The king, or *raja*, moved like the chess king, one space either diagonally or orthogonal to any space not attacked by an enemy piece. The object, as Rex had assumed, was to checkmate the raja. Rather than a queen, the piece that began next to the raja was called a *mantri*, or minister. Unlike a queen, it moved like a chess bishop, diagonally, but only one space at a time. The piece shaped like the head of an elephant was called *hasti* or *gaja*. It moved diagonally, two spaces at a time, leaping over the intervening space.

Most familiar to Rex besides the king were the horse, or *ashwa* and the chariot, called *rat-ha*. They looked like and moved like the knight and rook, or castle, respectively. Except that the chess move called castling, where the king and a rook exchanged places in a specific move, was not a legal move in Chaturanga.

Finally, there were the foot soldiers or *padati*, known as pawns in chess. It could move one space forward without capturing, or one space diagonally forward to capture, but it didn't have a double move. And it could be promoted only to *mantri* when it reached the last row on the enemy side.

The last difference that surprised Rex was that a stalemate was considered a win for the stalemated player, rather than a draw. With the moves in mind, the old Indian and the young American began to play. Rex lost the first game rather quickly, which Gyan politely told him was because he was trying to play it like chess. However, when he lost the second game, Gyan put the board away and called his wife out to see Rex's magical dog.

By then it was past midnight. Rex marveled at the stamina the older people displayed. When he stepped outside, he had something else to marvel at. Dozens of people were sitting on the bare ground outside, completely silent. Middle-aged men and women, younger adults, and children from teens all the way down to babies were waiting in a crowd. The moon had come out, and Rex estimated there were probably forty or more individuals, not counting the small children who were held in their mothers' arms.

What the hell is this? And why did Digger not alert us about them?

Gyan answered his unspoken question with pride. "These are my sons and daughters, their children, and their children's children. A few of the babies are their children's children's children."

Rex's head was spinning. *Three generations of Gyan's family came...for what?*

And once again, Gyan answered his thoughts.

"Please, show them your magic. With the dog. Show them how you speak to the dog and he answers you."

Rex groaned inwardly. Digger was going to get a big head, performing for an audience this size. But he owed it to his host, for the banquet he'd enjoyed. He started with the basic command, "Digger, come."

Digger obeyed instantly, of course. He appeared at Rex's side out of the shadows of the veranda, to a murmur of surprise from the audience. Rex assumed it had looked to them as if Digger had materialized beside him, summoned from another dimension. As he put the dog through his paces, sitting, rolling, jumping over Rex's extended arm, sticking out his right paw to 'shake hands' with Rex, the children clapped, and the adults gave soft sounds of admiration. Rex looked around for a suitable tree for Digger to climb as his last trick of the evening. A gnarled and stunted rosewood grew near the roofline of Gyan's house.

"Digger, roof."

Exclamations of surprise went up from a few people in the audience when Digger leaped into the tree, and when he appeared on the roof, the entire crowd shouted and clapped.

Gyan's wife, Akshara, broke her silence for the first time since Rex arrived at their home earlier as she poked Gyan in the side and said, in Hindi, "Now you must not tell me you cannot repair the roof, old man. If a dog can climb the tree, so can you."

Rex tried to suppress his laugh and ended up snorting, an inelegant sound that attracted Gyan's attention.

The old man laughed and shrugged his shoulders. Women. What can you do?

After Digger came down from the roof, Rex told them it was okay for the children to pet him if they wanted. Digger stood patiently while a few of the braver children approached gingerly and patted him and spoke to him in a dialect Rex couldn't quite follow. But their tone was approving, and Digger soaked it up. Then Gyan said something in the same dialect and made a shooing motion with both hands. The crowd dispersed into the night.

Back inside, Rex wondered if it was too early to take his leave, but Gyan had one more thing to show him. He pointed to the pictures on the wall near the bed. "My children," he said again. Then he named them, one by one. When he came to the last one, a picture of a beautiful young woman, he said the name with great sadness in his tone. "This is my youngest child, the jewel in my crown. Rehka."

The young woman was stunning. Long, thick, wavy black hair parted in the center framed an oval face of perfect proportions. Her brown eyes were accented with liner, mascara and shadow, making them appear large and soulful. Her nose was strong but straight and not too large for her face. Most attractive of all were her lovely lips, full, lush, and colored with a dusky, deep pink lipstick that complemented her caramel-colored, flawless skin. Rex felt certain he'd have noticed if she had been present. He asked where she was, because he hadn't seen her among the clan members earlier.

"We do not know where she is."

Sensing a story behind the words, Rex knew it might be polite to ask to hear it, but on the other hand the sadness could mean she was dead, and he didn't want to make his host any sadder. He hesitated. But then Gyan began to tell the story without prompting.

"We have not seen her in months. You must understand, though the caste system has been outlawed, it is still very much honored. We are of the Vaishya caste, honest, but poor farmers. Rehka, however, wanted more. She was able to attend school, but we could not pay for her to go to a university."

Rex followed the narrative, wondering how it would end. He made an appropriate noise of understanding.

Gyan continued. "She was stubborn. I blame myself. I indulged her, as she was my last child. She went without my knowledge to a money lender. She entered Kurukshetra University and graduated with top honors." Gyan said the last with pride. "She got a respectable job but living in Mumbai is costly. She could not pay to live and pay her debts, too. She entered indentured servitude to work off her debt, and she is not allowed to visit us."

Rex commiserated. He knew the practice was forbidden, but it was still alive and thriving and part of the Indian economy. "I'm sorry," he said. The first thought was he could only hope the young woman would soon be free of her debt. The second was that it was unlikely. Unscrupulous creditors piled costs of housing and food as well as interest on top of the original debt to keep their virtual slaves indebted forever. Even worse, a woman as lovely as she would probably have been pushed into the sex trade in a city far from her home.

Bullying and exploiting the defenseless. Rex felt the rage building in him.

Gyan brightened. "She would have loved to meet your dog. If you are ever nearby again, please come to visit. Maybe my Rehka will be home by then."

Rex took the statement to mean that he was now free to say goodbye. He thanked Gyan and promised to visit again.

He collected Digger from his place on the veranda and left.

Four

THE NEXT MORNING, Rex intended to continue the journey that had been interrupted the day before. Kapal Mochan was only a couple of miles up the road from where he had stopped for Digger's needs the day before, but it was miles apart in atmosphere. Where Bilaspur gave every evidence of a modern city filled with cheaply-constructed apartment houses and a faltering economy, Kapal Mochan was a city steeped in history.

Before leaving, he had a breakfast brought up to his room, where he also tried again to feed Digger the prescribed dry food along with fresh water. Digger once again preferred Rex's breakfast, but Rex was vigilant and managed to finish it himself without sharing. Digger crunched at his own food, but he punctuated the task with reproachful looks at Rex.

By nine a.m., late in the morning by Rex's standards, they were on the road.

The temple of white stone or brick, Rex couldn't tell which from his first sight of it, rose on the banks of a sacred pool, where pilgrims rid themselves of sin by taking a dip. Rex didn't feel particularly sinful, as he'd always acted in support of his country's freedom from terrorism and drug dependency. As far as he was concerned, he'd been justified in every killing.

Now he was a few weeks into a new life, no longer a soldier in that fight. He was burned as an undercover agent, he knew not by whom. So, his dip in the pool would symbolically mark the death of his old persona and the birth of the new. From this time forward, he'd be a nomad, searching out places that interested him because of their history, living nowhere and traveling where the wind blew him.

He didn't intend to dip his entire body in the pool as devotees did. He was certain that such an action would mean Digger would want to join him, and that might be a serious offense to the Indian pilgrims who might consider dogs unclean. For his money, the pool might just as well make an unclean animal clean as wash away sin, but that was his opinion only. He was mindful that he was a guest in this country.

When he arrived at the parking lot, he considered leaving Digger in the van. More than a hundred vehicles were already parked there. However, the temperature was already rising. Rex reckoned he'd rather offend a few people than let Digger bake in a closed car. He apologized to Digger for putting the leash on him again. But Digger seemed okay with it.

Rather than walk through the building to the edge of the pool where hundreds of people were waiting their turn for a dip, Rex walked Digger around by a path that led through the parklike grounds and headed for an edge where he could dip just his hand – the right one – in the waters. By the time he got there, he felt a little silly.

He'd initially thought the gesture would mark his transformation from quasi-legal assassin to tourist without a plan. He didn't consider his previous actions as sins, precisely. Certainly not on the order of killing a Brahmin, though he also didn't think those hundreds of people he'd avoided on the other side of the pool had all killed Brahmins, or anyone else, for that matter.

The Brahmins were the top tier of the outlawed caste system. Like everything else he'd observed about India, the law that had made it illegal to discriminate against anyone because of their membership in a lower caste might work in principle. But in action, the caste system still ruled. The Brahmins, traditionally priests and teachers, were thought by the ancients to have sprung from the head of Brahma, the Creator.

Four main castes below the Brahmins were Kshatriyas, warriors and rulers originating from Brahma's arms; Vaishyas, like Gyan's family, were farmers, traders and merchants, originating from the Creator's legs; and Shudras, or laborers, from his feet. The Dalits, or Untouchables were not considered a caste. They had the lowest, dirtiest jobs and for that reason were untouchable. Rex, in his insatiable quest for knowledge especially of history, knew it wasn't that simple. Dozens of sub castes existed, especially those that were based on specific jobs, almost like unions.

Rex got on his knees and looked down into the water. An inexplicable feeling descended on Rex as he prepared to dip his hand in the water. It was not spiritual, it stirred some emotion in him, but he couldn't quite define it yet. He shook himself from his reflection on the caste system. No, all those people were not killers. Bathing in this pool had come to mean washing all sin away, like baptism, not just the sin of killing someone.

But to Rex, now that he was right there, and he gave it some thought, he felt as if he were to go ahead and do it, it would wash away his oath of revenge on the terrorists who'd killed his family and hundreds of others at the railway bombing in Madrid in 2004. It meant going back on the oath he'd taken upon joining the Marines, to defend his country from enemies, and on the one he'd taken more recently next to Trevor, to avenge the deaths of his friends. There were still a lot that had to be done, evil people that had to be held accountable. He had names from the hard drives of the drug lord who'd arranged the ambush that night, and there was still much to be decrypted.

I'm not ready to wash away those oaths.

He sat back, unfolding his legs and then crossing them in front of him, still staring at the water. Digger watched with evident interest as Rex reviewed his life.

Have every one of my killings been justified?

There were many, and he remembered them all. Sometimes his near-perfect memory was a blessing, often a curse. He could recall in vivid detail, for example, the broken bodies and bloodied faces of his mother and sister as they lay dying.

Yes. Every one of them was justified.

Rex was not a religious man. He considered himself an agnostic, at best. If there was a God, He might have a different opinion of those acts, but Rex's conscience was clear. Nevertheless, even though he had consciously set his life on a new course, he knew it was not the end of the path, at least not until he'd completely fulfilled all his oaths. Only then would he be ready to bathe in this pool.

Slowly, Rex pushed himself to his feet, turned away from the water, and started to retrace his steps along the path. About halfway to his van, Rex deep in thought, he and Digger met a lovely young woman with an entourage of several more. She was dressed in white traditional robes edged with red and richly jeweled. A veil of the same cloth draped her head, anchored by heavy pendants of what appeared to be rubies and diamonds, and a choker-style necklace of the same surrounded her throat. The other women were also dressed in traditional garb, all alike.

Rex took them to be a bride and her bridesmaids on some errand having to do with the wedding. He stepped politely off the path, leading Digger to his opposite side.

The bride smiled at him, and the bridesmaids tittered with delicate laughter.

Lucky man, the groom.

***

WHEN HE REACHED the van, Rex decided to let Digger have some time in the forest before they got on the road for a long trip. He still needed to decide where they were going next, anyway. A little time with a map and his list of other historic sites would give him some ideas. He took his lunch from the cooler and stashed it in a small knapsack, along with Digger's bowls and food and extra water bottles. The map and notes he wanted to consult went into a pocket in his cargo shorts.

Digger had been on his best behavior, so as a reward, Rex let him off the leash. When they were ready, he said, "Let's go play in the woods, buddy. Stay close."

Digger for once had the same idea, so they made it to the edge of the woods without incident. Rex couldn't help but compare this forest with the woods back in Connecticut, near his Sandy Hook childhood home, which were quiet, peaceful places. Back there, the only noises in the woods were birds, insects, and his family or other campers. In India, however, the howls and other utterances of the wild monkeys made a cacophony he didn't find so peaceful. Nevertheless, he ignored the noise, certain it would fade into the background of white noise like the noise of a city did for its residents.

Rex found a fallen tree and used it for a place to sit, telling Digger he was free to go and explore and play. The dog immediately took off, nose in the air, taking in all the scents and stopping at trees to lift his leg and demarcate his domain. Rex took out the notes and map to decide where they were off to next. His stomach was beginning to growl when Digger came back, bringing a company of irritated monkeys with him.

"Digger, what did you do?" he asked. He was more than a little worried. Contrary to anything that made sense to him, Rex knew the monkeys were protected, considered sacred by the Hindu religion. There were signs everywhere saying that the monkeys were protected under the Wildlife Protection Act of 1972. It was a crime, punishable by fine, incarceration, or both to hunt, capture or kill them. Rex assumed he'd be in trouble for even trying to scare them, though, from what he had observed so far, the WPA was honored more in the breach than observation in the cities.

Digger had no answer for the irritating creatures. He crawled under the tree where Rex was sitting to get away from the monkeys. Some of them were so audacious they would run up pull his tail and then run away. Digger's snarls and growls didn't scare them. They followed him into his hiding place. He whined, no doubt expecting Rex to do something about it.

Rex laughed in spite of himself. He looked around, making sure no one was watching, took a chance and shooed the most persistent monkeys away. After that, the whole troop retreated to the high branches of nearby trees.

"Are you ready for lunch?" he asked Digger. He took off his knapsack and poured the usual feast for Digger – dog chow and water – and opened the bag with his own sandwich in it. Digger lapped at the water, but as usual disdained the food. Until a bold monkey swung down from the nearest tree and scrambled to the bowl. Digger barked fiercely at him.

Rex chuckled. "Come on Digger, you didn't want it. Let the poor monkey have it then."

Digger, though, was determined to protect what was his, even if he didn't want it. He rushed at the monkey, snarling. Before Rex could intervene, the monkey retreated, chittering angrily. Digger sniffed the food and then turned away.

Rex was certain Digger wouldn't eat the food, now that it had the monkey's scent on it, but he didn't remove the bowl right away. To do so would require him to put down his food, and he remembered what had happened yesterday. He continued eating his sandwich. But within seconds, the bold monkey was back with two companions.

Rex admired their tactics. Two of the monkeys tormented Digger, though they didn't do anything that led Rex to believe they were about to hurt him. They worked in a team. One would snatch at his tail, then retreat when he whirled around. Then the other would do the tail thing and retreat. Meanwhile, the third monkey was stuffing his cheeks with the food from Digger's bowl.

Rex couldn't help but laugh loudly at the sight.

Digger must have been offended when he realized that Rex was entertained by his dilemma and was not going to do anything to help him. He stalked away, putting his back to a tree and sitting with his tail curled around his feet, just like a cat. And just like a cat, the end of his tail was twitching with irritation. But no monkey could get at it without risking Digger biting its head off.

Rex was so busy watching the comedy that he failed to notice one of the monkeys sneaking up on him, until it snatched the remainder of his sandwich right out of his hand.

"Hey!" he shouted. Whereupon the monkey with the stuffed cheeks began spitting soggy dog food into his paw and throwing it at Rex. Then it became a full-on attack. The monkeys surrounded him, separating him from Digger, and pelted him with dog food and other soggy stuff, the origin of which he didn't want to know.

Abandoning his food, his knapsack, and Digger's bowls, he beat a hasty retreat toward the van, shouting "Come Digger!"

He hadn't gone ten steps before the leader of the unruly troop rushed up from behind and jumped on his back. Rex was not unaccustomed to a pack weighing thirty pounds or more hanging from his back, but an angry male monkey of the same weight, and ten or more following in support of the one on his back with bared teeth and making angry, high-pitched noises, was a different matter altogether. He didn't even have time to worry the animal would bite him, before in the corner of his eye he caught something moving from his left side in a flash and hitting the monkey on his back, carrying it sideways.

Rex whirled to see Digger throwing the monkey on the ground.

"Digger, leave it!" he yelled, but it was too late.

Digger ripped the monkey's throat out with one savage jerk of his head.

46

"Oh, shit!"

While all the other monkeys in the vicinity set up a howling like a whole herd of banshees, Rex looked around. There were no witnesses except the monkeys. He and Digger were in big trouble if they stayed. He didn't even think to go back for the knapsack and bowls. They could be replaced. Digger couldn't.

"Come on, boy, let's get out of here!"

He ran for the van, with Digger on his heels. The monkeys followed, but at a respectful distance. They were still howling with rage. Rex opened the driver's door, urged Digger to jump in, and jumped in after him. He peeled out of the parking lot like the devil was pursuing him, and indeed, the monkeys might have been possessed. Some of them chased the van, jumping from tree to tree at a rate Rex couldn't believe. He was forced to slow for the speed limit and because he didn't want a constable to stop him and inquire why twenty or thirty pissed-off monkeys were following him.

The monkeys gave up their pursuit, just as Rex entered the village of Bilaspur and pulled into the nearest parking lot to check on Digger to see if he came out of it unscathed. He was good.

While scratching him behind the ears to comfort him he said, "Digger, thanks buddy. But let's not kill any more monkeys while we're here, okay?"

As if he understood, Digger growled low in his throat which could have meant, "Okay, but only as long as they don't attack one of us."

Rex looked around to get his bearings and noticed a restaurant across the street. "I can't get you a steak in this country where cows are holy animals, boy, but you deserve a chicken at least. I'll be right back."

A few minutes later, he was back, with two orders of chicken baked in a tandoor oven in a to-go bag. He drove leisurely to the park where they'd had lunch the day before, or rather where Digger had had Rex's lunch the day before. Rex didn't remember seeing any monkeys, but he took the precaution of eating inside the van, anyway. He took out his chicken and then handed Digger the other bag. Digger took it delicately in his teeth and jumped over the seats, into the cargo compartment, where he ripped the bag apart and devoured the chicken inside.

While he ate, Rex thought about his morning, which led him to think about families. He'd had a family – a mother, father, sister and brother. Terrorists killed them, as he'd remembered in depth he didn't often afford himself today. It wasn't just about oaths. He often felt isolated, alone in the world, and save for Digger, he literally was alone.

When he'd joined the military, his family had been his military brothers and a few sisters. The rigors of basic training had made them fast friends, even while it made them rivals. He'd lost those friends, except for Frank Millard, when he was plucked straight from basic and transferred to Delta Force training. He hadn't known at the time just how extraordinary that had been, but he learned soon enough. It was unprecedented.

He'd made other friends during his Delta training, but fewer. All those men had been focused on surviving the toughest course there was, or so they thought. They saw him as a threat to their own successful journey to become elite Delta Force operators. When the time came for the survivors to be assigned to a squad, they'd become even closer than brothers, but that time never came for Rex. Once again, an inexplicable circumstance had washed him out. He'd spent more than half a week drunk before CRC caught up with him.

CRC turned out to be even tougher than Delta Force, and Rex hadn't minded. Someone, he thought maybe the Old Man, John Brandt, had been behind the scenes since his dossier had crossed his desk, right at the beginning of his Marine enlistment. He'd funneled Rex through his initial training and then cut off his choices. And Rex had become, he thought, a valuable asset.

He didn't know what to think about CRC now. His orders that led to an ambush had come from the Old Man himself. Rex didn't want to believe that he'd become a liability that needed to be sanitized, but he *had* gone against his orders not to interfere with the drug trade he'd been monitoring. If Brandt had wanted to be rid of him, he'd have preferred a shot to the back of the head to an ambush that killed his friends. Frank Millard had turned out to be the head of Phoenix Unlimited, his assigned logistics resource. And

Trevor, the irrepressible Aussie he'd met on a previous mission had been there, too.

All were lost to him. Even Frank and Trevor were gone, killed in the ambush, and leaving him only Digger. And Digger had just risked his own life to save Rex's.

Okay, maybe it wasn't quite that dangerous, but maybe it was. Rex knew monkeys had killed people in the cities of India. They were big, smart, dangerous animals with fangs the size of a big dog's like Digger. A bite could get infected, and a troop of monkeys could have brought him down, if Digger hadn't intervened. If they'd all turned on Digger they would have ripped him to pieces.

Digger is my family.

It was the first time he'd thought in those terms, and the first time he'd missed his CRC family since the explosion that killed his friends.

His thoughts kept on being occupied about family, and about sacrifice. About Gyan's broken family, with a daughter missing.

No family should go through that kind of pain just because of a merciless moneylender.

Five

WHEN HE PASSED the beautiful and beaming young bride, he knew what the feeling was that bothered him at the pool earlier and gave him pause and prevented him from continuing with the 'cleansing act' — it was rage. The young woman reminded him of the Gyan's stunning daughter. Overcome by the contrast in her situation and the lovely bride's, he accelerated his pace to get to his van, let Digger in and got behind the wheel.

He called Digger to come up front, looked at the dog sitting in the passenger seat, staring at him. "We should help them, right?" he asked, nodding his head.

Digger smiled. Rex doubted he had any idea what the question meant, but he took the smile to mean, "Why do you even ask? Of course, we have to."

"I thought that's what you would say." He started the van.

Half an hour later, he found himself at the door of Gyan's little house again. In the daylight he could see that the plaster on the outside walls was of assorted colors, no doubt patched from time to time rather than painted all at once. In his hand was another small box of candies, this time in apology for dropping in without an invitation.

Digger sat at attention by his side.

This time it was Akshara who answered the door. When she saw Rex, her eyes grew round before she cast them downward.

Rex was embarrassed. "I'm sorry to intrude," he said in Hindi. "Is your husband at home?"

In broken Hindi interspersed with a familiar-sounding but unintelligible dialect, she answered that he wasn't. Could she give him a message?

Rex handed her the box of candy. He spoke slowly, hoping she could understand him, and not sure that he should be speaking to her at all in her husband's absence. But it had occurred to him that Gyan might wave him off if he offered to help the daughter. Maybe her mother wouldn't.

Akshara had stepped back into the house, leaving the door open, but she hadn't invited him inside. He felt certain it would be improper to follow her in, so he waited. A moment later, she came out with two folding stools that had three legs and a seat of sturdy cotton canvas. She set them down and sat on one of them, gesturing for him to take the other.

When he was settled, she told him she had enjoyed watching his clever dog the night before. He was catching on to the dialect. It was definitely related to the more formal Hindi he knew.

After a few pleasantries, during which Rex thanked her again for the best dinner he had in many years, he broached the subject he'd come for. "Mrs. Gyan, tell me more about your daughter, Rehka."

Akshara's face instantly changed to a mask of grief. "My daughter is dead," she said.

Rex knew it wasn't literally true. "She indentured herself," he responded. "Surely she is still alive."

"We can only hope that she is alive. We don't know if she is. We haven't heard from her in months. I'm afraid we might not see her ever again."

Rex asked gently why Akshara thought that. The story poured out of her quickly, so fast Rex could barely follow her, and it wasn't at all what he'd been told the night before.

"My daughter was ashamed to tell my husband, but she was worse off than what he told you. That was her fiction. What really happened was she lost her job. Her supervisor wanted her to give him her innocence. You understand?" She waited for Rex to answer.

He understood, and the rage was about to erupt in him. "She refused, and what then?"

"She was dismissed, of course. India does not protect women as it should." Akshara's defiance showed in her raised head. She looked directly into his eyes for the first time. "My baby was unfairly dismissed, but that was not the worst of it. Her boss falsely accused her of stealing money and even showed her some documents to prove it, all falsified, of course. But it was a woman's word against a man's. She had no chance. He demanded she submit to him or pay him an impossible sum, more than she had saved or could ever hope to gather on her salary. With no job, she could not pay, and if he told anyone she had stolen money from her employer, she would not get another job and probably end up in jail. His word against hers.

"So, she borrowed the money."

Akshara's face was now streaked with the tears she couldn't hold back as she told him the rest of it. "Yes. She borrowed the money. But then after her boss got the money, because he couldn't have his way with her, he went and told people about the stolen money anyway. My daughter did nothing wrong! But she ended up with no job, and she could not pay the money lender. That was when she entered servitude to the money lender rather than dishonor our family by sleeping with her despicable boss."

"Why then are you saying that you don't know if she's alive?"

"Because she is not with Dhruv, the money lender anymore. We don't know where she is and what happened with her."

She broke down completely and sobbed into her hands.

Digger had been watching her as she spoke, and now her tears seemed to distress him as well. He whined softly and moved closer, until he was leaning against her legs. He put his head in her lap.

Akshara gasped when she felt the weight against her legs. Tears still streaming, she clapped her hands over her mouth, suppressing a small scream.

"It's okay, ma'am, don't worry," Rex said. "He knows you're sad. He's trying to comfort you."

Akshara tentatively touched Digger's head, between his ears, where his long hair was softest.

Digger groaned, which Rex knew for a sign of pleasure, but Akshara snatched her hand away.

"He likes that," Rex said, reaching over to demonstrate how to pet the dog. "His name is Digger, and he can understand you if you praise him. I can see he likes you very much."

Akshara followed his lead, stroking the dog's back and murmuring what sounded to Rex to be baby talk. Before long, she forgot to cry and was giving all her attention to Digger.

However, Rex's blood was about to reach boiling point. Unscrupulous money lenders who victimized the vulnerable had just joined his list of human vermin, which already contained terrorists, arms dealers, and drug dealers.

"This Dhruv, he lives in Mumbai?" Rex asked.

"Yes."

"And how long ago did your daughter indenture herself?" he asked.

55

"Four months."

"When was the last time you heard from her?"

"Six weeks ago. But not directly. One of her friends sent us a letter to tell us that her 'owner', Dhruv has been arrested and is now in jail but that Rehka has disappeared.

Rex was quiet for a moment. When he spoke again he had made up his mind. "Do you have something she wore? Perhaps a scarf? May I borrow it? Also, the picture of her?"

Bewildered, the old woman went into the house and brought out a finely-woven cotton scarf. "This is the only thing I have of hers and here is her picture." Rex had second thoughts about that. Gyan might miss it. He took his cell phone out of his pocket and snapped a few pictures of it and made sure they were of good quality. He handed it back to her and asked her to hold up the picture close to her chest and took a few more pictures. She was intelligent enough to know that the reason why he did that was to show those pictures to Rehka, if he found her, as proof that he knew her mother.

He held up the scarf. "My dog will get her scent from this to find her if we get close," Rex said. "I can't promise I'll find her, but I will bring this back to you, and if I do find her, your daughter will be wearing it."

Akshara cried even harder and made the extraordinary gesture of hugging Rex tightly. "May your journey be blessed," she sobbed.

Gently, he extracted himself from the embrace and wished her peace until they met again.

Digger curled around Rex's legs to reach Akshara's dangling hand and nudged his head upward, against her palm.

She smiled and petted him a last time. "You, too, my new friend," she said. "Thank you for comforting me."

To Rex, she said, "When we meet again, Digger is welcome in my home."

Six

BRANDT RETURNED TO his Arizona headquarters the day after the Senator's death was reported. There was nothing more he could do there until someone found Carson or Carson's successor was appointed. When the former happened, he hoped it would be in a foreign country and it would be his team who found him. He'd know the job would be done right if that were the case.

When the second happened, he'd have to go and introduce himself and his group to the new DCIA. But the revelations about Carson had shaken up the old guard, and Brandt assumed the successor would be vetted six ways from Sunday before the announcement was made. Then would come the Congressional hearings before approval. It would be a while. In the meantime, the National Security Advisor would lead the CIA, and he already knew Brandt.

At the end of a long day, made longer by waking up in the Eastern time zone and working through to dinner in a time zone three hours behind, Brandt invited his friend and CRC's lead psychologist, Rick Longland to his quarters for a nightcap. As he poured a generous shot of the eighteen-year-old smoky amber whisky for Longland, he casually asked, "Do you also find it difficult to believe that our boy is actually gone? It doesn't feel like it to me."

"You mean Rex Dalton." Longland said.

"Yes." Brandt said.

"It's hard to believe," Longland said. "If ever we had a recruit who I believed could take care of himself and beat the odds to live to a ripe old age, I'd have put my money on Dalton."

"Why? Have you heard something to convince you otherwise?"

"No. It's just inconceivable that he walked into an ambush. Add to that the fact that no one has been able to identify his body with certainty."

Longland played Devil's Advocate. "Well, neither were the bodies of his team mates identified. Apart from that he hasn't reported in. Surely, he would, wouldn't he? If he were alive?"

Brandt stared at Longland for a short while before he spoke. "I'm not so sure about that. Consider the circumstances. He'd been over there for just about a year, and he sent back report after report, begging to do something about the drug trade rather than just observe who was doing what. But the CIA wiped their asses with his requests.

"Then we get word that someone has started disrupting the trade. No idea who. A few weeks pass, maybe not even that long. And suddenly, his orders are reversed, by the same CIA who had been ignoring his requests. His orders are to take out a bunch of the bastards together as they have a pow-wow, but it turns out to be an ambush. Now if he was indeed killed it doesn't matter what he thought.

Does it? However, if he somehow survived… what's he going to think and do?"

Longland took a beat, and then answered. "That he was set up. If he had time to think anything at all."

"That's my take on it, too. If it were me, I would not have been contacting us and I am sure neither would Dalton. Only he doesn't know who did it or why. His orders came from me, which I passed on directly from Carson.

"In his shoes, if I survived, I would have started by not trusting CRC, me, John Brandt, the man who gave me my orders. In other words, to answer your question, no, I don't think he'd report in."

While Brandt was talking the blood had drained from Longland's face, leaving him pale. "Holy shit! That means…"

"Right." Brandt nodded. "What you said, back before we sent him over there."

Longland didn't need a reminder, he recalled vividly what he'd said. They had been discussing how Rex seemed to handle stress better than any other agent. He'd warned Brandt about the consequences, should Rex decide to remember the part of the soldier's oath that went, '*I will support and defend the Constitution of the United States against all enemies, foreign and domestic…*' and realize not all the bad guys were in the Middle East, or south of the border. He'd told Brandt that one day the stress factor might get to Rex and he would 'snap'.

Brandt had asked what they should do about it, and he'd answered, "Nothing for right now, other than that it is mandatory to monitor him. If it ever becomes necessary to eliminate him, make sure it's done properly, because if you screw that up and he survives... we're dead... all of us. He will hunt us down and kill us all first. And then he will go after the politicians, officials, and other scoundrels—the domestic enemies. There won't be any stopping him."

Brandt was contemplating his Scotch as if he could read the future in it.

Longland quickly finished his shot in one gulp. "Then, my friend, you must certainly find him. Otherwise, we'll wake up dead one night, and after that many others, bureaucrats and politicians will have the same experience."

"My thought exactly," Brandt answered.

***

THE NEXT MORNING, he summoned Josh Farley, one of his agents whom he judged to be nearly as good as Rex Dalton, to his office.

"I have a special assignment for you. Go pack your stuff. Wheels up in half an hour."

The agent didn't ask any questions. He'd have no doubt he would get his orders in the air. Twenty-four minutes later, he was back with a full duffle bag in tow. He still had no questions. However, he was surprised when he climbed aboard the helicopter to find Brandt there before him.

"Sir?" he questioned.

"Sit down and strap in. I have a story to tell you," Brandt said as he put on his headset when the pilot started the engines.

A few hours later and several hundred miles to the east, Brandt introduced his man to his best female agent, Marissa. The move was unprecedented. None of the male agents had known of the female CRC agents and vice versa.

Over dinner, Brandt gave them their orders, finally satisfying the agents' curiosity. Before doing so, he gave them the history and explained in no uncertain terms that Rex Dalton was an exceedingly dangerous man to cross swords with. They should avoid it at all costs. He gave his assessment of what was going on if Rex was still alive, and why they needed to not approach or confront him in any way.

Their only priority was to find out if he was still alive, as Brandt suspected. If they found him, they were to stay out of his sight and get in touch with Brandt immediately. He'd take it from there. That was it. Do not, repeat do not, approach or confront him in any manner.

If they discovered he was indeed dead, Brandt would like them to bring whatever remains they could find back for proper burial.

The pair of agents listened without interrupting. When Brandt was finished talking, Marissa asked just one question. "Where in the world would we start looking for him?"

Brandt responded by handing her a thin file. "It's not much, but this is what we have on him." In the file was the brief description of how his family had died, the missions he executed in the past, the known contacts he'd made during those missions, information about where he'd vacationed when on leave from CRC, and his orders for Afghanistan. It also contained information about the Phoenix Unlimited personnel and his use of them for his logistics while in Afghanistan.

A single page gave the names and contact details for the few Phoenix agents who hadn't been killed in the ambush. They had dispersed when their CEO, Frank Millard was killed, but they were the last known good guys to have any contact with Rex. Brandt suggested his team start with them.

"In my opinion, if he did survive that explosion and he was capable of moving, he would have left Afghanistan. He could have gone to China — he speaks Mandarin like the Chinese. He could be in India — he speaks Hindi and Urdu like an Indian. He could be in Europe — he speaks several of their languages like the locals. I guess what I am saying is, he could be anywhere. I suggest you first establish whether he is dead or not. For that you must get to Afghanistan, go to the site of the explosion to collect samples, and get them analyzed and compared to the DNA we have.

"But this is your investigation, I'm not going to run it from my desk. I know what you're capable of. Therefore, I leave it to you to decide the best way to go about this. If you need my opinion or help you know how to get hold of me."

Then he wished them Godspeed, told them again to be extremely careful, and left them sitting at the table to plan their first move.

Seven

REX WAS NO stranger to Mumbai, though on his previous visit, in December of 2008, he'd been focused on terrorists and not money lenders. At the time, he didn't care who had financed the previous terrorist bombing in 1993 when the city was called Bombay, and the Indian Mafia, as some called it, was involved. For what reason, when that organization was busy corrupting Bollywood, the Indian version of Hollywood with the cutesy name, no one ever knew. Maybe it was simply a money transaction.

In 2008, it had happened again. This time, the terrorists had targeted victims with American or British passports. The price for their return without further harm was for all mujahedeen in India to be released. Following the lead of the US, the Indian government had refused to negotiate, leading to a bloodbath. One-hundred and sixty-four victims had lost their lives in the initial attack and what followed.

In any case, someone above Rex's pay grade – in the CIA, he assumed — had a lead on some Pakistanis who were involved, via a journalist who'd had some exclusive facts. Rex had questioned him, killed him and then led the mission to hunt the Pakistanis down across the border and mete out justice more expeditiously.

As he drove away from Gyan's house, burdened with Akshara's sorrow and his own assessment of where he'd find Rehka, he mentally reviewed what he'd learned when he'd last been in Mumbai, in 2008. Though it turned out that the Indian Mafia wasn't mentioned in conjunction with that attack, he'd still made a study of the organization. Like the Camorra in Italy, it was more loosely organized than the American version of La Cosa Nostra. And like the American version, there was strife among the various branches.

If he could somehow locate where Dhruv had been incarcerated, he'd start there. He could tell him who to contact in D-Company, the oddly-named cartel originally controlled by Dawood Ibrahim. Some argued that it wasn't a stereotypical organized crime cartel, but rather a collusion of criminal and Islamic terrorist groups. Rex knew it to be a hotbed of criminals that included specialists in extortion, murder, smuggling, and drug trafficking, in addition to finance of terrorist operations. All covered in the seemingly-legal involvement in film financing. The link was moneylending. Unless he missed his guess, Dhruv was connected to D-Company somehow. And if he wasn't, he'd still be able to tell Rex what happened to Rehka. Given her extraordinary beauty, it was probably to someone in the film industry.

Rex was troubled by the thought that he'd find Rehka being forced to act in the seedier side of the film business – porn. Rex didn't mind if he had to mess the guy up, break an arm or two, whatever it took, to get his answer. In fact, he was inclined to do that even if Dhruv cooperated. While he was at it, he intended to get the name of Rehka's supervisor who'd driven her to borrow money. He'd like to mess that guy up, too.

Rex used his laptop to search for Dhruv's name, in the hope they'd say where he was jailed. By a lucky happenstance, the guy was incarcerated in New Delhi, which was on a direct route to Mumbai, only about a four-hour drive from Bilaspur. He'd get there around dinner time, and it would be a good place to stop for a quick meal and to let Digger out to relieve himself. While he was on the way, Rex would think of some way to get immediate access to the former moneylender.

"Let's go, Digger," Rex said, looking at the clock on the dashboard.

Digger turned at the sound of his name and tilted his head.

"Right," Rex said, "Of course. What am I waiting for?" He started the engine and drove away with no evident haste. But as soon as he was out of Akshara's sight, he stepped on the pedal and sped to the highway.

According to his GPS, the trip to Mumbai would take twenty-seven hours. A six-week-old trail wasn't really an emergency, but it felt that way to Rex. An extra hour might just mean another degradation for that poor girl.

Not if I can prevent it.

In his mind, the speculations about how her masters would use her had first morphed into assumptions and then became truth. The best of the images in his mind were grave, but not as ominous as the ones where, in his mind's eye, he saw her being injected with drugs to make her compliant and then sent her out to walk the streets as a prostitute. He could only hope they'd see her beauty and conclude she was too valuable for that.

Even so, in some corner of his mind, he knew there was virtually no difference. He'd make it to Mumbai in twenty-four hours, tops, counting the stop in New Delhi.

***

BY THE TIME he reached the first destination, the Tihar prison system in Delhi, he knew he'd been too optimistic. When he pulled up at the prison he still hadn't been able to formulate a plan to quickly gain access to Dhruv. He was going to wing it.

As prisons went, especially in South Asia, Tihar was not the worst. It could even be called progressive, in that its declared aim was to convert the inmates to model citizens, by equipping them with marketable skills, education, and respect for the law as well as improved self-esteem.

Rex was a bit cynical about the chances of success to achieve those noble goals. Maybe for some, one or two percent, if they're lucky. For the rest of them? Not a chance.

Naturally, like everywhere else in India, the prisons comprising Tihar's complex were seriously overcrowded. It took too much of his self-allotted twenty-four hours just to find Dhruv in the nine prison buildings. He was finally located at a venue where he was attending a concert, part of the music therapy designed to rehabilitate the inmates.

Yeah right. Tell me about the kind of music that could turn a low-life like Dhruv into a model citizen.

With no legitimate reason to get an interview outside visiting hours, Rex resorted to the universal currency — bribery. For the princely sum of three-thousand rupees, not quite fifty US dollars, Rex gained an interview.

Dhruv sat in an interview room when Rex entered and was surprised to discover he had no restraints – no shackles or handcuffs – and the room was not locked. This must be a progressive prison after all, or the money shark was not considered an escape risk. Rex wasn't too worried about that. It would be with great pleasure that he would help the Indian prison authorities to keep this scumbag behind bars if he would make Rex's day and try to escape during the meeting.

When Rex walked in, the moneylender's face showed surprise, but he quickly composed himself. His expression became neutral, and he waited for Rex to speak first.

"You were expecting someone else," Rex stated.

"Yes."

Oh okay, so that's how it's going to be. Good let's do it that way then.

"To whom did you sell Rehka Gyan and when?"

"I can't remember." The smallest ghost of a smile twitched Dhruv's lips.

"Can't or won't?"

"Yes." Dhruv replied, obviously thinking that was a very smart answer.

Rex didn't respond, he just looked the man in the eyes and suddenly Dhruv's macho demeanor changed. He must have seen in Rex's eyes what so many bad guys had seen in those eyes shortly before exchanging the temporary for the eternal.

Dhruv's face was pallid. He started talking. "I'll tell you what I do remember. I remember that policemen came to my door, frightened my wife and my elderly mother, and took me away. I remember wondering how my wife would support herself and my mother, as was her duty."

Rex said nothing. There was nothing to say. He had no sympathy with this guy.

Dhruv spoke again. "My wife got a good job after my former associates framed me and put me here, but it does not pay enough to hire someone to watch my mother, whose mind has become weak as she nears death. My wife is torn between her duty to my mother and keeping her job."

"Okay, let me see if I understand you correctly. You are worried about your wife and mother. Right?"

Dhruv nodded.

"Good. Seems to me your time in here has already taught you some compassion for humans.

"I'm also a compassionate man. I'll lend your wife the money every month until your mother dies. At a very modest interest rate of say twenty percent per month. Then, when she can't pay, I'll take her indenture and sell her. How's that?"

Dhruv's head dropped to his chest in defeat. "I will give you the name, if you promise you won't interfere with my family."

"I'm prepared to forget my new business idea," Rex said, "assuming I can find this man quickly. Give me the name."

"First, your assurance that you will leave my family out of this."

"No, you don't understand the business principal here. It works like this: First I get the name. Then, if my search for him is successful, I'm prepared to leave your family alone. Who knows, if I'm really happy with the information you're about to give me I might even consider a little monetary gift to your wife.

"Not that *you* deserve it, but maybe your wife is innocent and needs to be rewarded for putting up with a slimeball like you."

Dhruv shrugged. "It is nothing to me. I will never leave here to see my mother again, and my wife does not have the money now. She can't be worse off than she is already.

"The name is Kabir Patel."

Patel was one of the most common names in India. It would be like trying to find John Smith in the US or UK. He prompted for more details, got the address, and was told that Patel was a member of D-Company.

Rex was a man of his word. If he found the right man, he'd deliver a thousand dollars to Mrs. Dhruv.

"Where will I find your wife?"

Dhruv declined to give his wife's name or address.

"Okay, no worries. I'll find her if I need to."

Rex left the room, informed a nearby jailer he was done, and went out to the van.

Digger's head was all the way out the partially rolled-down window.

"Sorry, boy. I know it's hot. Let's go find a place where you can have a run and some cold water."

The prison was a couple of miles out from the city limits, and there was a nearby park Rex had made note of as he passed it earlier. The visit had taken longer than he'd hoped, and he still had some investigation to do before he found the target, but Digger's toilet needs were urgent, and they both needed food. Rex needed a bucket of coffee, too, because he planned to drive through the night.

Eight

REX AND DIGGER were on the road again by six that evening, with the cooler full of snacks and water, and a large to-go cup of coffee for Rex. He'd found a pet shop as well, and finally made good on his promise to let Digger ride in the front seat. Digger didn't seem to mind the new harness. Rex had to admit it was better to have a companion in the front seat next to him instead of an empty space.

His GPS advised him it was just over fourteen hundred kilometers to Mumbai, and it would take nearly twenty-four hours to get there, at the posted speed limits. He calculated the miles – about eight-hundred and seventy. He figured he could make that in under twenty hours if he could stay awake.

"Digger don't let me sleep, okay?" He didn't think the dog could understand that statement. Commands were supposed to be positive, not negative, but he'd taken to speaking to the dog like he would to a human. He was family after all. Most of the time, it was just about speaking aloud, as if he had a human companion. He didn't expect replies or understanding. Sometimes, though, Digger surprised him with a sound or facial expression or motion just at the right moment which always left Rex with the impression he understood.

Every few minutes at first, the GPS voice, which he'd programmed to be a pleasant female voice with a British accent, would tell him to take this turn or that, or notify him there was a gas station on the left or right in a few kilometers. As he passed Jaipur, however, he could see that he had a long stretch with no directions before 'she' would speak again. By then, it was ten p.m., and though he wasn't sleepy yet, he knew he'd better have another coffee. He pulled into the gas station, let Digger out, and filled the tank. His business inside concluded, he got back into the car with another large take-out coffee and prepared for the long, dark, drive ahead.

He hadn't factored stops into his travel time, so he tried to make up the time by ignoring the speed limit, but he was at times forced to slow down through long stretches of road construction zones, though there were no workers in the middle of the night. It kept him on his toes, fortunately, since Digger was neglecting his companionship duties for long naps. The dog woke only when they had to make another stop for gas and coffee.

It was just past midafternoon when they drove past the first houses on the northern edge of the sprawling city of Mumbai. It took another hour to wend his way through the tangle of streets to the address Dhruv had given.

He parked and reconnoitered. The building was tall, no doubt housing the commercial interest on the ground floor and an apartment complex above. There didn't seem to be a back door on the ground floor.

Rex gave his approach some thought as he watched the front of the building. The mobster seemed to be doing brisk business. The sign said it was a tobacconist shop. Cash transactions only, it appeared. The clientele appeared well-heeled. The men and women who went in wore modern clothing rather than the traditional styles favored in the northern villages.

Money laundering.

Rex couldn't see a way to enter and confront the owner without the risk of causing a public scene. There were too many 'customers'.

Promptly as six p.m., a last handful of customers came out the door one after the other and the lights went out in the shop.

Rex was relieved.

Digger was getting restless, and they both could use some food, but first he wanted to question the proprietor.

However, no one else came out after someone he couldn't see on the inside flipped the Open sign to Closed.

***

REX WAS ABOUT to get out of the van when his attention was drawn to a commotion a few doors from the shop he was watching. He looked over and saw a man dressed in jeans, cotton shirt, and black denim jacket, surrounded by what looked like a bunch of rough guys. As he watched, one of them hit the man in the denim jacket with a cricket bat between the shoulders. He went down, and three of the thugs jumped on him, punching, and yelling. Two of them, one short and fat the other tall and skinny, remained on their feet dancing around kicking at their victim.

The man in the denim jacket was hopelessly outnumbered and if the attack continued he would soon be dead. Rex jumped out of the van with Digger on his heels. A desperate scream rang out, and he broke into a run. Digger shot forward like a bullet out of a gun. By the time Rex got to the scene, Digger already had the short fat man by the arm, holding on as he screamed in shock, shaking him, and trying to get away. The tall skinny one was hightailing it down the street, apparently wanting none of the fight if a dog was involved.

Rex yanked up the first guy he could get a hand on from the scrum on the ground. He held him by the front of his shirt and clocked him with a vicious right hook, which lifted him off his feet and smashed the back of his head into the wall behind him, where he slowly slithered to the ground. Minus a few of his teeth.

One down, two to go.

Digger's screaming fat man finally broke free, turned and followed the skinny man down the road. Digger didn't give chase. The fight was still on, so he ignored the retreating thug and went for one of those on the ground, a man with a red shirt, grabbed him by the leg and started pulling him away.

Rex reached into the pile for another one, picked him up by his hair, but as he drew back his fist to land an almighty punch, the guy yelled "Police!" Rex saw it was the man with the denim jacket, the victim.

He didn't have time to ask for a badge. The last man on the ground was rising in his direction with a huge knife in his right hand. Rex let go of the guy's hair and kicked the guy with the knife in the nuts. His contribution to India's birth control efforts. As the man doubled over, Rex stepped up and hit him with the right knee in the face. Game over for this hooligan.

Rex looked around to see if there were more and saw the man who yelled that he was a policeman chasing after the fat man waddling down the street. He was about thirty yards away. Rex pointed at the fleeing man and said to Digger, "Get him!"

Digger let go of the man with the red shirt and headed down the street. Rex took a step towards the man in the red shirt who was now on all fours trying to get to his feet and kicked him in the face, breaking his jaw and laying him out flat on his back on the pavement.

The fight was over.

Rex looked down the road and saw Digger had passed the policeman and caught up with fat man, jumped from about two yards away and caught the poor sod by the same arm he had him with before. The guy went down face first onto the pavement and Digger jumped onto his back and grabbed him by the neck.

The policeman caught up with the two of them but stopped a few yards away, too scared to get near the growling dog and its prey.

Rex was sure his three guys would not move soon, so he followed Digger and the 'policeman'.

"Digger! Leave it!" he shouted.

Digger let go and stood back, allowing the policeman to get his hands on fat man. The policeman grabbed fat man by his healthy arm and hoisted him to his feet and shoved him back toward Rex. Fat man was moaning and groaning, sporting a lacerated arm and very little skin on the right side of his face.

"Thanks for the help. Good dog you have there. Is she licensed? You can't have an attack dog here, even though I'm grateful to her and you." The policeman said between heavy breaths.

"She's a he," Rex corrected.

"Huh?"

"The dog is male not female."

The policeman looked at Rex then at Digger and apologized.

"And yes, he's licensed," Rex said. "My service dog, not an attack dog." He started to reach into his pocket.

"I'll take your word for it," the cop said. "I'm lucky you were here. As you can probably guess, I'm undercover. Or I was. Someone ratted me out, and these guys were going to kill me and make it look like a bad drug deal. I owe you and your dog my life."

"It's cool," Rex said. "I don't much like drug dealers, and I really don't like cowards who send five guys to kill just one. It really isn't sporting."

The cop laughed. "You're right. Now I need to ask you to stay here while I call for backup to pick these dirtbags up. You'll need to make a statement."

Rex wasn't particularly keen to get involved with the police. However, it would only create suspicion if he refused to give a statement. Realizing there wasn't much he could do about it, he said, "Okay."

Back at the spot where Rex had felled three of the attackers, they found them all still unconscious. Fat man was shoved to the ground, face down, hands behind his head, and told to stay that way.

"Guard," Rex said to Digger.

Digger took up a position with his front legs on fat man's back, which kept him unmoving and quiet.

"Funny command for a service dog," the cop remarked.

"Yeah. Well, sometimes he needs to guard me," Rex replied.

Within fifteen minutes, two police cars arrived, and the would-be murderers were cuffed and stuffed into the back. The undercover officer hitched a ride with Rex and Digger.

***

WHEN THEY GOT to the police station, Rex was offered some coffee. He took one sip and decided it was probably the worst coffee he ever had. He thanked the person and took another sip. It wouldn't alleviate his hunger, but it had caffeine in it and that's what he needed. He'd been awake since early the previous morning, and it would help keep him that way. He and Digger were sitting in an interview room when the undercover cop came in and closed the door.

"We didn't introduce ourselves. I'm Aarav Patel. And you are?"

"Randall Dalvi," Rex answered smoothly. It was the ID he was carrying. He just hoped the paper would stand up to examination if it was needed. He couldn't help but notice that the officer had the same last name as the gangster he was hunting.

Hopefully not related.

"Interesting name. I'd have thought you were British, from your accent." Patel said.

"I am. My parents emigrated before I was born."

"Okay. Now I'd like to take your statement. How did it happen you were there when those guys jumped me?"

Rex began to spin a story about hearing the tobacconist shop had the best cigars and arriving just in time to see the shop close. "I was just about to drive away when I saw the scuffle in my rearview mirror," he concluded. "You know the rest."

Aarav, whose name meant 'peaceful and wisdom', nodded but gave Rex a knowing look. "And your service dog just happens to know how to take down a dangerous criminal."

"Yes. Lucky, that, wouldn't you say?"

"Right. Very lucky, I would say."

Rex almost laughed, the guy's tone was so sardonic.

Aarav looked at the closed door and lowered his voice.

"Mr. Dalvi, seriously, I'm grateful that you came to my rescue. I've also been a policeman for long enough to know there's more to your story, but you seem to be an honorable man. At least in this case you were on the right side of the law. I won't trouble you. If there's ever anything I can do for you…"

Rex smiled. "Now that you mention it. There is one thing. Do you know who owns that tobacconist shop? Does he run it himself? I need to talk to him."

The cop shook his head. "I know him, and yeah, he's there some of the time. He's dirty, we know it and we've been trying for a long time, but we can't pin anything on him. You don't want to do business with him, or even talk to him. He's bad news. You won't be able to get close to him, anyway. He keeps four bodyguards around him all the time."

"I want to talk to him about a business deal he recently made."

The cop shook his head again. "Bad news, I'm telling you. I just hope you don't intend to do business with him. That would land you on our watch list."

"Nope. No such intentions, I just want some information from him and I'll be on my way. I was waiting for him to leave his establishment," Rex said. "But I don't think he came out. Is there another way out of the shop?"

"The shop has a hallway in back that leads to the apartments above. He didn't come out – just went home. He lives up there. You'd have to go through the bodyguards to get to him. Suicide mission."

Rex had been up since early the previous morning. He didn't think four bodyguards would be a problem, even without Digger. With Digger, it would be a piece of cake. But he was hungry and tired, not at his best, and getting himself injured or killed wouldn't help Rehka. He considered the situation for almost a minute, with the cop staring at him, wanting to know his business with the owner, no doubt.

"If they're anything like those clowns who attacked you earlier, I doubt I'll have a problem," he said looking at Digger. But Digger didn't respond.

"They aren't. Trust me, you don't want to take them on alone. Those guys are big and mean."

"I'll cross that bridge when I come to it," Rex said. "Besides I am on a peaceful mission, I just need some information. That's all.

"Can you recommend a place to stay and maybe someplace to eat around here? My business with him will keep until morning."

The cop named a hotel and told Rex they had a good kitchen.

"Thanks, man. I'm beat. I'm going to check in and rest tonight. But I could use some help tomorrow."

"I'll meet you there at eight. The shop doesn't open until nine, but maybe you'll get lucky and see your man on the way to breakfast."

"Thanks. Much appreciated."

Nine

REX WAS ABLE to get a room where he could have Digger with him. He ordered food from room service and gave Digger his rations. Too tired to argue, he let Digger have half his food, showered, and then crawled into the bed at an unfashionably early hour. He set an alarm on his watch, in case catching up on missed sleep kept him too far under to sense the time.

At six a.m., he woke refreshed, pulled on his clothes and went in search of a place to eat on an outside table, where Digger could be next to him. This time, he ordered a double breakfast, convinced Digger would talk him out of half of it again. He wasn't disappointed. The first chance he got, he needed to put his foot down about the food situation. Digger may not understand it, but it was for his own good.

He arrived at the spot where he was to meet the cop at seven a.m., an hour early. He wanted to check things out before the cop arrived. He immediately noticed that although the sign still said closed, people were coming out the door in droves.

Rex reached under the dashboard, below the steering, unclipped a part of the panel and retrieved his Sig Sauer P226 where he'd stuck it with Velcro tape. He checked that the gun was loaded and put in the small of his back where it was covered by his denim jacket.

During a lull in the traffic coming out of the building, he went to the door and tugged it open.

Inside, another door immediately to the right led into the tobacco shop. However, the hallway ran back the full depth of the building, and on the other side from the shop, halfway back, two sets of elevators discharged a steady stream of residents. He walked to the end of the hall and discovered it teed into another hall leading to the right, behind the tobacco shop, and to the left, where it ended in a locked exit door.

Rex had noticed the notch in the wall when he'd checked for a back door, but he hadn't thought it led from the shop – it was almost half a block away. Now he could see that, if one had the key, one could enter the shop, come out in the hallway, and exit through that other door unseen.

Rex mentally kicked himself. For all he knew, his target had left by that way the previous night. He didn't want to pick the lock, alerting anyone who had a key that there was an intruder in the building. Instead, he retraced his steps, counting them for each leg of the journey, and walked to the end of the block where he'd gone around the night before. He entered the narrow opening and walked up the alleyway to the notch he'd observed yesterday, counting his steps again. He'd been right. The notch was approximately where he'd end up if he'd been able to go through the locked door. It had a door in it, oriented in the right direction.

Now he didn't know whether his target was in the building or not. He walked back around to wait for the cop.

The cop was right on time, which Rex had learned was a rarity in this country. He greeted Rex with another caution. "I can't condone violence, you understand. We have nothing concrete on this man. It wouldn't be proper for me to engage in a fight with him. Or his bodyguards," he added. Then he winked.

"I wouldn't ask you to. Just watch the back door and let me know if I miss him, all right?"

"Okay," said the cop.

Rex grinned. "You knew there was a back door. Why didn't you tell me?"

The cop shrugged. "I thought you knew."

Another time, Rex might have set him straight, but he'd been bone-tired the day before. He missed something obvious.

You're on a mission Dalton, better shape up.

He watched the cop walk toward the end of the street and turn the corner. He was still dressed in street clothes, not a uniform. It was a good thing. They'd stood here talking in full view of many apartment windows. He could only hope that they hadn't raised any suspicions.

Rex melted into a shadow on the other side of the street, where he could loiter unseen. Digger wriggled in behind him and lay down at his feet, between his heels and the wall. It made Rex have to lean a little further than he liked, but at least the dog wasn't conspicuous that way. Rex crossed his arms and waited.

Another wave of people exited the building, maybe going to jobs that started later, or maybe the others were heading out early for breakfast. None of them seemed to be a criminal mastermind, but who was to say? Rex didn't know what the guy looked like, but the chances were high that he wouldn't exit the building without his bodyguards, and Rex hadn't seen anyone with four people who seemed to be guarding him. A few people also entered.

Precisely at nine, the disembodied hand reached for the sign and flipped it again. The shop was open for business. That was Rex's cue to go in, before the shop got busy.

A bell tinkled as he stepped into the shop through the interior door. Rex couldn't see anyone but heard a female voice asking if she could help him. He searched for her. Rounding the corner of a bank of shelves, he found himself face-to-face, or rather face to his chest, with a diminutive Indian girl, maybe eighteen he reckoned. He'd expected a man, and one who was at least his size. The surprise left him stumbling for words for a moment. "I… uh…"

The girl switched to English. "May I help you?" she said again. Rex realized he'd left himself at a disadvantage by blurting out English words. To cover, he continued in English, but with a London accent.

"I'd like to speak to the proprietor. That is, to the owner, if they are not one and the same." He tried an owlish look, working himself into the persona of an Oxford don, or what he thought one would say.

The girl didn't answer. Instead, she was staring at Digger as if she'd never seen a dog before.

"My service dog," Rex explained. He tightened his hand on Digger's leash, taking up a bit of slack.

"I see. I'm sorry, the proprietor, who is the owner, yes, is not here. May I help you?" The third time she asked.

Rex had finally regained his composure. He asked for a pack of Indian-made cigarettes and, while the girl was getting them, asked when the owner might be back.

The bell tinkled again, and Rex turned to see a grossly obese Indian man of about forty waddle in. "I'm Kabir Patel, the owner," he said in English. "How may I help you?"

He must have heard me ask her. And what's with this 'how may I help you?' Is that the only English they know?

Rex switched to Hindi. "I'd like to speak to you on a matter of some delicacy."

He got no further before the man brushed past him and approached the girl. He bent and whispered into her ear, and then kissed her on the mouth. From her expression, she was as disgusted by it as Rex was. But she nodded and left without another word to Rex.

"I have sent her on a small errand. She'll be back in a moment. What is the nature of your business?"

"Rehka Gyan," he said, "Where is she?"

"I'm sorry, but I don't know who you're talking about." The guy didn't break a sweat, and his expression gave away nothing. Maybe he was telling the truth, maybe not. Rex didn't think so, and he wasn't in the mood to play games.

"I think you do. Let's go up to your apartment and see if she's there."

It was a calculated risk. The guy's bodyguards were somewhere nearby, he assumed, but they weren't in the shop. Maybe the errand the girl had been sent on was to collect them to come and get rid of Rex. The truth was, it would be better if they were there. He'd rather have them where he could see them.

The fat guy's mouth twitched.

Almost a smile. So, the bodyguards are up there.

Rex kept his gaze steady. Digger's low growl was enough to let the crime boss know the suggestion was not merely a suggestion.

"All right," he said. "Let's go to my apartment. Perhaps I can convince you you're mistaken."

He waddled out to the hall again, the bell in the empty shop tinkling as he opened the door.

Rex wasn't concerned about the business. The girl would be back soon enough, he reckoned. From what he'd seen, she might need rescuing, too, but first, Rehka.

He followed the man out and down the hall toward the elevators. They waited a minute or so, and then the doors opened, disgorging the girl and yes, four large men with bulky muscles, in turbans.

Why is it that criminals always pick bodybuilders to protect them? As if steroid infused muscles somehow made them good guards.

The fat man spoke in rapid Dravidian, which Rex now knew was the dialect spoken by most of Gyan's family, thanks to the helpful clerk back in Bilaspur he'd asked while getting supplies for his trip. The fat guy had told his guards to get out of the elevator, and then crowd back in after he and 'the mark' had stepped in.

The guards obeyed and got out, followed by the girl. Patel told her to go back to the shop, speaking Hindi this time. Then he stepped into the elevator holding his arm out to keep the door open and gesture for Rex to follow.

Rex had already decided those steroidal boneheads weren't getting back into the elevator if he had anything to say about it. Trusting Digger to act without a command, he turned himself around and delivered a forceful chop with the side of his right hand to the throat of the guard closest to him. The others didn't have a chance to move before the first man was out of commission, gulping for air, sinking into unconsciousness.

Digger went into action. He leaped for the throat of one of the others, bearing him down to the ground as he landed. Rex took advantage of the confusion to land a well-placed punch on the tip of the chin of the third guard, with his left hand. Just then, the fourth guard grabbed him from behind.

With Digger still engaged with his target, Rex had to resort to a time-honored street fight move to defend against the guy who was trying to crush him in a powerful bear hug from behind. A head-butt.

The arms surrounding him fell away, and the guy they were attached to dropped like he'd been pole-axed. Rex might have a headache later, but his target had a broken nose and was unconscious. He spared a look at Digger, decided he was doing fine, and turned back to the guy he'd punched on the chin. He was trying to get up, but his legs were too wobbly to carry his weight, and the elevator doors were trying to close. Rex was in the way.

Fat dude, Patel, was wringing his hands. He probably hadn't had to fight since he came up from the ranks, so Rex ignored him.

He stepped over to Digger and his man and told Digger to leave it. Digger let go and stepped back. The man tried to get to his feet, but Rex kicked him in the side of his head and he slumped to the floor.

But a scream from practically right under him gave him assurance that Digger was now engaged with the guy he'd punched on the chin.

"Excuse me for just a moment, while I get the trash out of the way," he said to the boss. He turned and helped Digger drag the guy out of the doorway and just for good measure he kicked him in the ribs. The man fell to the floor and curled up in pain. Then Rex called to Digger, "Guard" and stepped back into the elevator and hit the Close Door button.

"Good, now we can go to your apartment. What floor?" he said politely to the boss.

The guy folded. Fainted dead away, without answering.

"Shit," said Rex. He made a guess that a guy with the means to have bodyguards around him all the time would probably have the top floor. Maybe it was a penthouse, like back in the States. He shrugged and pushed the button for the highest floor, then he turned and started trying to revive the bastard.

When the elevator stopped, and the door opened, Rex had only managed to partially revive Patel. He was too heavy for Rex to even drag him out, so Rex pushed the button to keep the doors open and slapped him sharply. That made him open his eyes.

He gasped. "Where... Who?"

Rex grinned. "Your place, and I'm your worst nightmare. Get up." Ever since watching Rambo III, he had always wanted to say that part about the worst nightmare.

Patel rolled onto his side and struggled to push himself to his feet. Rex helped by grabbing the back of his collar and pulling, which caused Patel to start gagging and choking. He found the strength to shove himself to standing in a hurry after that.

"Good job. Now, move your fat ass to your apartment."

Rex shoved Patel out of the elevator. Stumbling, Patel caught himself on the opposite wall and looked around to get his bearings. As Rex had guessed, there was only one large apartment on this floor. Patel staggered to the door and reached in his pocket for a key.

"I'll take that," Rex demanded in a whisper.

Very quietly, he unlocked the door and turned the knob gently, so that not even a click betrayed his presence. He drew his gun from the back of his pants, pointed it at Patel, and gestured with it for him to go in first. With his other hand, he mimed zipping his lips.

Patel nodded and pressed his lips together. He started toward the door, and as soon as his bulk was directly in front of it, Rex propelled him in with a shove to his back. Rex followed, his gun ready, sweeping the room for threats.

"There's no one here," Patel protested.

"We'll see." Steering his captive with one hand, Rex cleared the rooms. Patel had been telling the truth. No one else was there.

Patel was gaining a little confidence, though. He turned toward Rex, raised his hands, and backed away from the gun. "What do you want?"

"Rehka Gyan. That leech, Dhruv, sold her to you, or maybe you took her when he was jailed. Where is she?"

"I don't know who you're talking about."

Rex was getting tired of this dodge. He pointed the gun at Patel's nose. "What have you done with her?"

Patel's hands shot higher into the air. "All right! Don't shoot. You're too late. I sold her."

"To whom and when?"

"A few weeks ago."

"Listen Patel, I don't have the time or patience for your bullshit. I'm not going to ask you again. Start talking, tell me the whole story and nothing but the whole story or your brains will decorate the wall behind you."

Patel shivered and started talking. "Dhruv owed me money. I took the girl as payment, but I sold her to a Saudi friend of mine. She's probably now in his harem. He enjoyed her performance so much that he overlooked the fact she was no longer a virgin. He took her as a pleasure wife."

Rex literally saw red. The casual and arrogant way Patel revealed Rehka's rape pushed all of Rex's buttons. He still held the gun pointing at Patel in his right hand, but his left fist shot out and landed squarely on Patel's fat, ugly nose. Blood sprayed, and Patel went down, but Rex wasn't through. He dropped the gun on a nearby chair and went to work.

He'd encountered pure evil before and kept his cool even while he meted out justice. He'd exposed a child pornographer, killed drug dealers, terrorists, arms dealers, and anyone who helped them, all in the name of avenging the deaths of his family and protecting his country. But this time, he could contain his rage only long enough to get the name of the Saudi, before he let it loose.

He kicked Patel in the ribs and stomped on him where his legs met his torso. Patel curled into a fetal position and Rex landed a kick to his kidneys. He didn't stop until Patel stopped screaming.

Rex stood back, breathing heavily, both fists clenched, and looked at the wreck of a body at his feet. Patel was still breathing.

Good. They can't get me for murder, at least not yet.

Rex picked up his gun and looked at it. Pointed it at the quivering lump of flesh on the floor. Put just enough force on the trigger that another twitch would fire it.

And then, he took his finger off the trigger and turned away.

The bastard wasn't worth it. If he took the shot, the other Patel – his new cop friend – would hear. He'd have no choice but to arrest Rex, and then Rehka would be enslaved in a Saudi harem forever, or until she committed suicide. Rex landed one last kick to Patel's face which broke his jaw in a few places, wringing a gurgle from him.

"You'll be having your food through a straw for the next six months asshole. It might just help with your obesity issue. You can thank me later." Rex hissed as he turned and left.

He took the elevator down and found Digger still guarding the casualties. "Stay. Guard," he said, and walked out to find Aarav.

"I happened upon a big mess inside," he said. "I have no idea how it came about and who caused it. When I got here that's what I found. One thing is plain as daylight — someone out there must have a serious grudge against your namesake."

The two of them went inside, and Patel just shook his head at the carnage. He looked at Rex inquisitorially.

"I'm afraid I won't be of much help to solve this one. Like I said, I got here after the fact. And I've got a plane to catch, so I won't be able to stay for a statement. Although I think I just gave you one — I don't know what happened. I take it that would be okay with you then if Digger and I leave now?"

"I'll call for backup. Go on, get out of here."

Rex said, "Digger, come." He and Digger walked out the door, leaving Aarav to scratch his head and figure out how to explain what had happened.

If Rex had looked back, he would've seen a smile on Aarav's face.

TEN

REX WAS SPEAKING metaphorically when he said he had a plane to catch. The truth was that he had no ID that would get Digger into Saudi Arabia without a long quarantine, if at all. The Saudis recognized only Seeing-Eye and Hearing dogs, not service dogs for the 'invisible' maladies, like the PTSD that Digger's papers claimed. In fact, they had gone so far as to ban ownership of dogs as pets in 2008, but a quick check of the internet revealed that was no longer the case.

What Rex needed was a new identity, and various documents for Digger that included valid health and vaccination certificates, which he could provide thanks to having Digger checked by a veterinarian as soon as he'd reached India. Other documents Saudi Arabia required, he'd have to have created by the same forger who'd create his. Using the forger he'd used before wasn't an option. Everything in India was for sale – including the intel that a savvy guy with a big roll of money had entered the country with no ID and paid for a complete legend, only to be back a month or so later looking for a new one.

The bottom line? He had to find a new forger, one as good as the old one, and he had to give the guy enough time to create flawless papers. Rex went back to his hotel to shower, change clothes, and cool off. He hadn't broken a sweat for his efforts in beating Patel and his goons, but his rage had left him tense and unsettled.

A warm shower followed by a cool rinse put him in a better frame of mind. Digger needed a walk, so Rex took him downstairs and let him run on the grounds of the hotel while he thought about the quickest way to find a good forger. Then he had an idea. Patel – the cop, not the gangster – would probably know of someone. He already knew Rex wasn't what he claimed to be, but he'd chosen to keep that to himself, partly in gratitude for Rex and Digger saving his life. Just maybe, it was also partly because he suspected Rex could get things done that the police couldn't. What would it hurt to ask him? Asking wasn't a crime.

Rex took out his phone, looked up the number of the police station where he'd given his statement the evening before, and dialed. When the phone was answered, he asked for detective Aarav Patel.

"He's tied up with a case," came the answer.

"Will he be long?" Rex asked. "I just have a quick question."

"I'll give him the message. Right now, he's with the captain. There was some gang violence early this morning and five members of D-Company were badly beaten." The man on the other end of the phone sounded like he was delighted to share the news.

"Okay, I'll call back."

"I could take your number, have him call when he's free."

"That's okay."

Rex was willing to take a chance that Patel would still help him after being left in a precarious situation. But not so big a chance that he'd hand out his cell number on a silver platter to anyone who asked.

He called Digger, went back to his room, and waited an hour.

This time, he was transferred to Aarav Patel right away.

"Aarav, it's Randall."

"Please don't tell me you have stumbled upon another half dozen beaten up crime syndicate members. I had a hard-enough time explaining the last five. I thought you would be on a plane by now." Patel laughed.

"That's the reason for my call. You see, that plane I need to catch. It will take me out of the country."

"I would hope so." Patel chuckled. "What can I do to get you on it as quickly as possible?"

"I need someone to help me with papers… for me and my dog," Rex said.

"Ah, that kind of papers. Just a moment."

Rex heard footsteps and then a door closing, before Patel came back.

"You mean some artwork, right?" Patel said, emphasizing 'artwork'.

"You got that right."

"Would you be coming back to India when your errand is finished?"

"Yes."

"If I were to give you a name, would you be willing to drop off the, ah, papers to me, when you're done with them?"

With only a little regret, Rex said, "Sorry, man, I don't think I could do that."

"It was worth the asking." Patel exhaled. "Okay, we know this man is an *artist*. We just can't get any evidence against him. It tends to walk out the door with his customers.

"Is your errand something I'd approve of?"

Rex answered, "I'm hundred percent sure you would. You have my word on that."

Patel sighed. "I've broken more laws in the less than twenty-four hours I've known you than all of my life to this point. What's one more?" He gave Rex the name and address. "Don't get me in trouble, my friend."

"No chance. And thank you." Rex ended the call.

"Come on, buddy, we have an urgent assignment," he said to Digger.

***

THE NEW FORGER confirmed Rex's guess that he'd need several days to complete the work. In fact, he'd said a week. Rex offered a premium on top of the already expensive order if he could do it in three days. The extra money did the trick, and his order was fast-tracked.

While he waited, he gathered the gear he wanted to take with him. It felt familiar. He bought a computer carrying case and a camera bag. One of his weapons had a few pieces that could be broken down and camouflaged as camera or computer parts. What couldn't be camouflaged that way, he concealed in a lead case marked 'film'.

At a shop that had the same name as the one in New Delhi where he'd found Digger's kongs, he bought a large crate for the flight. Rex was nervous about how Digger would react to the crate, but it was a necessary evil. Digger looked it over when Rex put it in the back of the van, but he didn't growl at it. That was a plus.

Rex inspected Digger's combat gear, including the harness with the night-vision camera, and decided it was still in decent shape. Using the make and model name of the camera, he researched what software he'd need to interface with it on his new iPad and installed it. That night, he got Digger into his gear and took him out for a test run. It worked perfectly.

Next was deciding how to explain his night-vision goggles, if anyone asked. Chances were that if everything else was in order, an x-ray wouldn't flag them. If it did, Rex would have a story ready. Something along the lines of needing the night vision gear to take pictures out in the desert at night time.

Getting his gear in proper order to take with him also put him in mind of what he wouldn't need – or necessarily want – to have with him on the trip. The laptop and hard drives he'd taken from the Afghani drug lord, for example. He hadn't finished exploring the information in them and probably wouldn't finish for a good long time. Some of it didn't need immediate action, but he might want to act on it later. However, he wouldn't be doing anything with them until he got back. It would be too hot for them in the van in airport parking, not to mention the potential for theft. He started a checklist, and the first thing on it was to find out what bank might have a large enough safety deposit box for the hard drives.

Then there was the question of his cash, some of which he'd need with him, but certainly not the bulk of two-hundred-thousand dollars that remained. He'd been frugal except for the purchase price of the van and of his and Digger's two sets of identity papers. He made no apology to himself for spending on those – the best was required and came at a price. He decided to deposit the cash in several international banks, so the amount would not be questioned anywhere, and he'd be able to access it in almost any country.

Finally, the diamonds. It was easy enough to place them in a safety deposit box, but he decided perhaps not the same one as the hard drives would occupy. Nor in a bank where he also had a major cash account. Those, he'd put in a Deutsch bank safety deposit and leave just a few hundred dollars in a checking account there. When he got back, he'd look for a buyer. He'd carried them around long enough. It was time to turn them into a more useful asset – cash.

When all that was done, he started researching the Saudi who'd acquired Rehka's bond and learned how he was connected to the royal family and where he lived. The connection to the royals was tenuous. He was probably about somewhere around number three hundred in the line of succession, but still wealthy beyond any reasonable measure.

By the time the new ID and Digger's extra papers were ready, so was Rex. He knew where he was going and who to see, his equipment and his partner, Digger, were in top condition, and he had a ticket for the next flight to Riyadh.

Eleven

REX NEEDN'T HAVE worried about Digger's reaction to traveling in a crate on a plane. Whether it was because he recognized they were at an airport and realized they were going to a new place or because Trevor had trained him well, he made no objection to being placed in it directly from the van. Rex had obtained a flat-bedded luggage cart and loaded the crate, his duffel bag and carry-on on it.

Then he opened the crate's door and said, "Get in, Digger." To his surprise and gratification, Digger leaped over the seat back into the now-cleared cargo space and jumped to the ground before climbing onto the luggage cart and walking calmly into the crate.

"Sorry, buddy, but I have to close the door. Will you be okay?"

Digger's expression couldn't be described as a smile, Rex thought, but he didn't look upset, either. His mouth was open, tongue hanging out, but it wasn't stretched into that wide, happy smile Rex associated with assent. It was going to be okay, though, at least until he had to surrender Digger to the baggage handlers to be placed in a cargo hold.

Rex left the van in a long-term parking area and paid in advance for a week. He hoped the search for Rehka wouldn't take that long, but he didn't want to advertise when he'd be back. If it took longer, he'd pay online for more time. Mumbai's airport was brand-new, and it boasted not only everything anyone would want in an airport, but also it was the most beautiful airport Rex had ever seen.

Shining floors of granite or marble tile, Rex didn't know or care about the difference, reflected the interesting ceilings. In the concourses, giant petals disbursed the indirect lighting in some places. In others, the petals were pierced with lattice-work, and the light above guided the pedestrians below. Lounges that punctuated the area could have been directly transported there from luxury hotels. Room dividers of lace-like panels, richly-upholstered furniture in red, gold, and amber colors provided a visual feast, along with artwork and even shelves bearing books and small sculptures.

Rex was tempted to stop at every shelf to examine what looked like genuine historic artifacts, but he was prompted by overhead announcements to hurry along. His flight wouldn't wait for him to explore the opulent acres of airport terminal.

Six weeks ago, Rex wouldn't have been able to imagine that he'd ever allow a dog to get close to him, let alone own a dog, or rather that a dog would own him. Even four weeks ago, he and Digger were so often at odds with each other he wouldn't have imagined he'd now miss Digger if they were apart for four hours, as they would be on this flight. As it was, he surprised himself when he admitted to being grateful as he took his seat in the aircraft that the forged papers held up and he'd see the pooch when they arrived in Riyadh. In his carryon, he had one of Digger's kongs already stuffed with special treats of dried meat to be given to him as soon as practicable after they've landed, to make up for having to ride in the cargo section.

Rex exercised his motto – sleep when you can, you never know when you will get the next chance – to spend most of the flight in slumber. He watched out the window only long enough to get a glimpse of the Arabian Sea far below before closing his eyes and falling instantly asleep. Halfway through the flight, he woke long enough to request a sparkling water with a twist of lime to hydrate as the plane passed over the coast of Oman, but by the time they were in the airspace of the United Arab Emirates, he was asleep again. An hour later, he woke to the captain announcing in Arabic, Hindi, and English that they were on the glide path to Riyadh.

King Khalid International Airport proved to be as impressive as the airport in Mumbai, though not to Rex's eyes quite as beautiful. The theme here was shades of white and desert tans, with the décor supplied by greenery that couldn't have survived in the harsh conditions outside. One wall of large copper plates into which sculptures of enormous silver-colored hands intrigued him. Were the positions of the fingers saying something in sign language perhaps? He had no time to contemplate it. Digger was waiting for him in baggage claim and was no doubt waiting to be released from the confines of the cage.

On his way over to the baggage area, he'd had time to think about why Digger was so willing to go into the crate earlier. Obviously, the dog had flown before. Trevor had told him so. In fact, Trevor had told him stories of parachuting on training and real missions into target areas with Digger strapped to his chest. He was an old hand at flying, and Rex guessed that a crate had been involved at least some of the time, though perhaps not always on military planes. Rex had even remembered Trevor telling him about a few high altitude-low opening, known as HALO, jumps where they both had to wear oxygen masks. Yes, Digger had his own oxygen mask, but no more, as Rex had left it at Phoenix headquarters in Kabul, along with most of his own gear and everything Digger hadn't been wearing on the night of the fateful mission.

It didn't matter. He didn't anticipate any HALO or other parachute jumps now. And if there was ever an occasion when one would be required, he'd find a way to get the equipment to do it, including an oxygen mask for Digger.

Rex eventually arrived at the baggage claim, where Digger spotted him first and let out a yip, which attracted Rex's attention. Immediately followed by a couple of higher yips from two chihuahuas in much smaller crates chiming in. Rex looked in the direction of the noise and made eye contact with Digger. The spike of relief and pleasure he felt when he saw Digger was safe and sound was new to him but not entirely surprising.

"Hey, boy! I'll have you out of jail in just a few minutes," he called.

Digger relaxed his muzzle and let his tongue loll out.

Rex located his duffle bag quickly and secured a cart to carry everything again. Digger would have to stay in the crate until they picked up the rental vehicle Rex had pre-ordered, a roomy SUV like the American Ford Explorer, with plenty of cargo space. Rex didn't know whether he'd need the four-wheel drive, or whether he'd need all that room, for that matter. But he suspected he'd need to get out of the country without parading Rehka through an international airport. The SUV was perfect for a border crossing in a remote area, if that became necessary.

However, those were things he'd worry about later, he first had to find her.

The minor Saudi prince that Kabir Patel had sold Rehka's bond to lived in Dammam, a lovely city on the Persian Gulf, about an hour by air from Riyadh. Rex could have flown directly there, but he didn't want to use the ID he'd flown in with while he searched for the Saudi. He'd switch back to the ID he'd been using in India instead. It was as good a cover as any, and if he ran into trouble, he'd still have the new one to help him get out of the country. So, no flights. He'd do the four-hour drive instead.

Pushing his luggage cart through the nearly-empty airport, he wondered where all the travelers were. Most of the nicer restaurants were closed, too, and he was hungry and so was Digger. He shrugged. They wouldn't let him bring the cart in with Digger, anyway. Best to grab something from one of the convenience shops in the airport. Leaving the cart outside the wide opening that served as an entrance to the next one he saw, he bought a road map in case his cell phone couldn't find a signal in the wide-open desert, several bottles of water, and two pre-made sandwiches.

Rex found the car rental counter and handed over his ID for the clerk to match up with his reservation.

"Everything is in order, sir. You may take the shuttle to our lot. Your vehicle is waiting there."

Rex thanked the man, accepted the return of his ID and a receipt, and pushed his cart out the door, where a shuttle waited. By the time they reached the rental car lot and he took delivery of his vehicle, his stomach was growling loudly enough he thought others might be able to hear it. But he waited to eat. Digger needed a run, so he'd eat in a park, if he could find one.

Once inside the vehicle he used his Swiss Army knife, which he had in his luggage, to quickly remove the inside cover of the side panel of the driver's door and hid his second ID, some cash, and the Sig Sauer P226.

A quick search on his cell phone revealed there was a national park half an hour north, and Rex could see a green space even closer, though it wasn't identified on the map. He decided to head in that direction and stop where the green space was to see if it was a park. If not, Digger would have to wait another twenty minutes.

Ten minutes later, Rex discovered the nature of the map's green space. It was a racetrack. But he could see trees, and beyond them a grassy field with a fountain. It would do.

Rex turned in, found a parking space, and put Digger on his leash.

"Sorry again, boy, but we don't want to fall afoul of any laws. This country has a history of not approving of dogs or their owners."

At the last minute, he decided to take the food and water as well. The trees he'd seen shaded a small brick courtyard with tables, clearly meant for picnic lunches.

The parking lot was also strangely devoid of other vehicles. Rex assumed there were no races today and couldn't help but think about the contrasts between wealthy Saudi Arabia and destitute Afghanistan. It was definitely two different worlds linked by a single religion. Saudi Arabia was said to be the birthplace of Islam. The two holiest Islamic shrines were located in Mecca and Medina. Even the monarch's formal title — the King of Saudi Arabia, Prime Minister, head of the House of Saud and The Custodian of the Two Holy Mosques, made reference to the important shrines.

But the main difference between the countries was the rich oil deposits under the desert sands of Saudi Arabia.

The world coveted that oil and the kingdom had profited. Saudis' average annual per capita income was about twenty-seven times more than that of Afghanis. Yet, the Saudi's paid no taxes, as opposed to Afghanistan's twenty percent top tax rate. In response to their lot, Afghanis protesting it risked death at the hands of their Taliban-influenced government. King Abdallah on the other hand, had in March of 2011 announced a series of benefits to Saudi citizens, including funds for affordable housing, salary increases, and unemployment entitlements.

While Afghanistan wallowed in ancient social norms and utter poverty, Saudi Arabia was taking steps to enter the modern era, even in women's rights. Much could be said about the reforms, some said it was too little too late, some said it was a step in the right direction and must be encouraged. Whichever way one looked at it, it meant some improvement in the quality of life for the poor in the Kingdom of Saudi Arabia. Of course, the improvements didn't extend to the personal lives of the ultra-wealthy, especially considering most of that class were the royal family. For them, life continued as usual — luxurious and abundant.

Rex knew with certainty that there were still many reprehensible practices that weren't widely advertised. The practice of putting toddlers on racing camels, for example, where they would be killed if they fell off their perches. It happened. The practice of starving and abusing the boys as they grew bigger, so they'd have longer utility for racing.

That thought certainly soured his enjoyment of the beautiful gardens surrounding the race track, though this one was for horses, not camels.

And of course, there was the practice of enslaving women, not only their legitimate wives, but also the 'pleasure wives' they were entitled to and other women who didn't even hold that dubious distinction, all hidden behind harem walls, wealth, and tradition. The circumstances he was expecting he would find Rehka Gyan in.

Rex let Digger off the leash, and the dog raced for a nearby shrub, pruned in the shape of a child's toy top. Rex followed at a more leisurely pace, the plastic bag for pooh collection stuffed in his left pocket.

Once Digger's relics were taken care of, Rex said, "Chow?"

Digger grinned, turned and raced Rex back to the table where he'd left the sandwiches. Rex ran in spite of the heat, assuming correctly that if he didn't get there before Digger finished the first sandwich, he'd no hope of having even one bite of the second one. Naturally, Digger was faster. But Rex arrived in time to save his sandwich, anyway. He snatched it from the table just in time and took a big bite, barely waiting to tear the wrapping off it first.

Rex was finishing the sandwich when a Saudi in uniform approached him. The man was shorter than the average Saudi, maybe five-foot-six, Rex guessed. Like many shorter-than-average men in any country, he made up for his lack of stature with an arrogant swagger. He wore wraparound mirrored sunglasses, a belt with a revolver in a holster studded with extra rounds, a tan uniform with three green stripes of his rank on his sleeves, and a black beret with a gold patch matching his collar studs.

Rex wouldn't have called him trim, but aside from a slight bulge that strained the two buttons above his belt, he looked fit enough.

Between the beret and the oversized sunglasses, Rex couldn't see a frown, but the man's mouth was turned down at the corners between a mustache and neatly-trimmed goatee. He certainly wasn't smiling. Rex didn't need to identify the black patch above the rank stripes on his left shoulder or the name written on the badge above his right pocket to know who or what he was.

Uh-oh. Cop. And he's not happy about something.

He put his sandwich down and started to reach for Digger's papers, when the officer told him to raise his hands. Confused, Rex complied. He started to explain he was only reaching for the dog's papers.

"Silence! You are under arrest for failing to observe Ramadan. Keep your hands where I can see them."

The officer wasn't smiling. It wasn't a joke.

Ramadan! That's why all the restaurants at the airport were closed. Shit, how could I forget about that?

Ramadan — one of the Five Pillars of Islam. A period lasting twenty-nine to thirty days, depending on the visual sightings of the crescent moon, during the ninth month of the Islamic calendar. The month in which, it is believed, Allah revealed the Quran to the Prophet Muhammad. A time during which all Muslims and anyone in a Muslim country were supposed to fast — not eat any food between dawn and sunset. The only people excepted were those who were travelling, elderly, ill, chronically ill, diabetic, pregnant, breastfeeding, or menstruating.

Rex had arrived, so he couldn't claim he was travelling. He wouldn't get away with either the age or the illness excuse. And he was not dressed to even try to convince anyone that he might be pregnant, breastfeeding, or menstruating. Ignorance was his only remaining defense, but ignorance of the law, he was given to understand since a very young age, was no excuse.

He knew he was going to be arrested. The only unknown was the punishment. "Digger, run! Hide!" he exclaimed.

Digger took off.

That kicked the officer into action and he tackled Rex to the ground.

Rex knew he shouldn't resist, so he let the officer take him down, but he turned his head toward Digger as he was going down. Digger had stopped, no doubt because he didn't know whether to obey the command or come back and help.

"Go!" Rex shouted.

Digger turned and ran for the nearest hedge. Rex approved. It was the only cover he'd seen where Digger might evade capture. It was lucky the dog was smart – he'd be on his own while Rex sorted things out.

Rex lay passively on the ground while the officer cuffed his hands behind his back and told him to remain on the ground. For a few minutes, Rex was alone as the officer made a cursory search for Digger. But evidently Digger had understood the situation. The officer came back without him.

He tugged Rex to his feet and started marching him toward a building nearby. Just his luck, Rex had broken the Ramadan laws in a deserted place patrolled by police.

"What did I do wrong?" he asked the officer in Arabic.

"You were eating before sundown."

"But I'm not Muslim. I didn't know the laws applied to me," Rex argued.

"That does not matter. In public, everyone, Muslim and visitor alike, must obey the laws. And when you're in this country you're supposed to know what the laws are."

Rex assumed he'd have to pay a fine and that would be the end of it. He would find out later just how wrong he was.

TWELVE

AFTER JOHN BRANDT had left them, Josh Farley and Marissa Bisset talked at the table until the server came to ask them if they were finished. He needed the table. They ordered dessert and talked on. Both knew that John Brandt, the Old Man, wouldn't have put them together if he'd thought either could get the job done alone. They each knew the other was competent at the types of missions Brandt's outfit, CRC, took on. But they didn't know each other's specialties, languages, or experience. Before they could work well together, they'd need to know those things as if they'd been working as a team for years.

It took a few hours. Josh was a trained assassin like Rex Dalton, well versed in all aspects of spy craft and a weapons and martial arts expert. He spoke two languages besides English – Spanish and Italian. He'd met Rex Dalton, but they had never done a mission together. By the time he'd joined CRC, Rex was already a legend, a lone agent, working without a team and for the most part without backup or logistics support of any kind.

Marissa was an expert hacker and spy and could handle herself in a fight, but she hadn't ever been involved in a military-style mission. She was the best female agent Brandt had. She'd been Carson's downfall. She also spoke two languages besides English, and one was Arabic. She'd be an asset on this mission for that reason alone. Her other language was French, which she'd spoken along with

English since she was a few months old thanks to her French father.

Marissa was about ten years older than Josh, but one would have to have seen her birth certificate to know that. The choices for their joint legend had been Josh's sister, girlfriend or wife. After a bit of discussion about what circumstances they might encounter, they decided on girlfriend or wife. Josh was hesitant to bring it up, but Marissa casually mentioned that in some countries they'd want to be domiciled in the same hotel rooms for safety. That meant she'd pose as his wife, especially in Muslim countries.

Josh wasn't naïve. He knew she wasn't flirting. At the same time, he wouldn't have objected if she had. The only problem he had was whether anyone would believe an average-looking guy like him could have bagged a beautiful creature like Marissa as his wife. He kept his thoughts to himself.

By the time they finished their dessert and then coffee with a cheese platter the long-suffering server brought them afterward, they had the rudiments of a plan. That was all they could do. What happened after they got to Afghanistan would depend on what they could find, or not, about Rex there. Maybe they'd find his remains. Even though Brandt didn't think so, they had to start there and eliminate or confirm it.

Like Brandt, though, Josh thought it was entirely plausible that Rex could have escaped the ambush and left the country. Rex's legend in CRC was not based on rumors it was based on facts. Marissa said she'd take his word for it. Brandt had given them *carte blanche.* They were to keep searching until they found Rex or conclusive proof of his death. Privately, Josh thought it might be the work of years. He himself knew how to disappear and he was good at it, that was one of the skills they were taught at CRC, but he knew Rex was even better.

They'd take a week to develop their legend, get their gear together, and wait for Brandt's logistics team to get them the identity papers they'd need to move freely in Afghanistan and some of the neighboring countries such as Pakistan, India and China. After that, they'd fly commercial to Kabul under the guise of journalists. It wasn't a truly safe legend, but it was the only one that fit a husband and wife team asking questions about a paramilitary outfit called Phoenix Unlimited. With luck, they'd convince the informants they found that their interest was in persuading the West that those groups had a just cause. If they were seen as sympathetic, maybe they wouldn't lose their heads.

They arrived in Kabul on the same day that Rex flew from Mumbai to Riyadh.

***

MORE THAN A month had passed since the ambush that had purportedly killed Rex and the bulk of the Phoenix Unlimited employees, including the CEO, Frank Millard. In the meanwhile, Brandt had discovered the link between the two men, Frank and Rex, who'd been in the same unit in Marine boot camp. He couldn't find any evidence that they'd had any contact since. That didn't mean they hadn't, just that the evidence hadn't survived. But in Rex's first report he'd mentioned that he knew Millard to be a good man and a good soldier, so he was going to use the serendipity of Millard's outfit being present in Kabul to use them as his logistics team. Brandt had given no objection.

Marissa dressed up in full garb, full-face hijab and all, accompanied her 'husband' to the address they had. It was her first visit to Afghanistan. She had been to Saudi Arabia and a few other Muslim countries before and she hated their treatment of women and the edict about the clothes they had to wear in public. But she was not going to let her peeves get in the way of the mission.

She and Josh already knew that Phoenix Unlimited had disbanded and, as expected, the compound was deserted. Not a shred of evidence remained to testify to the presence of a multinational team of paramilitary agents ever having been there.

"What's next?" Marissa asked.

"Landlord?" Josh answered.

"Good idea."

However, there also wasn't a shred of evidence to tell them to whom the property belonged. They knew because they'd gone over it with the thoroughness of forensic investigators. Finding nothing, they were forced to ask at neighboring businesses and homes, jumbled together as if the city had never heard of city planning. Maybe it hadn't.

Neither of Brandt's operatives knew whether city planning had been a thing thirty-five-hundred years ago, when it was founded.

Their search took them several blocks away from the compound before they found the butcher shop where Millard's cook had bought their meats. There, they heard from the proprietor that none of the Phoenix people had remained after a tragedy killed most of them.

"Yeah, well, tell us something we don't know," Josh mumbled just loud enough so that Marissa could hear.

They already had names and contact information for the survivors, but they'd hoped to find at least one remaining who wasn't on the list. It was a depressingly short list, and the handful of agents had scattered to the four winds. Josh speculated they may even have joined another paramilitary group and not stayed where their last known addresses were. What they now knew was that the story of the explosion and the number of casualties had not been exaggerated. But the reason for the explosion had been covered up.

"The story is that they were searching the house and grounds for explosives," the butcher told them. "And they accidentally found some. May Allah receive them and give them peace. Our country will not be safe for our children and our children's children if these terrorists and their bombs are not discovered and eradicated."

Marissa thanked him gently. Not every Afghani citizen was a bad guy. But those who were surely succeeded in giving all the others a bad name.

"Can you give us the location of the explosion?" she asked. "We'd like to pay our respects."

The address the butcher gave matched the information they had. So far, they'd learned nothing to convince them their intel was false.

Marissa had a growing dread that the samples they took at the scene really would match Dalton's DNA. She had a fondness for John Brandt that had nothing to do with the fact he was her employer. He was a decent man who'd been dealt a hard blow in the death of his wife. He'd lost his faith in a career that had betrayed him and his old-school CIA cohort. He'd lost agents before, but none as personally close to him as Dalton. She didn't want to be the one to tell him his favorite agent, someone he looked on as the son he'd never had, had also died.

Thirteen

IF DIGGER'S THOUGHT processes had been like a human's, they probably would have run along the lines of, "What am I supposed to do now? My alpha and my meal ticket has been taken away, and I have no idea where I am."

Or maybe not. Digger was an exceptionally intelligent dog, not given to futile kvetching. So, what he did was follow the policeman as he marched Rex down the street at a discreet distance. Rex had commanded him to hide, but there was precious little cover in this desert environment. Digger wasn't hungry – he'd taken time to eat the rest of Rex's sandwich after emerging from the hedge and before following the scent of his human leader. He wasn't thirsty now, but the heat beating down on his thick black coat would make it imperative for him to find a source of water soon.

When Digger arrived at the building, he saw Rex being put into a car. Rex didn't see him, so he didn't give another command. Digger continued to hide. When the car began to move, Digger moved, too. At first, he was able to keep up. Then the car got to a road where it speeded up. Digger had to cross under an overpass with no cover, but there was also no traffic, so he made it without incident. After that, he ran as fast as he could, but the car was too fast.

All Digger could do was follow the road, hidden by some shrubs that appeared here and there. Within a minute, he was far behind the car, but he kept going in the direction the car went. The car slowed to turn a corner, and Digger caught a glimpse of it. Immediately, he turned and began dodging through a field of sand and rock to intercept the car. It was a mistake. He lost sight of it. Then thirst overtook him, and he detoured to the smell of water, finding a fountain where he drank deeply.

A sound overhead attracted his attention, and he looked up. Digger of course didn't have a word for the thing in the sky, but he knew what it was. Something like it had carried him to this place, not long ago. He lowered his head and looked in the direction from which it had come. He cut across another big field and saw the car that Rex was in, now pointed in the opposite direction on a road that led to the flying-thing place. He began to run faster.

By the time he reached the road, he was confused. There were many cars, and some looked like Rex's car. They were all going in one direction, though, so he followed beside that road and lifted his snout in the air to search for Rex's scent, but he couldn't find any. It was only the smell of gas coming from the cars.

At last, a faint trace was familiar. Rex was somewhere ahead. He moved closer, ignoring the people who saw him and yelling at him. His friend needed him. He crept closer, hiding while he did so, until he saw the right car. It was not moving, and no one was in it. He knew it was the right car because it had Rex's scent. He crawled under it to wait for Rex.

***

INSIDE THE AIRPORT police station, Rex was worried and angry as well. Worried because it was beginning to look like a bigger deal than he'd thought and concerned about Digger's whereabouts and safety. Angry at the situation and at himself for the misstep. He hadn't visited Saudi Arabia before, but he couldn't help but believe being arrested here was not a good idea.

When he heard the policeman who'd arrested him saying 'blasphemy', he got really worried. The punishment for blasphemy in Saudi Arabia was in the discretion of the presiding magistrate and could range from a warning, a heavy fine and lashes to the death penalty — public beheading. Despite his intention to be compliant and not make waves, he couldn't let that stand. He protested, loudly, that he had not intended to blaspheme. It had happened only because he was not Muslim and had not realized it was Ramadan. Of course, he had only the highest respect for the Muslim religion.

When his protests fell on deaf ears, he took another tack.

"I am here to complete a business transaction with a member of the royal family. I demand that I be brought before a magistrate immediately to plead my case. The prince is expecting me."

It might have worsened his plight, but his situation couldn't get much worse. He hoped it would make them show their intentions and speed up the process. He was not going to allow them to hold him for years, or months, or even weeks. He had a responsibility to Digger, and he'd made an implicit promise to Akshara Gyan to rescue her daughter. He intended to keep both obligations and if it meant to do so he had to break out of custody and in the process break a few necks and limbs, then so be it.

The policemen in this station were more familiar with laws foreigners were likely to transgress. They saw it happening every day, and most of the time it was overlooked, settled with the payment of a fine, or someone above their pay grade received a bribe and released the miscreant. Occasionally, it was more serious, and more often than not, it somehow involved a member of the royal family.

Rex had inadvertently cited the one circumstance that the police tried to avoid like pork — getting on the left side of a member of the royal family.

There was a magistrate on hand to deal with foreigners right in the airport. That way, their cases could be heard right away, and the offenders deported immediately if the infraction warranted it.

Rex was brought before the magistrate and allowed to plead his own case. Back in the US and other first-world countries the general wisdom was he who has himself for a lawyer has a fool for a client. Rex believed it to be very wise council, but in Saudi Arabia justice could sometimes be swift and attorneys tended to interfere with rapid legal processing. He wasn't given the option to call one.

However, he had an advantage over many Americans who'd found themselves crosswise with the law in a foreign country. He spoke the language. Fluently.

In eloquent terms, he apologized for his accidental offense. He admitted the infringement. There was no way he could truthfully say he didn't take a bite out of his sandwich – the policeman had caught him red-handed. Furthermore, he knew the law, at least the core of it. He wasn't a Muslim, as he'd said before, he respected their religion and would never consciously do anything to dishonor the religion. He knew Ramadan was holy and he knew what was expected of Muslims during this time. What he didn't know was that the laws pertained to non-Muslims. Had he known that, he would never have committed such a monstrous transgression.

The only lie he told was that he hadn't known it pertained to non-Muslims. Having lived in Afghanistan for more than a year, he did know that. He also knew the best lies had an element of truth. Everything else he'd said was true.

It helped also that in questioning him, the magistrate asked his business in Saudi Arabia. Truthfully again, he said he had a business transaction with a member of the royal family. He didn't say it would be a one-sided transaction.

At this juncture, he saw another opportunity to strengthen his plea, and solemnly promised to the magistrate that as soon as he met with the prince, he would make sure to apologize and ask for forgiveness for embarrassing the royal family and his eminence the King.

Whether it was his eloquence, the fact that he made his plea in perfect Arabic, or because the magistrate was impressed or perhaps intimidated by his claim of business with one prince Mutaib bin Faisal bin Saud, Rex would never know. All he knew was that his potential death sentence was commuted to five lashes, which the honorable magistrate suspended for a period of three years. Meaning, the magistrate explained, Rex would not receive the punishment now, but if he were to be found guilty of a similar offense in the next three years, the five lashes would be meted out to him on top of whatever sentence he would get for the new offence.

Rex was relieved. He had no intention to stay in Saudi Arabia for three years. However, he wasn't so sure he could promise that he wouldn't break any laws or anything else for that matter, in the next week or so of his planned visit to the kingdom. He intended to not get caught again, and if he got caught, not to submit to an arrest as timidly as he did earlier.

***

REX SUPPOSED IT wouldn't be good form to ask for a ride back to the park, a distance of perhaps eight or ten miles by road. His rented SUV was still there unless it had been impounded. He had no idea where Digger might be. After collecting his cell phone and other items that had been confiscated upon his arrest, he walked out by the same door from which he'd entered.

The sun was high in the west, and the door was on the south end of the northeast-oriented terminal of the airport. Rex, whose sense of direction was flawless even in a foreign country, figured the racetrack was almost due east or perhaps a little north of that, and maybe five miles as the crow flew. In the distance, he could see structures that might be an office park or light industrial complex, perhaps a mile away across the airport complex's roads.

He debated whether to call a taxi from his current location or to walk across to the other buildings first. He was about to walk through to the other side of the building where the passenger areas were, when a movement under a nearby squad car attracted his attention. Two black paws, followed by a familiar black snout, emerged. Rex looked around quickly, giving Digger a hand-signal to wait.

Seeing no one nearby, he gave the signal to come, and Digger wriggled out from under the car. He ran to Rex and jumped, landing with both front paws squarely on his chest. Rex staggered and then righted himself.

"I'm glad to see you, too, buddy," he said in a low voice.

Digger whined his agreement and then jumped again, landing a lick on Rex's cheek before gravity pulled him back down.

Rex kneeled down, took Digger's head in his hands and pulled it to his own face. Digger licked his face while he was scratching him behind the ears. "Thanks for waiting for me buddy. Okay, let's get out of here."

His decision was made for him. He couldn't take Digger through the building without a crate or a leash. The fact was, he probably couldn't get him into a taxi without a leash, either, even if he could find a driver willing to take a dog at all.

"Can we get back to the Jeep, boy?" He called every vehicle a Jeep, because Digger recognized the word.

Digger gave a soft *woof* and turned in what Rex had decided was the right direction. He walked a few steps, then turned his head back to look at Rex. The message was clearly, "What are you waiting for?"

Rex had walked farther in worse heat than this. It wasn't his favorite idea, but he could do it. "Lead the way," he said to Digger. He followed as Digger set out. A few minutes later, he regretted the choice, as Digger started to cross a wide area of macadam. If he wasn't mistaken, it was a runway.

"Digger, no!" he called, but he was too late. The dog was halfway across. Expecting to be shot, Rex sprinted after him. They'd never have gotten away with the stunt in America. Maybe because of Ramadan there were fewer planes taking off and landing. Rex didn't know. He just thanked his guardian angel when they made it without being run down by a plane or shot as a terrorist.

Across a wide expanse of sand, they found the onramp to a raised highway, followed it up and across, and back down the offramp on the other side to the road that led to the buildings Rex had seen earlier. Those turned out to be a private jet-port, almost deserted. They passed by and continued in a slight north-easterly direction. Digger seemed confident of his direction.

By the time they reached the racetrack and the small park on its grounds where Rex had been picked up, Rex was drenched in sweat. Digger had taken another drink from the fountain he'd found before, but Rex hadn't. He was parched. He saw his SUV where he'd left it and was soon drinking water from a bottle that had been in the cooler. He found it difficult to pace himself but knew that guzzling it would probably cause an equal and opposite reaction.

He was also half-starved, but the sandwich he'd been eating was gone. He looked at Digger. "Did you eat my sandwich?"

Digger dropped his head and avoided Rex's eyes. He recognized 'eat' and 'sandwich'.

Rex interpreted the gesture as "what are you talking about?" or "What sandwich?" But Digger's body language proclaimed his guilt. Either way, he didn't dare take another bite of anything, in case another police officer was lurking nearby. It wasn't yet sundown. If any policeman or anyone else had tried to bust him for drinking the water, also forbidden during daylight hours of Ramadan, he'd have done some busting of his own.

Fourteen

REX WAS BEHIND his planned schedule because of the interruption. He'd meant to be in Dammam by this time. It was a four-hour drive, with few options for stops along the way. Judah was his best option, but he could find no indication that there would be restaurants or that they'd be open when he got there.

He hoped to find a place where he could get food well before he reached Dammam. If there was no food to be had beforehand, at least he was certain to have some options in the resort city. He'd make the best of his delay, find a hotel, and begin his search for the prince tomorrow.

He tried to find some philosophical well-being in the realization he'd dodged not a bullet but a howitzer round. But hunger and philosophical musings didn't go together for Rex. He was grumpy. More than grumpy, he was ready to knock a few Saudi heads together.

Digger seemed to sense his mood. Instead of sitting upright in the passenger seat, he'd squirmed in the harness until he could get comfortable lying down and was now snoring. Rex was even grumpier not to have companionship. Still, Digger had done his best to help. Rex was still puzzled about how Digger was able to find him at the airport police station because he couldn't have possibly followed the police car the entire way.

As he drove, Rex tried to think of how Digger had done it. He concluded that Digger must have taken the route he led them back on, since he seemed to know exactly where that fountain was. He'd never know, not until Digger learned to talk in a language Rex could fully understand or vice versa. These thoughts made him feel a little better about the dog falling asleep. It had been a long day for Digger, too.

After seeing the difference dropping his target's name had made to the police and magistrate, Rex fleshed out his next steps a little more as he drove. Two hours later, he approached the village of Judah, or so the signs said. He could see no evidence of occupation, not even a light in a window. Dammam it was, then, and he hoped he didn't run out of gas before he got there. The indicator said he had half a tank. If the gauge was true, the SUV must have had a larger tank than he thought.

Maybe in Saudi Arabia they fit bigger gas tanks because of the long distances between towns. Ironic, come to think of it. The country is located on top of the largest lake of oil on the planet, yet I might run out of gas.

Two hours after that, it was nearing midnight when he entered Dammam. Several phone calls finally located a hotel where there was a vacancy and he could check in. He had to bribe the desk clerk to get Digger in despite his service-dog papers.

Nothing had gone right since I landed in this accursed country. Well, maybe I should be grateful I'm not sitting in a jail cell in Riyadh or worse, waiting for dawn to come so they could chop my head off in public.

***

REX WOKE IN a better frame of mind. He'd found a vending machine in the hotel and though he'd paid an exorbitant premium to the clerk to change some of his dollars for the Arabic coins he needed to purchase some sandwiches, nut and chocolate bars. Not entirely the meal Rex would have liked to have, but the food had been welcome.

Digger agreed.

Rex had also remembered the pre-stuffed kong when they got to the room, and Digger was transported by joy when he saw it. Rex had actually been able to break free of his somber mood and laugh at Digger's antics. Fortunately, they were on the first floor, so they had no one below them to complain about the thuds as Digger pounced on the toy, 'killing' it for the dried meat stuffed inside.

A long shower to clean the dried sweat from the afternoon's hike relaxed Rex enough to sleep, though he was keyed up about the next day's tasks. He managed about four hours before the alarm on his phone woke him in time to have breakfast at the hotel restaurant before sunup. This would be the last day of Ramadan, thankfully.

Rex spent another hour in his room after breakfast, taking advantage of the hotel Wi-Fi to research what else might be forbidden. He didn't see anything forbidding business, so he checked out of the hotel and went to explore the marketplaces in the city. In the Middle East, markets are where people meet and socialize and gossip. Markets are fountains of information if one knew how to ask the right questions, and Rex knew.

His research had discovered that Prince Mutaib was suspected of illegal arms dealing by Israeli and US authorities. Rex knew how to insert himself into that milieu, he had dealt with quite a few arms dealers in the past. None of them survived. But in this case, he hadn't had time to build a bullet-proof legend yet. He'd have to rely on his wits and if necessary other measures of persuasion to get an audience with the man and then take it from there to see what the best way would be to gain entrance to Mutaib's home and thence his harem. The task would have been called impossible by anyone else. Rex regarded it merely as a challenge, like a bump in the road.

Rex expected Mutaib would not be found hawking his wares in the market, of course not. His markets were more rarified, and his hands would never have touched the product. He had lackeys for that. Rex needed to find them and do so without more run-ins with police. It was a peculiar country, he thought, that would clamp down on terrorism so tightly in public, and yet overlook any pro-terrorist activity among the extended royal family, thought to be more than three-thousand strong.

Rex's research showed that in 2009 the Saudi government made a decision to grant licenses to private gun shops to sell personal firearms in an attempt to rein in the widespread illegal ownership of assault weapons and handguns. Rex thought this was the type of situation where a man like Mutaib would probably like to assert his influence. Perhaps he would play a role in the gun shops' licensing, pulling the right strings to assure whether the shop got a license or not, depending on whether the shop bought its stock from him or not.

It was a bit of a long shot but certainly worth checking out and it was not as if Rex had other options to get him in the presence of this scoundrel, short of driving over to his residence, knock on the door and say, "Hey I am here to pick up Rehka Gyan."

Therefore, Rex spent most of the day loitering near gun stores. He carefully observed the people coming and going, not sure what he was looking for but would know when he saw it. Perhaps a shipment of weapons would be delivered to one or more of the shops and he could find out who was the seller. In the meantime, he was trying to get a feel for how these gun shops did business.

He entered a few shops, struck up casual conversations with the staff and clientele, looked at their merchandise to find out what makes and models they stocked and who their suppliers were.

For hours, nothing caught his attention except the growling of his stomach. Digger was beginning to give him accusatory looks and make noises almost under the auditory range, like a kid who muttered about parental decisions they didn't like.

As the sun's rays began to fade in the west, activity picked up. Restaurants opened their shutters and more people were in the streets. A sense of excitement and delight was in the air. The end of Ramadan meant an opulent feast, and it couldn't come fast enough for Rex and Digger, and judging by the jubilant atmosphere, everyone else in sight felt the same.

Digger's head, which had been drooping for a while, came up. His tail waved tentatively, as if he wasn't quite sure whether there was cause for celebration.

When the last sliver of the sun sank below the horizon, there was a hush, and then the evening call to prayer began. Rex had heard the calls four previous times that day, but this one seemed loudest, with the loudspeakers of the mosques all over the city overlapping each other. He could now break his fast with an *iftar* in the nearest restaurant.

He was walking quickly in the direction of one of the restaurants he'd spotted earlier when visiting a gun shop. That's when his attention was drawn to a man dressed in western clothing but who looked Middle Eastern, on the sidewalk across the street, going in the opposite direction, towards the gun shop. It was his demeanor that caught Rex's attention on the near empty sidewalk. The man looked a bit like a rat scurrying away from a dog. His head was bowed so far that he looked directly at the ground at his feet, risking bumping into anyone in his path. He looked from side to side and over his shoulder furtively, but never in the direction he was hurrying.

If he was trying to remain inconspicuous, he was not at all successful. Rex thought he stood out like a Vegas stripper in church during the Sunday service. Something was bothering the man deeply and Rex thought it was worth finding out what it was.

Rex stopped and bent down to Digger, scratching his head and ears as he spoke softly. "What do you reckon buddy? I think that guy across the street looks a bit stressed. Maybe we should check him out?"

Digger's face turned into a big grin for the sudden and unexpected treat he got from Rex.

Rex allowed the man to pass and watched him reach the gun shop. He looked left and right before entering. Rex and Digger then crossed the street and took up a position in the shadows about twenty yards away from the entry to the gun shop and waited.

The street was much darker before the man came out of the shop, and Digger alerted him to his target's approach. When he came into Rex's view, he was even more oppressed-looking than before.

Rex waited until the man was two yards away from him before he stepped out in front of him and blocked his way. Just before the collision, the man must have seen Rex's feet. He stopped abruptly, then tried to go around. Rex stepped sideways to block his way.

"Excuse me," the man said in Arabic. "I wish to pass."

Rex answered in the same language, and with a hint of menace in his tone. "A question first. You are upset about something. What was your business in the gun shop?"

The man looked up for the first time. His eyes shot wide when he saw Digger staring at him, and then his gaze shifted and traveled slowly up Rex's person, until it reached his face. Because he was several inches shorter than Rex, and only inches separated them, he had to bend his neck back and look up. What he saw made him flinch back.

"I… I'm sorry. I don't know what you mean. Please let me pass."

Rex didn't relax his stern expression. "I think you do. My dog and I will know if you lie. What was your business in the gun shop?"

The man became indignant. "I merely gave a message to someone in the shop. It's none of your business. Now let me pass."

"What message?" Rex thought the man might become angry then, but he could handle it if so. However, the emotion he sensed from the man wasn't anger. It was defeat.

"I… No. I cannot tell you."

"You will tell me, or you'll regret it." Rex gave Digger's leash a slight pull. Digger took a step closer to the man.

"I'll regret it in any case," the man sighed, bitterness twisting his features. "Who are you? One of Prince Mutaib's men?"

"I might be." Rex dissembled.

"If you are, then you can tell his highness what I told the man in the shop, I cannot pay. He wins."

"I'm not working for the prince. Nor am I your enemy. You were not on the way to prayer, I assume."

"I'm too late now."

Rex had found evidence that Mutaib was an international arms dealer on a large scale. His commerce took place overseas, where he supplied weapons to people with an interest in protecting and enforcing their illegal activities, anything from terrorism, war, and drug trafficking to human trafficking. For Mutaib to be running a small-time protection racket didn't make sense.

But then, on the other hand, maybe Mutaib had been running an extensive Mafia-style protection racket across Saudi Arabia in addition to his major business. That could be fairly lucrative.

He'd take what information he could get from the little rat-man tonight, and then make a more pointed visit to the gun shop tomorrow. At least he now had confirmation that someone in Mutaib's organization was there.

"How did the prince's man respond to the message you gave him?"

"Not good at all," the little man answered. Tears filled his eyes. "I must hurry home to my wife and explain what will happen tomorrow."

"And what's that?"

They were passing under a lamp on the side of a restaurant entrance. The man looked up with haunted eyes. "My debt for this period will be paid with the only thing I have left of value. One of Mutaib's men will take over my business. After that, they'll take my daughter. Then my wife. Thank Allah, I have no son. After that, they will kill me."

Rex swallowed his outrage. He couldn't let it interfere with his judgement. "Wait. Before you explain this to your wife, explain it to me. I might be able to help you if you can help me. Can I buy your *iftar*?"

"No one can help. I begged them to leave my family alone and kill me now. They refused. Even if they had consented, they would not have kept the bargain, and after I was dead, they'd take my wife at the same time as my daughter. They wish to punish me before they kill me, so they prolong my humiliation."

Rex thought humiliation was a peculiar word to describe the situation. The man would be *humiliated* when they took his daughter? What about grief-stricken? What about enraged? He kept that thought to himself.

"Can you not enlist legal help? I don't know your laws, but surely this can't be legal."

"I cannot take my case to court. Mutaib is too powerful. He is above the law. I should not have become indebted to him."

"Prince Mutaib is a money lender, too, then?" Rex was certain of the answer and only asked the question to keep the man engaged. But the answer turned out to be a surprise.

"Not precisely, no. He supplies the stock for every weapons shop in the region and a large number of shops in Riyadh and other cities and towns across the country as well. He does not wish to own the shops. When it became legal to seek a license to sell weapons, he let it be known that people could approach him to help them obtain a license and he would not only help them with that — he would also supply them with stock on margin. You understand margin?"

Rex thought he did. "Where you pay less than the stock is worth, sell it for a profit, and then pay the remainder of the price, along with some interest."

"Yes. That is correct. However, my shop was not profitable. The Prince does not care about my struggles. He only wants his money."

"Friend, such men never care about the struggles of honest men. Look me in the eyes and tell me you are an honest man." Rex thought he might have an ally if he could trust the man.

The man stopped and faced him. "I am an honest man. And despite what you may think or think you know about me, I love my wife. I love my daughter. I would do anything to spare them from what the Prince has in mind."

Rex nodded. "Then let's see what we can do before you give your wife such awful news. *Now* may I buy your *iftar*?"

Digger waited outside. Rex promised him in a whisper that he'd have human food as a treat later.

While they ate, Rex gathered all the information he could about Mutaib, his odd little side business, his household, servants, and enforcers. He didn't tell his guest about his plans. But he promised himself that by the time this was over, the scumbag, Mutaib, would not be collecting any debts from anyone ever again.

Rex assured the man his wife and daughter would be safe.

They didn't exchange names, but Rex followed him at a discreet distance when they left the restaurant, after pretending to go in the opposite direction. He made a note of where the man lived. If things went wrong, he'd collect them and help them get out of harm's way, if nothing else.

Fifteen

THE NEXT MORNING, Rex explained to Digger that he had to go into some shops, and for that reason he was leaving Digger in the hotel room. Rex had given him a walk after his breakfast, and he'd set down his portable water bowl with fresh water.

"You'll be more comfortable here, boy. I'll be back to get you before any fun starts, okay?"

Digger appeared to listen carefully, but Rex had no idea whether he understood. Leaving him tethered by his leash outside high-end clothing and jewelry stores while Rex bought what he needed to execute his plan was not an option. With the sweeping discretionary powers the Saudi police had, Rex was not going to take chances. They could make up crimes on the spot and 'arrest' or, God forbid, shoot Digger for anything from being unclean to vagrancy. He would in any event not be welcome in the stores. Maybe if he could pass for a teacup poodle, he would. Out of fear that Digger could read his mind, Rex made sure he had the door closed before he smiled at the thought.

He was certain Digger would mind his manners in the hotel room, but to avoid any unpleasant surprises for the cleaning staff, he left the Do Not Disturb sign on the doorknob.

It felt strange to be leaving the hotel without Digger. Once again, he was startled at how quickly the dog had become a part of his life. Not having to worry about him out on the streets was a welcome change, though he knew without Digger to alert him he had to be much more vigilant.

His first stop was at a clothing store, where he outfitted himself with two sets of clothing that would immediately mark him as a wealthy man and paid an exorbitant fee to have the pants and jackets custom tailored on a rush basis.

His next was to a jeweler. He'd have preferred not to spend so much money on a watch, but his battle-scarred tactical timepiece wouldn't suit. He bought a Tag Heuer Carrera with a black quilted-leather band and gold accents, which left him over two thousand dollars poorer, and a heavy gold signet ring. He didn't want to come across as too flashy. He wanted to display casual but not obscene wealth.

Then he went back for the suits and added shirts, ties, handkerchiefs, and silk socks. He considered a gold-knobbed cane but decided that was a bit over the top, no matter how handy it might have been for cracking the heads of the people he expected to meet in the afternoon. He also upgraded his shoes at a shop next to the clothing store.

All in all, it was a lot of money, just shy of ten-thousand US dollars, but Rex didn't care too much about the price tags. It was kind of liberating to use the dirty money he'd taken from the Afghani drug lord to right some wrongs.

If it took more than two days to get into Mutaib's personal presence, he'd have to write a check on one of his new bank accounts to extend his wardrobe. He hoped it wouldn't come to that. He'd entered the country on one set of papers, but he was now carrying the set he'd had drawn up first in India. For all intents and purposes, he was ethnically half Indian, half Brit, and a citizen of the UK.

Rex hurried back to the hotel a little later than he intended. The tailoring had taken longer than he expected. When he entered the hotel room, he thought at first Digger had been a perfect gentleman. Only when he'd put down his purchases did he discover Digger had left him a big and malodourous 'message' in the corner of the bedroom, probably to signal his displeasure at being left alone in a hotel room. And just to make sure, Rex would think twice before doing it again there was also a large, yellow puddle right in the doorway of the bathroom where he'd have stepped in his stocking feet if he hadn't been looking where he was going.

"Digger! Shame on you!"

Rex had to step wide to get over or around it. He used some of the bathroom tissue to pick up the 'message' in the bedroom and then almost all of the rest of the tissue to sop up the second 'message' and flush it all down the toilet. Finished, he looked at Digger and told him in no uncertain terms what he thought of this kind of behavior.

Digger didn't hang his head. His demeanor and sounds made it clear he had something of his own to say and Rex interpreted that as something along the lines of "Rex

Dalton, let this be a lesson for you. Don't ever lock me up in a hotel room or any other room for that matter again while you take off gallivanting in the streets for hours."

"Okay, I'm sorry. I won't do it again, unless I'm forced to. If only you could have understood why it was necessary."

But Digger was already back on the bed, eyes closed, and paid him no attention.

Rex took his second shower of the day and dressed carefully in his new clothes. In the full-length mirror, he surveyed the result. His trim frame, just under six feet, looked great in the custom-tailored silk suit, if he thought so himself. With a little prep time, he could have passed for a citizen of most Middle Eastern and Mediterranean countries, and for that matter, most South American countries. But with no beard, he looked like what he was pretending to be – a man of some mixture of descent, but thoroughly British in attitude, dress, and appearance. The addition of the watch and signet ring lent an air of wealth, if not obscene wealth.

Digger needed to be groomed. Rex wished he'd thought of that. He'd have left him at a groomer's while he did his other errands.

He'd probably not be shitting and pissing all over their place and if he did they *could clean it.*

There was no help for it now. He'd have to find a groomer, as he wouldn't go sticking his head into the hornets' nest without Digger by his side. He knew it was going to cost extra to have the grooming done in a hurry, but it would be worth it, all for the greater good.

While Digger was getting his beauty treatment, Rex used his cell phone to search for a hotel more in keeping with the financial status he would portray when he gained access to Mutaib. He found it in the Dammam Sheraton, a high-rise hotel with acres of beautiful sea-blue glass to echo the Gulf setting. The amenities in the hotel were many, including meeting rooms, private banquet rooms outfitted with crystal chandeliers and pristine white covers on tables and chairs alike, and luxuriously appointed guest rooms with stunning views of the Gulf. There was more; none of which he expected to use. He didn't anticipate entertaining the prince or his henchmen, but if the need arose, his choice of hotel would not betray his humbler origins.

Midafternoon call to prayer was sounding over the city when Rex and a much more respectable-looking Digger went in search of a meal, with the hope of locating the first of the henchmen Rex's Saudi ally of the previous night had told him about. Apparently, there were three who made daily rounds of the weapons stores, dropping off new supplies, checking for signs of trouble, and of course, collecting payments.

Rex had a description and name for all three. He owed the sad little man his peace of mind, because his information had been quite thorough, except that he knew only first names.

Gara, meaning mastiff, was probably a street name. He was the muscle – the one who came to beat debtors or take their possessions. Iskandar usually accompanied one of the others and was there simply as backup. His name meant guardian. Alealjum, meaning toad, was spectacularly ugly, with an enormous hooked nose and ears that stuck straight out from the side of his head like a wingnut, was the collector of debts and the man Rex's new friend had spoken to the night before. Of course, no one called him by that mocking name. His given name was Alula, meaning first born.

It was Alula whom Rex expected to encounter some time this afternoon. He knew the Toad would be in a certain quarter of the city, either collecting from a gun shop or enjoying a meal. If Rex timed it right, he'd interrupt the meal. But he was already two hours late because of the morning's errands.

Unlike his first day in Saudi Arabia, this, the third day, although a little late with some milestones, went much smoother. And unlike the second day, things started happening relatively quickly. Rex had eaten and had given Digger an afternoon break in a park, followed by what was rapidly becoming a habit, a treat of half a roast chicken bone and all. Only a little spicy. Digger wolfed it down and followed it with a long drink from a nearby fountain. He eyed the koi in the fountain curiously and fortunately didn't try to catch any.

They were returning to where Rex had left the SUV parked when he spotted someone matching the description he'd been given of Toad, coming out of a shop whose sign indicated it sold hunting rifles and shotguns. In a country that forbade hunting, it was a puzzle. Rex knew that wealthy Saudis hunted in Africa and other foreign countries, though.

He hurried to intercept the man he thought was Toad, slowing as he came into the man's view so as not to appear to be trying to catch him. As they passed each other, Rex feigned a start of surprise.

"Alula? Is that you?"

The other man stopped, and his surprise was genuine.

"Do I know you?"

"Sorry, no, I doubt you do. However, I have business with your employer, and your name and description was given to me." Rex didn't bother to explain that the description included staggering ugliness. Up close, he realized his informant's description of Alula was actually a bit flattering. The man was unsightly, the enormous nose was covered in vile, blackened pores the size of the Grand Canyon. Clearly, he didn't indulge in skin care. Or baths. His stench was almost as odious as the bulbous nose.

Toad, whose nickname was now completely understandable to Rex, looked down that monstrous nose at him. "I doubt that."

"Perhaps you weren't read in on the deal," Rex said smoothly. "It happens in the best of organizations. I'm with Acme Imports."

"Don't know it," Toad said brusquely. He tried to brush by, but Rex grasped his arm. In America, it would have been considered aggressive. In Saudi Arabia, it was acceptable.

"Then put me in touch with Gara," he said. "He would know about my company."

At the sound of his compatriot's name, Toad paused. Rex could almost see the wheels grinding in his brain. After a moment, he acquiesced.

"Come with me," Toad said. "I'll take you to him."

Rex knew he wasn't out of the woods. When Gara failed to recognize him, he'd better be ready to take action. He'd cross that proverbial bridge when he came to it.

Toad appeared ready to continue on his previous course, so Rex turned and matched him stride for stride, Digger at his heels.

"Big dog," Toad remarked. "My employer keeps mastiffs." It was a veiled threat. Mastiffs would be bigger and heavier than Digger, and the plural suggested he'd also be outnumbered.

All Rex could think of, though, was that the man they were going to see was also Mastiff, by name. He presumed by temperament as well. Rex had every expectation that Mastiff would prove aggressive. If necessary, he'd have to cut the man down to size in a way that would get Mutaib's attention in just the right way.

He didn't want to make the princeling mad. He didn't want to humiliate his henchmen, but he did need to let them know who was boss so that he could get *their* boss's attention.

The meeting with Gara went about as he expected. Toad became suspicious when Gara said he didn't know the Englishman or his organization either. They both drew themselves up to their full stature and thrust their chests out to confront him.

Rex asked, "Where is Iskandar?"

It took a bit of the wind out of their sails. They couldn't figure out why he knew their names, when they didn't know him. Rex took advantage of the situation by assuming an air of importance.

"Look, your employer isn't going to be pleased that you have treated me rudely. Take me to him immediately."

Just then, a larger man, almost Rex's height and considerably wider, joined the other two. Rex almost sighed in relief, it was another steroidal body builder whose brain functions would have been slowed down to a crawl from all the shit he'd pumped into his body to make his muscles grow.

"What is going on?"

"Iskandar, this man says he has business with the prince," Toad said. "He knows our names, but I think he's an imposter."

Iskandar looked Rex in the eye and said without inflection, "You had best be on your way, if you know what's good for you."

That's an elegant way to say, 'get lost.'

Rex replied evenly. "I think you have it wrong. One last time — take me to Mutaib or suffer the consequences."

Toad laughed.

Rex hit him in the throat with his elbow. Gara moved in, but Digger growled. Iskandar stood back to watch the outcome.

Toad was gurgling something. It sounded like *kill him*. No one moved. Rex moved his gaze from one to the other.

Who's in charge?

A flicker of his eyes revealed Iskandar to be the alpha dog of his crew. Gara telegraphed his move just before his fist came flying at Rex's face.

Rex caught his fist in an immovable palm and started bending Gara's hand down, which made him go down to his knees in front of Rex. "You don't ever want to do that again," he said. "Now gentlemen, before any of you get hurt, let's all agree that I'm going to speak to your boss, one way or another. It would be much easier and of course less painful for all three of you if you cooperated."

Toad, however didn't listen. He rose from where he'd crouched to nurse his bruised throat and threw himself in Rex's direction. Rex stepped lithely aside, and Toad landed awkwardly on the ground, where Digger immediately took custody of him by putting his teeth around the back of Toad's neck. This took all the fire out of him and he remained very still.

Iskandar hadn't made an aggressive move, and it was apparent that he was considering the odds. Rex hadn't broken a sweat or dirtied his new suit. He'd prefer not to, so he watched Iskandar closely.

The decision came down in his favor. Iskandar nodded. "I'll take you to Prince Mutaib. If you are not who you say you are, or if you have no business to interest him, I will kill your dog while you watch, and then I will kill you."

Rex could find no fault with Iskandar's pronouncement. It wasn't said with bluster or threat. It was a promise.

"I assure you, I will not give your owner a reason to be angry with you." He chose the insulting word 'owner' purposely. Iskandar's demeanor didn't change, though Gara's eyes narrowed and his skin darkened at the implication that they were slaves. Toad had nothing to say. He was cowering on the ground, his arms covering his head, and Digger was standing over him close enough to drool on him.

"Get up, Alealjum," Iskandar said with great disdain.

Rex didn't envy the man his fate in their quarters later.

***

REX DIDN'T EXPECT to be taken to the prince's home, and in that he was correct. Instead, Iskandar accompanied him to an office building while Gara took Toad to have his injury seen to by a medic. When Iskandar indicated Digger could not enter the building, Rex pushed back.

"Wrong. My service dog goes where I go. Need I remind you…"

"No, no, I need no reminder. He may enter." Iskandar waved him toward an elevator and pressed the button for the top floor.

"These delays are wasting valuable time, which your owner might not appreciate. I trust you won't put any more obstacles in my path." Rex was enjoying the role he was playing.

"No sir, I won't but when we get to the top floor I must ask you to wait while I announce your arrival to the prince. Will that be all right?"

Rex didn't want that. He knew there'd be trouble when the prince didn't know his name. As they exited the elevator into a luxuriously-appointed reception area, he answered impatiently. "The prince is expecting me, and you have made me late. I will go in with you."

Iskandar gave a nod that was a half-bow and gestured widely with his right hand. "As you wish, sir. This way."

Rex walked ahead in the direction Iskandar had indicated, Digger on his left and Iskandar rushing around him on the right to open the door to the prince's private office. As soon as Rex and Digger walked in, Iskandar backed out, closing the door behind him.

The prince was lounging in a chaise situated among several lavishly upholstered chairs and ottomans. The prince, in his early to mid-fifties was about five-foot-five, with a rotund belly and the labored breathing of an asthmatic. An impressively-sized dark-wood desk with elaborate hand carved patterns, occupied the other side of the room. It was devoid of computer equipment, papers, or any other trappings of business. Rex's instant impression was that all business the prince did personally took place in the more comfortable side of the room, verbally. It was validated when the prince lazily waved him to come forward.

As soon as Rex stepped closer, into the bright square of light emanating from a large skylight in the ceiling, the prince sat up straight. "Who are you? What is the meaning of this?"

Rex gave Digger a hand signal to relax, and he obeyed immediately, sinking onto his belly, back legs under him and front legs stretched out, his noble head resting on them. He answered, "Forgive me for barging in on you like this, Your Highness. I have been told about your remarkable business acumen, and I had no other way of getting an audience with you. It is on a matter of exigency that I had to take advantage of your men to get the opportunity to meet with Your Highness. Please don't punish them."

The prince, somewhat mollified by Rex's sycophantic demeanor and explanation, relaxed. "I appreciate your candor and courage. I forgive your unorthodox method.

Did you have any motive besides standing in my illustrious presence for wanting to meet me?" He smiled as if in self-deprecation at his own little joke.

Rex had no doubt it was a double entendre. By pretending to mean the opposite, the prince thought to be charming. However, he truly believed he was illustrious. It was evident in his expression. Many a truth is spoken in jest.

"As a matter of fact, I did." Rex raised one eyebrow and subtly rubbed the fingers and thumb of his right hand together.

Mutaib's expression sharpened. "I take it you have a business proposition to discuss? Sit down, my friend. Tell me your name."

Rex had a split second to remind himself that subterfuge was not his strong suit. He was good at finding the bad guys and dealing with them swiftly. Usually he didn't have much to say to his targets, his tactics were surprise and overwhelming force. This one he had to play very carefully.

Thus, began an elaborate dance of inuendo. Rex knew the players, knew the names Mutaib would recognize. Guns, armaments, weapons – none of those words would be used.

"My name is Ruan Daniel," he began. "But it is not the important name. Perhaps you remember Viktor Anatolyevich?"

The Russian he referred to was Viktor Anatolyevich Bout, a notorious arms smuggler who had been extradited from Thailand to America in 2010 to face numerous accusations stemming from his trade, tried, convicted, and serving a twenty-five-year sentence for conspiring to sell weapons to a U.S.-designated foreign terrorist group. In dropping his name, Rex's intention was to imply that he knew Bout, perhaps was a person who'd done business with him. If Mutaib bought it, Rex would have instant credibility.

Mutaib bought it.

"Of course, I remember him. A sad fate he faces."

Rex schooled his face to commiserate. "Indeed."

His true feelings were that the bastard deserved more than the minimum sentence for all he'd done. The blood of countless numbers had flowed, and many had died because of Bout's delivery of arms to terrorist groups, rebels, and criminal gangs. But Rex had a role to play, so his thoughts didn't reach his expression.

Rex continued. "Anatolyevich's absence has created a void in the market which had to be filled. And that, Your Highness, is the reason I'm here to seek Your Highness's wise council and astuteness.

Mutaib was enchanted. "Let us not be formal. You may address me as Mutaib. It is time for tea, my new friend. Will you join me?"

Though it was quite early for dinner and late for lunch, Rex remembered he was posing as a Brit and assumed Mutaib was honoring his custom. He allowed a grateful smile to answer. "Thank you, Your Highness."

"No, no – you must call me Mutaib."

Iskandar was waiting outside when Rex and Mutaib emerged from the office. Mutaib instructed him to call his driver and bring the Town Car around. "Wait downstairs," he said.

Iskandar took the elevator down, but Mutaib hung back, so Rex did as well.

"I understand your concern for my men," Mutaib said. "But surely you understand I must show them the consequences for allowing a stranger to reach me unhindered. If you had been an assassin, I would now be dead."

Damn straight your royal scumbag. If I didn't need you alive for a while longer, you sure would.

Instead of speaking his mind, Rex nodded his assent without answering. It didn't matter to him if Mutaib docked their pay, had them flogged, or killed them. They weren't going to survive his mission anyway. If Mutaib executed them, it would save him the trouble.

Not much later, the prince and Rex were enjoying a sumptuous meal in a private room in an exclusive restaurant where only the ultra-wealthy were served. Rex hadn't even recognized it as a restaurant until they got inside. From the street, it appeared to be a large private residence. Inside, Rex spotted a prominent American actress wearing a *shayla* with her unusually modest western clothing, women in silk *abayas* paired with *niqabs*, and many self-satisfied men.

Few of them even noticed Digger, who was making himself as inconspicuous as possible. The doorman had raised his eyebrows, but said nothing when Mutaib sailed through, mentioning that the man behind him was his guest. Digger had crept under the table in their private dining room.

Rex surreptitiously fed him tidbits under the table while listening in apparent fascination to Mutaib's monologue. The man liked his own voice. Rex's mention of an infamous arms dealer's name had led to the prince reminiscing about several others from the recent past, all from the Middle East.

Rex periodically murmured his admiration as Mutaib claimed close association with one or another of them, no matter how unlikely the claim.

Sixteen

THE PRINCE HAD apparently been impressed by Rex with his implication that he knew the notorious arms dealer. After detailing his close friendship and business dealings with several others, he began boasting about himself and how shrewd a businessman he was.

Rex played along and encouraged him to keep on blowing his own trumpet. It was obvious the prince enjoyed talking about himself, probably the result of his short-man syndrome, aka the Napoleon complex.

As Mutaib droned on about his wealth, his three wives and thirteen children, his beautiful home, and the business dealings that he claimed afforded him those luxuries, Rex mused on the insecurity that made some men who lacked the average physical stature of their neighbors behave like bantam roosters. Mutaib's behavior smacked of it.

His expressive eyes and soft hands might have attracted *some* women to him, but that would have been the exception not the rule. As his discourse moved to the subject of his 'pleasure wives' as he called them, Rex couldn't help but believe his wealth was the real attraction, not his eyes or hands or any of his other physical features. Assuming any of them had been drawn to him rather than purchased on the black market, like Rehka.

Rex sharpened his attention when he heard the term. Mutaib must have noticed it, and he began to expound on the beauty and exotic sexual talents of those he'd taken into his harem. Others, he explained, were his display pieces in Western countries, where beautiful women were an essential accessory, like expensive jewelry.

Rex kept his expression neutral. Distasteful as it was to hear the crudeness of his host's conversation, this was going much, much better than he could have hoped. His original plan, such as it was, called for him to be invited into Mutaib's home, where he could study the layout, and then to get into the women's quarters and extract Rehka.

Rex was still waiting for an opportunity which would get him the invitation to the residence when Mutaib offered it. He didn't blurt out an invitation to enjoy one of his slave girls. He hinted at it, then hid the hint in braggadocio and subject changes.

The meal was one of the longest Rex had ever endured. When the muted sounds of the city's *muezzins* calling the faithful to *salat al-maghrib*, the prescribed prayer just after sunset, penetrated the restaurant's walls, he was relieved to see Mutaib rise.

"You must join me at my home for supper," the prince said. "I can promise you a most entertaining evening."

That was what Rex had been hoping for. "Thank you, Mutaib. I'll be honored to join you for supper. I hope you will excuse me for a few hours so that I can see to my companion," Rex pointed to Digger, "and of course I'll want to dress for dinner. May I be excused?"

"Of course, of course. I will send a car for you. Where are you staying?"

It wasn't ideal. Rex would have preferred having his SUV handy. But he couldn't quickly think of a way to decline the offer without insulting his host. "The Sheraton," he replied.

They said their goodbyes, and Rex went outside to get his bearings. He was ten or more blocks from his rental vehicle by then, but the sun had gone down, and the walk would be pleasant. Digger needed the exercise anyway, along with a good treat for behaving so well in the restaurant. On top of the human food Rex had already given him. Today, he had his backpack in the car, and Digger's kong was available. He stopped between the restaurant and his destination to buy some dried lamb for it.

After reaching his SUV he took out Digger's kong, stuffed it with the dried lamb and walked across the road to an open lot where he unleashed the dog and gave him a chance to go for a quick run and toilet before handing him the kong. Half an hour later he was at the Sheraton and went to his room to prepare for his evening with the illustrious prince.

Under his impeccably-tailored suit, he wore what he privately thought of as his ninja clothing. Tight black pants with zippered pockets that lay snug against his skin when not in use, but folded outward like cargo pockets when he needed them. A tight, long-sleeved black knitted shirt went under a thin white shirt to cover the black one under his white dress shirt.

His dress shoes weren't the best option, but he could hardly carry in a second pair that would have been more suitable for a combat operation. His near-black hair didn't need a cover, but he put some dark greasepaint into a plastic zip bag and tucked it in flat in his suit jacket's inner pocket. There was no way to conceal a weapon, not even a knife.

Fortunately, he'd never felt a weapon was indispensable when it came to hand to hand combat. If he had need of a gun later, he'd obtain one from Mutaib's guards after disabling him.

He surveyed himself from all directions in the mirror. Nothing bulged. Regretfully, if he got the opportunity for the stealth operation tonight, his pricey suit might have to be left behind.

Before the hour for his appointment approached, he packed his duffle bag and took a back stair down to his vehicle. It might not be necessary, but a quick getaway option dictated that he be ready, and there were items concealed in the duffle bag he didn't want to lose if he didn't come back to the hotel tonight.

At the appointed hour, his room phone rang, and the operator gave him the message that his car was waiting. He let it wait just a few minutes longer. He didn't want to appear too eager. When he thought the right balance of arrogance and good manners had been achieved by the delay, he led Digger out of the room.

A pleasant drive to what Rex might have called a villa, had it been located on the Mediterranean instead of the Persian Gulf, gave him a chance to reassert the persona he'd projected to Mutaib. On the way, he murmured in English to Digger. When the time came to enter the house, he left Digger in the courtyard and gave him the hand signal to wait, then scout. He trusted Digger to figure out the rest, and to be where he was needed if he was needed in a hurry.

Both were wearing some of the comms equipment that had survived the explosion in Afghanistan or replacements for the missing pieces. Digger's special harness with the night vision camera that could be attached, his earbuds, and the battery pack to run both concealed on his collar and the leads threaded through his thick hair had all survived. The laptop that allowed whoever was handling Digger to 'see' what the camera saw had not, but Rex had replaced it. However, he had no plausible reason to bring his laptop to a social engagement, so he'd be 'blind' to what Digger was doing.

Digger's earbuds were Rex's only communication option. Naturally, he had his own earbuds and a throat mic concealed in his collar, so he could direct the dog. The earbuds would be of little use when he couldn't see what was making whatever noise he was hearing, but they would allow him to know if the dog ran into trouble of any kind and Digger would respond if Rex needed him.

He might even be smart enough to make a sound, so I'll know he's coming.

It was precisely ten p.m. when a robed manservant announced 'Ruan's' arrival. Mutaib, lounging among dozens of pillows of embroidered silk, welcomed him. There were no other guests. Mutaib gestured for Rex to seat himself and clapped his hands to summon a discreetly-waiting woman with a bowl of rose-scented water and a towel. The woman knelt beside Rex and without making eye contact bathed his hands and then dried them. Rex submitted to the ritual as graciously as if he'd been born to it.

After that, a parade of serving girls appeared. Some, Rex surmised from their undeveloped bodies, were as young as twelve or thirteen. Some were perhaps in their twenties. All were only partially clothed; their breasts bare of any cover but their long hair. They seemed unaffected by the gaze of their master and his guest. Rex was at first uncomfortable, and then, when the younger girls appeared, outraged. But his mission required he hide his attitude and act nonchalantly, as if this were his usual lifestyle.

Mutaib kept up a steady stream of commentary on the physical attributes of the girls. Rex assumed he'd sampled all of them, though his religion forbade fornication. It was sickening.

Halfway through the meal, Rex was startled to be handed a Bordeaux goblet. A girl of sixteen or so poured the ruby-colored wine into his glass while another who might have been her twin filled that of his host. Rex kept his mouth shut. If there'd been anything more than the decadent use of the serving girls that demonstrated Mutaib's contempt for both the law and his religion, this would have been it.

He sipped sparingly from his glass.

Mutaib had already downed one glass and was gesturing impatiently for the girl to refill his glass.

As the night wore on, Mutaib became more and more jocular. He didn't seem to be in danger of passing out from drunkenness, which made Rex understand he was a serious and experienced drinker. Being neither, though he could hold his liquor when required, Rex took opportunities to empty his glass in the large brass pot incongruously holding a Boston fern inches from his left elbow. He chose times when his move would be unnoticed by his host, particularly while the latter was engaged in conspicuous sexual harassment of his servers.

When not fondling the girls, Mutaib recounted his sexual exploits. The stories were vulgar, but so exaggerated that Rex could listen to them without being affected. Fiction had never interested him.

Around midnight, a girl came in with a glass tray holding two white lumps, a small silver tube, and a gold knife. Mutaib gestured for her to put it down on the table beside his reclining form and then picked up the knife. He expertly chopped the cocaine into a fine powder and then used the silver tube to snort a line of the coke.

He closed his eyes in apparent ecstasy for a moment. When he opened them, he waved the girl toward Rex.

Momentarily caught in a dilemma, Rex wasn't about to snort cocaine, nor could he graciously refuse. With a movement designed to look as if he was about to pick up the knife, he managed to upset the tray and lose the remaining powder and the second rock into the cushions. He made a horrified face and began to apologize, but Mutaib was laughing uncontrollably.

"No matter, my friend. There's more where that came from. But you must be a novice, no? No more of the good stuff for you."

He leered at Rex and leaned forward as if in confidence, though his voice was loud enough for the nearest serving girl to hear.

"No more cocaine, I mean. But for my new friend, nothing but the best of my women."

Rex tensed. Was Mutaib going to expect him to perform right here? Was he going to offer him a child? For a moment Rex considered how he could decline without insulting his host. Maybe he could claim to have a disease he wouldn't want to pass on. Humiliating, but not as bad as the alternative, which was killing his host prematurely.

However, to Rex's relief, Mutaib called for a manservant. The man, even though dressed in traditional robes, had an appearance that appalled Rex. Bald, beardless, and overweight, the man was the very picture of *soft*. Soft hands, soft high voice, soft bare feet. What had been done to him, no doubt as a child, infuriated Rex even more.

Once more he had to swallow his affront for the sake of the mission.

"Take him to Zoya," Mutaib said. His speech was slurred so the name came out as Zhoya, but Rex knew it was probably an Ethiopian name, meaning dawn.

To Rex, Mutaib explained. "Zhoya is not a servant. I have already three legal wives and she's not suitable for the fourth. It is *misyar*. She is yours for tonight."

This speech, Rex took to mean several things Mutaib hadn't said outright. For one thing, *misyar* was a type of Sunni marriage contract that was sometimes used for the convenience of not committing fornication in a legal sense. Typically, it was temporary, for as little as one night. Most men who entered *misyar* marriages were already married. This type of 'wife' would be called a mistress in America and most other countries.

However, he had his doubts that Mutaib's claim of *misyar* would stand up if it ever came to a court of law. Saudi marriage contracts were, by law and polite fiction, carried out by equal consent on the part of both parties. Maybe the Ethiopian woman he was being led to had entered a contract by choice, but more than likely she hadn't.

Second, he assumed she had fallen out of favor, either because she hadn't kept her beauty or was older. Mutaib would never have offered a woman he still considered valuable or had any sort of respect for, even a twisted sort, to another man.

Third, he assumed Mutaib was drunker or higher than he'd thought. He was being led into the sanctity of the prince's harem. It wasn't lost on him that entry into the harem in any circumstances other than by the prince's explicit invitation would have cost him his head.

It all played into his plans except for one thing. Zoya wasn't the woman he'd come to rescue.

***

THE MANSERVANT – REX didn't think the term eunuch was in vogue anymore – led him to a room that had evidently been prepared for him. A large bed and a single reclining chair were the only furniture in the room, and the bed was made up in luxurious fabrics, which also draped and mellowed the walls. Low, indirect lighting bathed the room in pink and gold hues. The manservant told him to make himself comfortable and backed out, half-bowing, and closed the door.

Rex remained standing and moved to the side of the room, near the door. What he did next would depend on who came through it next. He was ready for anything from a naked kid to armed guards.

When the door opened, Rex caught only the woman's profile before she passed him. His impression was of high cheekbones, a straight, well-formed nose and square chin, topped by a mass of black curls. Her form was slight under draped silk, and from her movements, Rex deduced she was still young. How young, he hadn't had time to notice.

Only a few seconds passed before she turned, and her eyes widened when she saw him. He didn't know why. Maybe she'd expected Mutaib, or if she'd been told she would be entertaining a guest tonight, maybe she was shocked he was still dressed.

Rex took only a couple of seconds to observe her lithe figure before his eyes flicked back to her face. She was clearly of East African origin, probably Ethiopian as he'd surmised from her name. It was impossible to tell her age. She could have been anywhere between fifteen and twenty-five. Not much older, he thought. She was lovely.

Her skin glowed in the amber light, and as she smiled tentatively, he noticed big, doe-eyes and full lips. If she'd come to him willingly of her own volition, he would have considered himself a very lucky man. But she hadn't, despite the smile.

Rex addressed her gently in Arabic. "You are Zoya?"

She cast her eyes downward and stammered her answer in broken Arabic. A sentence or two, which Rex could barely understand. She was asking him if she should undress.

"No. I want to talk to you."

She looked up again, quickly. Rex thought he saw hurt and confusion in her eyes. This could be more difficult than he'd thought.

"Tell me how you came here," he urged. More broken Arabic left him confused, so he switched to English and asked again. She shook her head.

Okay, she doesn't speak English, and I don't speak Ethiopian – what is it, Amharic? Arabic it is then.

Speaking slowly and without raising his voice, he asked and gestured for her to do the same. "Please tell me again where you were born."

She seemed to understand his Arabic better than she spoke the language. This time, she got it across that she was from Ethiopia, as he'd determined already. She explained that she'd been taken by 'bad men' when she was only eight years old, she showed with her fingers. She continued and explained with more gestures, single words and short phrases that she'd been sold to someone who brought her here, and at first, she'd been made to clean the harem and serve Mutaib's wives. Some of them were kind to her, but they turned against her when she became a woman, as she put it.

Then Mutaib had noticed her and gave her a room of her own and started visiting her at night.

Rex questioned her further. "Why has he sent you to me?"

Tears formed in her eyes and spilled down her cheeks. "I do not please him anymore. He wants me to do…"

She opened her mouth to say more, but Rex held up his hand in the universal gesture for *stop*.

"Would you leave, if you could?" he asked.

A flood of words in the language he didn't understand ensued, and she threw herself at his feet, embracing his legs. Rex hadn't expected that and took a moment to collect himself before he lifted her to her feet. Holding her by the upper arms, he said, "I came to help someone else, but I will take you, too, if that's what you want."

It was a more complex thought than he'd tried to convey before, but she understood.

"Who?"

"Her name is Rehka. She is from India and may have come here about four months ago."

"I know her."

"Can you show me where she is?"

She explained that it was still too early and that she'd have to wait until the prince had left the harem. She'd wait for him to leave and then go to Rehka.

Rex agreed, and then pointed to his watch and explained to Zoya that she should wait with him for an hour or so not to raise any suspicions. He sat down in the chair and pointed to the bed for her to lie down. The language barrier made it difficult to continue a conversation. Zoya closed her eyes and took a few deep relaxing breaths.

About ninety minutes later, Rex stirred, Zoya opened her eyes and Rex nodded for her that it was okay to leave now.

She slipped out of the room soundlessly. Rex risked a quick look outside the room to watch her glide down the hall and turn a corner. No one was within his sight, so he pulled his head back inside the room and closed the door. He looked at his new watch and decided he'd wait another hour. That should give the prince plenty of time to finish his amorous exploits and return to his quarters. Unless he'd passed out in the room of the woman he was with. Then there could be a problem.

While he waited, Rex lay down on the bed to think about how to get out of the compound with two women. He gave the problem and as many of its possibilities as he could imagine to his subconscious, set his internal alarm for an hour, and went to sleep.

Seventeen

HANDE AVCI ENTERED the room with only the passage of air around her moving body making any sound and went to shake the sleeping man awake. She cried out in fright when his hand shot out like a striking tiger and grabbed her wrist. He hadn't been sleeping at all, only pretending to, to trap her.

Zoya had come to her in her room and told her about the stranger, the prince's guest, and that he was not like the others. They'd both been threatened before with being sold away as prostitutes if they weren't accommodating to such guests. Here in Mutaib's harem, at least they were fed and well cared for at other times, and the times when they were expected to entertain were infrequent.

Zoya had told her the man would take her away, along with Rehka, the new one. She'd asked if Hande wanted to go as well. Was that a serious question? It was difficult to understand Zoya, but Hande was certain she had offered to take her with them. She asked where to find the stranger and Zoya told her which room.

When she reached to touch him, and he grabbed her, she tried to dodge back, fearful he'd hit her. His face softened, and he addressed her in Arabic.

"I won't hurt you. Who are you?"

"I am Hande," she answered simply, reassured by his calm and his words. "I'm going with you."

His expression turned guarded. "What do you mean?"

It had been a long time since she'd been so bold. Not since she'd left Turkey. Overcoming the beatings, she'd endured to learn to be a properly respectful pleasure wife to the prince was not easy.

She had come to Saudi Arabia, a young and inexperienced seamstress from the Turkish countryside, six years before. A man had come to her village to recruit factory workers, and Hande had responded, tired of her father and brothers treating her like a child who could not make her own decisions.

The agent told her many lies, wooing her with tales of independence and a good living in Saudi Arabia. She wished she'd been less trusting, less ignorant of the world outside her country. The agent sent her to the factory owner under the *kafula* system, meaning the factory owner had paid the agent, and she was now obligated to pay the owner for her passage to Saudi Arabia and the room and board he provided.

Far from a good living, the wages she was paid didn't even cover the growing debt. When she went to him to beg a lower interest rate, so she could someday pay it off, he laughed.

"I have a suggestion," he'd said. "You can pay off your debt and make your life better at the same time. No more long days of labor in the factory."

She should have known, by then, that the factory owner was not honest. He agreed to help her if she would spend one night with him. She refused to sleep with him. He'd raped her that night, and the next day he sold her to a wealthy man. She had to admit, her life was better with the rich man, Mutaib, than in the factory.

She despised Mutaib, though, and like Zoya, she'd fallen out of favor and had been relegated to the duty Zoya had been expected to perform tonight – a toy for the prince's guests. It was only a matter of time before her looks were gone and she'd be abandoned to the streets or worse.

She lifted her chin. "Zoya told me you would take her and Rehka away. I want to go, too."

Rex didn't answer at first. She watched as his eyes went blank, as if he was seeing something on a different plane. His lips thinned, his shoulders lifted and fell slightly. Moments later, he answered.

"How many of you are there? Mutaib said eleven."

"He lied. He lies always. Like all Arab men. There are many more."

Rex blew an exasperated sigh out his pursed lips. He muttered in English, "This is a problem."

She didn't understand the words, but she did understand the position she'd put him in. How could he justify telling one woman he'd take her away, and leave others who would bear the punishment for the escape? If he was a good man, as Zoya had told her, he'd have to take anyone who wanted to leave. When he spoke to her again, she knew she'd been right.

"How many would leave?"

"Six, seven… maybe."

Hande's hesitation worried Rex. His moral compass would not allow him to rescue only Rehka and leave six or seven women or however many there were, all in the same situation as Rehka, to their fate. He just couldn't bring himself to the point where he would leave any of them behind. His dilemma was taking that many was not in his plan. He had prepared himself to break Rehka out tonight and be gone, but the situation now called for a complete overhaul of his plans, including how he was going to get out of the country. He'd need a bigger getaway vehicle, for one thing. He didn't see himself sneaking that many women into his hotel room or driving out of the city with them crammed into a vehicle meant to seat only six people, plus Digger, and there could be more women, in the end there could be eight or nine.

Speaking of Digger, he wished he had the dog with him right now. It would make what he had to explain next a lot easier.

"I can't do this tonight. I didn't plan for so many. Can you give the others a message?"

"Yes. What do you want me to tell them?"

"Do you have the freedom to walk in the courtyard?"

"We have a courtyard for our use. We can walk freely there."

"Show me."

She went to the door and cautiously looked out. She motioned for him to follow. "I think it is safe."

Zoya hadn't come back, so Rex wasn't sure Mutaib had left the harem quarters yet. He cautioned Hande to walk quietly and peek around corners to check for guards, then followed her as she walked swiftly through the corridors. She pushed open a door and they were outside in a walled garden.

Rex looked up at the stars and oriented himself. "This is the northeast corner of the compound?" he whispered.

"I think so," she whispered back.

They returned to the room where she'd found him.

"Come to that courtyard at two a.m. tomorrow," he said. "A big black dog will lead you out and bring you to me. You aren't afraid of dogs, are you?"

Hande was gazing at him in astonishment. "A dog? Why a dog? Why will you not come yourself?"

"I'll be driving a big vehicle. If I can't get close, and I don't think I can, you will have to come to me. The dog will lead you."

She shook her head. Rex didn't know if it meant she wouldn't do it, couldn't believe it, or wasn't afraid of dogs.

"Do you understand?" he asked.

"I don't know if I understand why you want to do it like that, but I will do as you say."

Just then, there was a light rap on the door.

"Hide," he hissed at Hande.

Hande dived to the floor on the side of the bed away from the door and rolled partly under it, concealing herself in the bedclothes.

Rex stood to the side again and opened the door. Zoya walked in.

Zoya whispered urgently, "Guard comes. I answer."

Rex interpreted that to mean let her do the talking. She was undressing as fast as she could, throwing the silks here and there.

"Quickly!" she said, urging him to do the same. Inside a few seconds, she'd pushed him into the bed, only partly undressed, and sprawled across him.

A knock sounded at the door. With no appearance of embarrassment, she got up and walked to the door without covering herself. She threw it open, giving the guard a glimpse of Rex, who had snatched the sheets up to cover the fact that he was still wearing the pants of his ninja outfit.

The guard said something in a muffled voice, and Zoya answered. She closed the door. Loudly, she said, "You must leave. I will help you dress."

Rex understood that his night with Zoya was being orchestrated, and it was time to go. He put the clothes back on that he'd shed in haste, leaving the collar of his shirt open and his tie draped around it. He smiled at Zoya and whispered that Hande would tell her the plan. Then he opened the door and pretended to stagger a bit as he handed himself over to the guard to be escorted to the car.

Digger was waiting by the car when they came out the front door of the house. He rose to greet Rex, tail wagging and a goofy smile on his face. Rex said, "Good boy." He let the dog into the car and followed him into the back seat.

***

IN THE HOTEL room, he started talking to Digger, who had taken up his usual position on the bed seemingly listening, as if he'd been a human team mate, while Rex paced around the room. He couldn't know how much, if any of it, Digger understood, but speaking it aloud helped him detect flaws in the new plan he was formulating. There was one aspect he couldn't do anything about, which was that he didn't know precisely how many women to prepare for. It started with one, then it became two, now it may be six or seven, and there could even be more.

Everything else, he could deal with. In the morning, he'd trade in his rental SUV for a larger one, something like a Chevy Suburban. He'd buy a big cooler and stock it with water and food for the journey, and he'd plan an itinerary. He needed a less repressive country, somewhere he could help the women find asylum. Oman would do, but getting to Muscat, the seaport, in the most efficient way would require two border crossings in and out of the United Arab Emirates. Without papers for the women, he didn't have a prayer of making it.

He'd also want to take Digger to Mutaib's compound and try to show him the courtyard where he'd have to get to the women. That was a dicey proposition. He couldn't afford to be spotted or have Digger spotted. But he didn't know how else Digger would know what to do.

By the time Rex fell asleep, still thinking about the day ahead, it was closer to dawn than he wanted. His last conscious thought was to wonder if any of the women knew how to drive.

Eighteen

ZOYA AND HANDE didn't dare discuss their plans during the day. As soon as their would-be rescuer had left the harem quarters, the two young women discussed whether he was trustworthy. Zoya's imperfect grasp of Arabic made it more difficult, but it was the only language they had in common.

Somehow, Zoya conveyed her trust to Hande. "He didn't... use me," she said, though she used the crude version of the word for a sex act, the only one she knew in Arabic. She counted this as one of the main reasons, among others, to trust him.

Hande, being older and more cynical, counseled caution. "You must not hope. He may come to help us. He may not. We do not know why he didn't use you. I hope he is a good man. He seemed to be. But we don't know what his business is with Mutaib. Do I need to remind you what a wicked man the prince is?"

Zoya nodded. She wanted to tell Rehka only that they may have a way out. Hande was certain that if the man was not boasting, he would be willing to take them all. They also disagreed on when to break the news to the others.

Zoya thought they should tell everyone before the dawn broke, if they were going to give everyone the news, and not just Rehka. Hande again urged caution, giving her opinion that the less the others knew beforehand, the less chance of the plot being discovered by Mutaib or his legitimate wives.

In the end, they agreed to tell the others that night. They went separately to break the news, Zoya going first to one who knew both Arabic and Hindi, so she could tell Rehka, who knew even less Arabic than Zoya.

Each swore the women they notified to secrecy. "Do not speak of this to anyone else. Don't pack anything, that will raise questions. Just be ready to go to the courtyard at two tomorrow morning."

Despite the secrecy, the air in the harem quarters held a sense of electric anticipation that was almost palpable. The imposition of unusual quietness among the seven women who knew of the escape plan, and their lack of interaction with the others was soon noticed by the uninformed.

The harem had always been a place of shifting allegiances and intrigue. Mutaib kept about nineteen women besides his wives in the quarters. The wives had their own suites and didn't interact much with each other or the pleasure wives. They attended to their children, entertained their mutual husband at his whim, and followed a pecking order that roughly corresponded to the order in which Mutaib had married them, though each enjoyed favoritism from the prince at times, which temporarily changed it.

The others had only simple sleeping rooms of their own, and they spent their days gossiping with the others. They ate together, prayed together, even bathed together. There were a few children in the harem with them – boys only until they reached school age, and girls up to about the age of ten, after which they would go to the homes of husbands arranged for them by Mutaib. The children played together, often under the supervision of two or three of the mothers. That duty rotated among all the women, whether they had children or not. Those who'd been there the least amount of time might even have been the most often called upon for the duty, as there was also a pecking order among this group.

Neither Zoya nor Hande had children, and because Rehka didn't either, none of them thought to question what would happen with those who did. Among the seven were two whose sons had reached an age where they were sent to a boarding school, one who refused to bond with her child because of the way he was conceived, one who had a toddler — a little girl she adored *despite* the way she'd been conceived — and one who was pregnant with her first child.

After the midday prayer and meal, several of the women who planned to meet in the courtyard retired to their rooms for a nap, correctly believing they'd have a long night. After that, they submitted to being dressed for dinner along with the rest. No one knew in advance who the prince would summon or who would be commanded to entertain a guest. Their orders were to be always prepared, all of them, for they'd be beaten if they were not ready. As the hours advanced, the buzz in the air became more pronounced.

Hande was worried. She saw groups of women in twos and threes clumping together in whispered conversation. Her paranoia convinced her that they were talking about the escape plan, that they'd somehow deduced that was the reason for the perturbation in the harem environment. She regretted giving in to Zoya's insistence to tell the others so early.

She was particularly concerned that Zoya and Rehka had been in close contact all day. They'd never been close before, given the language barrier. Hande feared their unusual behavior had been noticed by women not included in the escape plans. Even her own nervousness could give the others a clue that something was afoot. She fought to keep it under control and concealed, though she couldn't get rid of the feeling of looming disaster.

***

EARLIER IN THE day, one of the women had carefully considered her options. The seventh woman Hande hesitated about when she told Rex the number could be six, perhaps seven. She was pregnant, about six months along, and still able to travel. She never considered abortion like some of the others. Abortion was an abomination in her religion, as in most, anyway. Despite her circumstances, she had secretly determined, once she'd known she was pregnant, to honor the baby's father and try to love him as was her duty.

She didn't speak of it to the others. Most of the pleasure wives either despised the prince or had become apathetic and resigned to their fate. But she was young and considered herself among the most beautiful. The prince had only three wives and was legally entitled to a fourth. Why should she not be the fourth? If she bore the prince a son and demonstrated her love for him when he visited her, would he not look upon her with favor and make her his wife?

And what would be her lot if she returned home? Her father and brothers, along with other men of her village would stone her as a harlot. She could not get rid of her baby and pretend to be untouched. She could not go somewhere else, pregnant and unmarried and expect to find a way to support herself. She'd die, along with her the unborn baby, whom she'd begun to allow herself to love.

After thinking on all the implications, she knew she could not escape with the others. But perhaps her knowledge of the plot would find further favor with her baby's father and secure her future. Therefore, right after morning prayer, she'd humbly requested an audience with her prince.

The prince had listened to her narrative with disbelief and then rage besieged him. He was so beside himself that a guest would betray his generosity that he almost struck the messenger. Only at the last moment before his hand connected with her cowering form did he gain control.

Instead of the slap she'd expected, he helped her up from where she'd fallen to her knees in terror. He kissed her on each of her cheeks and caressed her swollen belly. "You have done well to tell me," he said. "Thank you. You will be rewarded."

She gazed at him adoringly and said, "I only wish to please you, my lord." She didn't dare ask to be legally married. Not until their son was born.

***

MUTAIB CONSIDERED WHETHER to have the two conspirators brought to him and beaten. The woman who'd given him the information told him who they were, but she didn't know who else might be planning to escape. He decided to say and do nothing until they were in the courtyard. Then he'd have his guards round them up and bring them to him. In the meanwhile, he'd decide on suitable punishment. Perhaps beatings for the women who'd conspired with the imposter, Ruan Daniel. Maybe he'd let his guards have the others to do with as they wished. If any survived, he'd turn them out on the streets or maybe just dump them somewhere in the desert — let them die and the vultures have a feast.

Yes, that is the way to handle this. Then there will be no other attempts. I cannot be seen as weak.

The imposter however, required a different approach and the worse punishment imaginable. He called his henchmen, Gara, Iskandar, and Alula, the Toad.

"The man you brought to me yesterday has mortally offended me. You failed me. I should punish you, but I have to admit he was very good in his disguise. He even fooled me. And no one makes a fool of Mutaib bin Faisal bin Saud and lives to talk about it. The three of you have one opportunity to redeem yourselves. Bring him to me, alive. You may use whatever resources you need to fulfill your task."

Nineteen

REX HAD COMPLETED most of his arrangements when Mutaib's henchmen caught up with him. He'd exchanged rental vehicles, filled the gas tank of the new one, and purchased the supplies. He'd paid for another night in the hotel, though he'd only use part of it. He'd rest there after showing Digger where the harem courtyard was and imprinting Rehka's name and the courtyard in association in Digger's mind. Only when the rendezvous hour approached would he drive as close as possible to the courtyard.

Most Saudis who had the luxury would be indoors, avoiding the intense midday sun, when Rex decided it would be an appropriate time to take Digger to Mutaib's compound. Leaving the SUV in the hotel parking garage, he took a taxi to the neighborhood and then approached the compound on foot from a few blocks away. He and Digger were both looking forward to some shade as they approached. Rex was gratified to notice a tree close to the wall that Digger might be able to climb for access.

He was focused on his destination when three cars roared up behind him, one swinging around to block his way in front, and one stopping right beside him. Four men poured out of each car, three of them familiar. In no time, Rex and Digger were surrounded. Curiously, none of the thugs had guns drawn, though Rex wouldn't discount the possibility they had them concealed.

Rex didn't have to guess, something had gone wrong and he was in serious trouble. He was outnumbered. The best tactic would have been to get away, but it was too late — there was no escape.

The man Rex knew as Toad started forward, and Rex gave Digger the hand signal to attack. One of the principles of Krav Maga, was to attack first, before his opponent had the chance. With Digger's help he might have a chance to prevail, maybe. One thing was settled in his mind. He was not going to give up without a fight.

With the hand signal, Digger sprang at Toad, taking him down. Rex didn't have time to observe what happened next. He blocked a lunge from Gara with his left arm and slammed his right elbow into Iskandar's nose, breaking it and sending the Saudi reeling backward. After that, the others pounced.

In the ensuing melee, Digger got in some vicious bites and killed one man outright with his signature ripped throat offense. Another would be partially paralyzed from Digger's bite to the back of his neck.

Rex was a blur of motion, kicking here, slugging there, using his momentum to body-slam one thug even as another moved in. He dealt them heavy losses, but it was apparent he wasn't doing enough damage to win. There were just too many of them, and he didn't have the time to permanently disable all of them.

If there'd been only four, or even six, considering Digger was a help, he'd have been able to put them down with enough savagery that they wouldn't get up again. As it was, too many went down, recovered, and rejoined the fight.

Rex couldn't hope for anyone to call the police. There were no houses with views of this stretch of road, only compounds with high walls. It wasn't lost on him that the closest one was Mutaib's, and the fight was moving inexorably in the direction of a gate in the wall. At the rate the fight was going, he'd be dragged into the compound and beyond any expectation of discovery within a few minutes.

His hands, elbows, head, and feet were fully engaged in defense, and although he was causing damage the overwhelming numbers of fighters were still standing and attacking, too many for him to turn his actions into a proper offense to disable them. He realized he needed to get Digger away. But he couldn't use a hand signal; there was no time, and in any case, Digger wasn't looking – he was busy attacking whoever he could.

"Digger, run! Hide!" he yelled. The dog barked, a sharp sound that echoed off the surrounding compounds' walls. To Rex, it sounded like 'no'. He yelled it again, louder, he wanted Digger out of there. Just then he went down with four of the attackers hanging onto every limb.

He heard a yelp of pain from the dog and another from some human, and then someone slammed a fist into his temple which dropped him to his knees, a kick in the back of his head turned everything black.

***

AT THE SECOND command, Digger had disengaged. Someone had kicked him before he got clear, and he yelped. Then he turned and tore at the retreating leg with his bared teeth, laying skin open. He tasted blood, which roused his instinct to kill and feed, like his wolf ancestors. But his discipline was stronger.

He'd been commanded to run and hide, even though his alpha was in danger of being captured or killed. He fought his nature to protect, obeyed the clear command and reluctantly ran to hide.

From beneath the car that had blocked them in the rear, he watched as his alpha went down in a crowd of enemies. He growled, low in his throat. He'd know these enemies again if he met them. He would kill them. But for now, he'd obey. He stayed hidden.

***

ISKANDAR WAS THE only member of the team of the original three henchmen to remain standing after the fight. Toad was dead, his throat ripped out by the demon dog. Gara would recover, but not for a few weeks. He had a broken arm, a mangled right hand, and a soft-tissue injury that was causing him to cough up blood. He'd been taken to the hospital along with five other seriously-injured foot-soldiers from Mutaib's staff.

Iskandar had directed the others to carry Rex into the compound, secure him with ropes and handcuffs, and guard him while he, Iskandar, let the prince know of their victory. He then doubled security within the compound and outside. He thought the dog would have fled and would not return, but after seeing what it had done to Toad and some of his men, he didn't discount his thought that the dog could still be lurking somewhere, ready and able to do severe damage to get to its master.

"Shoot that dog on sight," was his order.

He was looking forward to the interrogation of the prisoner. Not only did this man insult him more than once, but Gara and Toad were also his closest associates. Friends. Now Toad was dead and Gara incapacitated for the near future. He was hoping, might even request, that he be the one to perform the interrogation. No doubt Mutaib would wish to deal the death blow. That was his privilege. Iskandar just hoped he'd get an opportunity to deal a few of his own before that.

"Your Highness, the prisoner is secure," he reported. Normally, he would not have been so formal. However, his disheveled state and the necessity of reporting that six of the prince's security force were dead or disabled made him nervous to assume any familiarity with the prince. Messengers with news such as this often bore the brunt of the prince's displeasure.

Twenty

REX REGAINED CONSCIOUSNESS slowly enough to suppress any groan or movement that would telegraph it to whoever was guarding him. He was lying uncomfortably on his back, his arms and hands under him and secured with handcuffs. His legs were tied together at the ankle. He opened his eyes just a slit and surveyed what he could see of the room. No one was within his field of vision.

He shut his eyes again and quieted his breathing. When he didn't hear anything to indicate he was being observed, he made one more test. He made a gagging sound deep in his throat and then held his breath. He'd been trained to hold his breath for up to five minutes with little effort. It would be enough for anyone who might be watching him to become alarmed and check on him. But when the five minutes passed with no effect, he breathed again, opened his eyes fully, and started to sit up.

That's when he heard a familiar voice.

"I am glad you could join us my friend," sarcasm was dripping from Mutaib's voice. "It's almost time for the party."

Here it comes.

He sat all the way up and placed his bound legs on the floor. He wouldn't give Mutaib the satisfaction of seeing him worried. So, he smiled. "Thanks for the invite."

Mutaib's face darkened with rage. "Bring in the women," he commanded.

Someone outside opened the door and thrust Zoya and Hande inside. After them came someone Rex had never met, but he knew who she was. Rehka looked exactly as she had in her picture. Her almond-shaped eyes were dark with fear, her face paler than he'd expected but understandable — the fear would have robbed her of her normal complexion. Her dark brown hair was straight and hung to her waist unbound. Her full lips were also bloodless.

All three women were naked, and their hands were bound in front of them. Rex's heart beat faster with the fear of what would happen to them and what he'd be forced to watch.

Did Zoya or Hande tell Rehka why she's here? Does she know it's my fault? Mutaib will want to know who sent me, and there's no name to give him. I better think of a name quickly.

Iskandar followed the women into the room, closed the door and leaned with his back against it, his arms crossed over his chest in triumph. He carried a short-handled whip with several thin, plaited leather strands attached to it.

Rex averted his eyes from the women, unwilling to add to their degradation by looking at their nakedness. Instead, he focused a fierce glare on Mutaib.

"They are innocent. Punish me. I'm the one who seduced them into my plot."

Mutaib's lips curled in a cruel smile. "All in good time. You will be punished, make no mistake. But first you *will* watch their punishment. You *will* watch, or it will go worse for them. Look at them!"

A snap of the whip against flesh, followed by a sharp cry, forced Rex to comply with Mutaib's demand. He swung his head back toward the women and saw Zoya's arm bleeding. The cuts would scar. Rex despaired at the thought of what he'd brought on these poor women.

"Tell me who sent you," Mutaib demanded.

He blurted out the name of Rehka's creditor, Dhruv. Rehka flinched when she heard the name and Mutaib noticed. He addressed her directly. "You are the reason for this rebellion?"

She didn't understand all the words, but she understood 'you'. She paled even more and shook her head mutely in denial.

Mutaib nodded and Iskandar laid the whip vigorously across her back. She cried out and fell to the ground.

Rex saw that her back was bleeding and gritted his teeth in rage. "I'm sorry," he half-whispered. "Rehka, I'm so sorry."

"Which one of you showed this camel dung the courtyard?" Mutaib asked.

Hande gasped. Iskandar's whip snaked out and cut her, but she didn't fall.

To Rex's surprise and admiration, she turned a contemptuous look on Mutaib and pressed her lips together.

Mutaib made a gesture to Iskandar to move towards Rex. "Your fists only," Mutaib said. "I want this to last."

To Rex, he said, "Who is this Dhruv you speak of? I do not know him. Is he the girl's father? Her husband? A boyfriend?"

Rex stayed silent and stared at Mutaib in defiance. He'd done Rehka enough harm by opening his mouth. Mutaib nodded again and Iskandar stepped forward. He yanked Rex to his feet and slammed his fist into his stomach as hard as he could.

The blow would have doubled a man in worse physical shape than Rex. Rex, however, tensed his stomach muscles and absorbed the blow.

"That's it," he said, smiling. "Pick on someone your own size, not defenseless women. How about you take these restraints off and the two of us have a go at it? Just the two of us. The winner gets the women. Or are you a yellow belly who can only hit women and men who are tied up?"

The interrogation went on for several hours. Mutaib would ask Rex something, and each time the answer or lack thereof would earn a blow whether it was truthful or a lie, answered straight or with sarcasm. Iskandar had learned to hit him where he couldn't defend himself with clenched muscles, so he was covered in bruises, maybe a few cracked ribs, one eye swollen shut and blackened, and his nose was bleeding and interfering with his breathing.

Iskandar's beatings shifted between Rex and the women. Soon they weren't in much better shape than Rex. Though Mutaib had Iskandar leave their faces alone, perhaps intending to sell them after the beatings, the enforcer was allowed to hit them anywhere else. Their torsos and breasts were covered in bruises and not one of them could stand when Mutaib called a halt when the sound of the Imam's voice over the loudspeakers at the nearby mosque calling the faithful to evening prayer reached their ears.

Rex couldn't help but marvel at the hypocrisy of a man who would degrade a woman by having her stripped and beaten, and then turn around and pray to a deity he thought of as merciful and just.

A just god would strike him with lightening and that would've been merciful compared to what I have in mind for you scumbag.

As Iskandar led the bleeding and bruised women away, Rex made a vow. If he survived this and escaped, and he had every intention of doing so the moment he was given the opportunity, Mutaib, Iskandar, and any man left in this compound would die.

Meanwhile, while Mutaib and Iskandar were appeasing their pious consciences, he had a bit of time to plan his breakout.

He wouldn't be left alone for long.

Twenty-One

JOSH AND MARISSA had exhausted their investigative leads in Afghanistan without discovering anything new.

Visiting the site of the explosion convinced them there was no point in taking samples, even if they could have done so without starting another riot. They reported to Brandt that it was a very real example of scorched-earth philosophy on the part of the Afghani rabble that had rioted after the explosion.

When he asked what they meant, they said, "The place is literally scorched. We asked a few people who were guarding the place, not allowing anyone to enter the property, what had happened there. They said they and others had burned a place where infidels had attacked them."

"That's the same party line we got at the time. And it's bullshit," Brandt said.

"Doesn't matter, we can't take samples. We can't get in, and even if we could, they won't let us take anything out. Also, the scene's been compromised. Evidently, they dumped tons of flammable material on it before they set it on fire. No telling how far down we'd have to dig to get to any human DNA. And then we'd probably have to remove a hundred or more cubic yards of material and ship it home to even have a hope of finding or not finding human DNA."

"You're saying it's too big a job for you."

"I'm saying it's too big a job for CRC, or anyone, for that matter. It would require invasion and occupation by military force, massive effort, and months if not years of analysis. Let it go, boss."

"I understand. But we still need to exhaust all efforts to find Dalton if he survived. Go ahead and hunt down the remaining Phoenix Unlimited employees. I'll email their dossiers."

They'd been a tight group in the first place, and more than half, including Frank Millard, the CEO, had been killed in the explosion. The others, only six, had left Afghanistan to find employment somewhere else. To find them, Josh and Marissa would have to travel to at least four hot spots in the Middle East and Africa. They discussed the options to determine which outfit they'd visit first.

Whether Rex was dead or not was only one of two major questions Brandt had. The other one was who had betrayed him. Obviously, Bruce Carson had been the final messenger in the chain. Brandt didn't think he was the primary source of the kill order.

With Carson gone and out of Brandt's immediate reach, Josh and Marissa would have to unravel the threads of the conspiracy from the other end. That meant they had to at least consider the notion that one or more of the former Phoenix Unlimited employees could have been part of the treachery. They needed to find them and look into their eyes when they questioned them to judge whether they were telling the truth or not.

Two of them had gone together to a logistics provider in Egypt. The crisis there that had begun three years before was winding down with the *coup d'état* and subsequent stabilization. However, there was still some unrest, attacks and bombings against the police to protest the imprisonment and death sentences of members of the Muslim Brotherhood.

Some of Egypt's troubles spilled into Iraq's, with Muslim extremists joining ISIL at the beginning of the Iraq war. That was still very much a danger zone and expected to remain so for some time to come. One member of Millard's remnant team rejoined the US Army, said to have been absorbed into Delta Force and acting as an advance observer. If that proved true, they had little hope of tracking him down and even less hope of getting within a country mile of his location. For the Army to allow that would be to compromise his mission.

Another buddy pair's last known movement had been to the Sudan, where they could be anywhere. Marissa argued that it could take years to track them down and it would be extremely dangerous to do given the ongoing civil war.

The last member of Millard's surviving group had simply vanished. They had no information on him at all. Brandt suggested they look for him in Afghanistan first, among the other paramilitary organizations active there. If that didn't prove fruitful, they could go on to try to find the others. At the end of their discussion of the options, Josh and Marissa agreed that might be the best use of their waiting time.

Josh had been right about his safety argument. Every time they questioned a local, they risked blowing their cover, which in Afghanistan was already thin. They could point to no articles coming out of their 'journalistic' research. If anyone questioned them, they'd have to explain they hadn't completed their research, but if anyone dug deeper they'd find that these journalists made no notes and took no photos.

Falling afoul of any law, and there were many that they were sure they just couldn't even anticipate, would get them thrown out of the country or worse. The further they dug, the better they understood what Rex had been up against when he'd been assigned there for over a year. Eventually, though, they asked the right person the right question.

It was in a coffee shop in a poor quarter of Kabul, on the edge of a teeming marketplace. Unbeknown to them this was the market which Rex frequented to pick up on gossip and befriend informants. Marissa overheard someone sitting at a table next to theirs with some men, talking about a friend he thought was dead. He was explaining that he'd given the friend a lead on a job loading a truck, but the truck had exploded the next day. Fearing his missing friend was the one who had caused the explosion and that the subsequent investigation would lead back to him, the speaker, he'd fled Kabul and only just returned.

To Marissa, who understood every word the man was saying, the story sounded vaguely familiar. She translated for Josh. When they'd come to Kabul, they had a full briefing on Rex's mission and his reports, and they'd seen how frustrated he was at the inaction he'd been under orders to maintain. *Observe and report* – that's all he was supposed to do. But Josh had known of Rex's reputation, and he knew Rex had a reputation for being a rebel at times, an agent who sometimes followed his own council, not the orders he was given. They'd also been briefed by Brandt about the mysterious bombings and other raids against the opium industry, which Brandt thought was the work of Rex Dalton. With the wisdom of hindsight, Brandt speculated it was probably what led to the false flag mission ordered by Carson that killed the mission team and maybe Rex. Or not.

The truck bombing described by this man to his friends at the table sounded like one of those that could have been pulled off by Dalton, though it took place in Kabul rather than in the opium fields and factories around the country. But it was no secret that the truck was loaded with drugs at the time of the explosion.

Marissa eavesdropped until the man she overheard expressed the opinion that he'd always been suspicious of his friend's sudden appearance in Kabul. He was explaining that the friend had a story about where he'd been before, but the accent was slightly off, as if he'd been brought up in Kabul instead of where he said he was from. And the man would disappear for days at a time, then show up again asking questions about drug trade jobs.

"If you ask me, he was an undercover policeman," the man finished. "I liked him, though. I wonder where he's gone now. It's been weeks since I saw him."

One of the other men at the table wondered if his friend could have been vaporized in that explosion. It was a really big one. He'd seen the wreckage afterwards and said no one who was close would have been left recognizable.

Marissa had quieted Josh's prattle with a firm hand on his wrist. When the man stopped talking, she nodded toward him and squeezed Josh's wrist.

"Follow my lead. I'll explain later," she said in English.

Josh nodded once.

Marissa got up and went to the table where the man was still sitting. His companion had left, leaving the coast clear for her questioning.

"I'm sorry," she said in Arabic, "but I couldn't help overhearing what you were talking about. Do you really know an undercover policeman?"

The man looked offended. "It is not proper for you to speak to me. Tell your husband to come over here and ask me. I will *not* talk to you."

Marissa smiled. They'd chosen the right cover, though the only reason the man had for assuming Josh was her husband would have been that they were out in public together.

"My apologies. I didn't mean to offend you. My husband does not speak Arabic. Would it be okay if I translate for him?"

The man though about it for a moment and nodded.

Marissa asked Josh to join them and told him how it should be done. He'd need to ask her the questions while looking at this man, and she would translate the conversation. But it was imperative that he must always have the conversation with this man, not with her. She was just a sideshow.

Josh nodded his agreement and fired the first question.

"We are journalists, and if you could tell me what you know about that policeman, it would help our story."

"But I don't know much about him."

"Can you tell us what he looks like? How tall is he? What is the color of his eyes, his hair? Any marks and features on his face or body?"

Their informant shrugged. "Hair almost black, dark brown eyes. I noticed no blemishes on his face, and of course I did not see anything else except his hands. He has large hands, working man's hands. And his nose, now that I think of it."

"What about his nose?"

The man turned his profile to them, and then looked directly at them again, displaying a nose shaped rather like an arrowhead when viewed from the front, and a hawk's bill from the side. "His nose looked like a youth's." He took the fleshy part of the end of his own and wiggled it. "This part was thinner. Like a European's nose."

"Is that unusual?" Marissa forgot to let Josh ask the question first, and the man became offended again.

"Tell your husband what you asked me. If he wants to know, I will answer."

Marissa, angry with herself for the mistake, told Josh what had happened. "I think that may be our answer, but I'm not certain it's all that unusual. Pretend to be angry with me, and then ask him."

Josh put a bit too much authenticity into it for Marissa's taste. Her eyes told him there would be consequences when he yelled, "How dare you address another man! You belong to me, and you'd better get that into your head."

Then he turned and asked the informant the same question Marissa had. Marissa translated after explaining that her husband was very angry with her for her mistake and apologizing.

Mollified, the Afghani graciously accepted her apology. "It is not unusual among our youth. But this man is older. Perhaps my age."

Marissa's guess was that the man was between thirty-five and forty, so if he was describing Rex, he was about right on the age estimate.

She translated the answer for Josh and then asked, "Is there anything more to be gained from this man?"

"I can't think of anything. He's just described fifty or a hundred million men of Arabic ethnicity. Rex was passing for native, so it could have been him, but I'd say best case scenario would be about fifty-million-to-one."

Marissa sighed, and her shoulders slumped a little. "Well, at least the food and coffee here were good. Tell him thank you, and let's get out of here."

Josh addressed the man with a smile and nod of thanks, Marissa translated, and they paid for his meal as a gesture of good will. The upside of their effort was, if either of them ever had to come back here on a mission, they'd have a friendly native to start with.

Twenty-Two

REX HAD BARELY begun to consider the room, his situation, and the possible use of items in the former to help with the latter, when Iskandar returned. The tall Saudi strode straight from the door to Rex's chair and backhanded him with such force that the chair turned over and Rex banged his head on the stone floor.

So that's the way it's going to be. He's going to beat me to a pulp while his boss is making atonement to Allah for doing so.

He was relieved in a way. Being forced to watch the women being beaten had been far worse torture to him than anything this pig could do to him. Even if that included killing him.

Rex wasn't afraid of dying, he just didn't have in mind doing so now.

But it wasn't enough for Rex to endure the beatings. Sooner or later, Mutaib would get tired of playing with him and kill him. Worse, when they killed him, they'd do the same to the women but probably rape and torture them before doing so.

I got them into this – it's my obligation to survive and get them out.

He was going to have one hell of a headache, but he hadn't lost consciousness. That meant no concussion, he thought. Then he started thinking about how he could turn the tables and stop Iskandar. He was on his own for now. He didn't know where Digger was, if he was in range of the comms unit with his head phones or not. All he could do was try, but not with Iskandar in the room.

Should have thought of that while I was alone.

Rex was already in bad shape. He barely noticed when Iskandar summoned someone to help set his chair upright again, with him still trussed to it. He forced his mind to ignore the pain and concentrate on what he was going to do when he got out. He never allowed himself to even think that he might not get out. He was thinking about what he could say to Digger when he had the chance, and how he could say it, to have the dog lead the women out of the compound.

He only paid more attention to what was happening in his immediate presence when the door opened and Mutaib returned. Silently, the prince walked close to him to examine his bruises and contusions. He stepped all the way around Rex's chair and then backed up toward the wall with the door.

"Continue," he said.

Iskandar had dismissed his helper. "Gladly, Your Highness," he said. He stepped forward and punched Rex square in the nose. More blood started streaming from it.

Rex smiled, allowing the blood to spill into his mouth, where he knew it would line his teeth and present a gruesome sight to anyone watching. "Is that all you've got?"

Iskandar looked at Mutaib with an unspoken question in his eyes. The prince nodded. Iskandar squatted to release the bindings from Rex's legs and his handcuffs just long enough to release the chair's arms from them. He yanked Rex up and shoved him against the wall, where he swiftly attached a handcuff to each hand and clipped them onto two rings in the wall above his head. With his torso exposed and unable to bend over to defend it, Rex felt the first blow to his liver.

He no longer had the ability to even try to tense his muscles to absorb such a blow. But Iskandar had made the mistake of leaving Rex's legs unshackled. When he approached again, Rex flexed with his core and drew both legs up. Hanging from the handcuffs, he shot his legs out and caught Iskandar in the solar plexus. The force of the kick lifted him off the ground and sent him flying backwards, his heels and the back of his head hit the floor at the same time. Lights out.

Despite his pain, Rex laughed out loud when Mutaib let out a girlish shriek and fled from the room. A moment later, two men came in and dragged Iskandar's limp form out. The door slammed, an electronic *click* told Rex he'd been locked in, and he was alone.

Time to return to his escape plan again.

***

WITH HIS ARMS extended far above his head and shackled, Rex could stand for hours, but there would be a toll on him. First his hands would go to sleep as the blood drained from them and couldn't return. They'd be useless if someone unshackled him. Permanent damage would occur if it went on for long. Furthermore, all his options for escape required the use of his hands.

Rex supposed someone would be in eventually to beat him some more or kill him. In the meanwhile, he was hungry and thirsty, his hands were beginning to tingle, and to make matters worse, he needed to take a leak.

It would have been laughable if he hadn't been so desperate, but he was not going to give them the satisfaction of pissing in his pants.

He took his mind off the urgency and searched the room with his eyes, taking note of everything in it, though there wasn't much. He did it methodically, starting with the door, its lock, and its latch handle. It was a lever-type opener. He visually took the measure of the distance from him. Could he lift himself like he'd done to disable Iskandar and jostle the door open? That would force someone to come sooner.

The chair he'd been sitting in was wood. If he could get loose, breaking one of its legs in just the right way would provide him with a fine weapon. He'd gladly skewer Mutaib. Iskandar's discarded quirt lay in the corner. Rex could see no use for it as an escape tool, maybe as a weapon once he was out of the restraints. His fists, legs, and head, his Krav Maga instruments of destruction, would be much better weapons, if they weren't useless blobs of tingling flesh by the time he had the chance to use them.

There was nothing else in the room. The chair, the quirt, the rings he was half-suspended from, which he couldn't see but knew were there. But the rings were not going to come out of the wall — he had already tried. And there was a lone lightbulb without a cover dangling from a wire stretching from the ceiling.

Go figure. They didn't put me in quarters reserved for honored guests. How many have gone through here before me? I'm willing to bet very few, if any, ever left here alive. But Rex Dalton will be going out on his own two feet.

Rex tried bellowing for help, on the chance that Digger could hear him, or annoy any guards outside into coming in to check on him. After a while he realized the yelling was only making him thirsty. So, now, he was thirsty, *and* he needed to take a piss.

"Not too bright, Einstein. Shut up and think," he chastised himself aloud.

Just when he thought there was nothing left to consider, the door opened. An impossibly old woman, Saudi he guessed, came in with a bowl of water and a crust of what looked like moldy bread. Her face was not covered by anything but ten thousand wrinkles. She was so stooped it was a miracle she didn't topple over on her face, and she moved with the arthritic stiffness of a nonagenarian.

He greeted her in Arabic, saying, "Thank you for the water, grandmother. Can you let my hands loose, so I can lift the bowl?"

She ignored him, refused to even look at him, as she went about her business. She set the bowl on the ground, and the bread beside it. She picked up the quirt and tucked it into the folds of her garment.

There goes one of my weapons. Do you mind? I wanted to strangle some asshole with that.

When she left again without acknowledging him, he started laughing.

"Hey! How the hell am I supposed to drink that?" he yelled.

To his surprise and gratitude, the door opened, and a man came in, much younger than his last visitor. Rex didn't wait to see what he would do. He spoke in rapid Arabic but deliberately mumbled and slurred his words to create the illusion that he was weak and crushed. "I must relieve myself. Can you let my hands loose, please? They have brought me water and bread, but I need my hands also to drink and eat."

The young man was short, but bulky. Rex estimated the man would outweigh him by fifty pounds or more, and it appeared to be all muscle.

I can take him even with my hands asleep. If I can just get them loose. But this is not the time to put up a fight, not yet.

Without speaking, the man reached to release Rex's left hand, staying as far away from it as he could while doing so. He kept one end of the handcuff around Rex's wrist and used the other to control Rex's movements and keep his swing short. Rex could have made a move to hit him in the throat with an elbow but controlled the urge to go into action.

The young man wrestled Rex into the chair and cuffed his hands together in the back with zipties but didn't tie them to any part of the chair.

"When I have gone, you may do as you wish. Drink from the bowl like a filthy dog if you want. Piss in your pants, I don't care. The prince wants to keep you alive for a long time while he tortures you, but the rest of us would gladly kill you. Enjoy your life while you can. What's left of it is going to be full of pain and suffering. I wish the prince would allow me to give you the deathblow, but I think he is keeping that privilege for himself."

Rex didn't respond, just sat there, limp in the chair, keeping up the ruse that he was spent.

The man stepped through the door, and Rex heard the distinct electronic click that told him the lock was engaged. He was in far better shape to make an escape now. His hands were as good as free, he had water, sustenance in the form of bread, and he could finally take a piss. And the guard had just given him the opportunity he was waiting for. The zipties.

Life was good.

Rex had been trained to defeat handcuffs, duct tape, ropes, and zipties. There were three or four ways to get out of handcuffs provided one had some sort of metallic pin or a double-jointed thumb. But he didn't have to worry about that now.

Contrary to popular belief, zipties are not invincible. There are many ways to defeat them. The first, of course, is to cut them, but Rex could see no rough edges in the room. He could break the chair but cutting the zipties with a rough edge of wood would likely be a good way to make a bloody mess of his wrists before he got the ties cut.

Another of the methods is to break the ties with brute force by raising one's arms above one's head and bringing them down with speed and force against the pelvis or stomach while pulling the elbows back sharply in the same move. Rex had enough cuts and bruises for one day, and he also didn't feel strong enough to try that. He decided to use a less violent and painful method — cut the ties with his shoelaces.

He dropped off the chair, climbed through his arms, and went to work.

Rex's CRC training had included survival skills, and he had taken it to heart. Every pair of casual shoes, boots, hiking footwear – basically, anything he wore on his feet except dress shoes and boat shoes – required shoelaces. And he replaced every pair of shoelaces in new shoes with 550-paracord laces. Paracord shoelaces were a miracle of modern engineering. They were incredibly strong. They were also incredibly versatile. They were typically made with a seven-cord core, each cord made of three strands of nylon parachute cord. The entire bundle was wrapped in lightweight kermantile rope, making a smooth rope surface.

Rex had never had a shoelace break at an inopportune time, but that wasn't the point. In an emergency, he could create a lengthy string for a snare, a support for a hanging shelter, and quite a few other handy uses, just by pulling the steel tip off the end (nice for creating a spark when needed) and accessing the inner cords. But he didn't need any of that today.

The laces would serve nicely as a friction saw to break the zipties holding his wrists together. Now that he had his arms in front, he sat on the floor and took out his shoelaces. He tied them together with a sheet bend knot, consisting of a loop in one end of one shoelace, into which he looped one end of the other shoelace and pulled tightly together.

His movements were a bit restricted by the ziptie around his wrists, but as soon as he'd seen that the guard was going to use a ziptie, he'd flexed his wrists to create a bit of slack. His fingers were strong enough to make quick work of the untying and removing the laces from his low-rise trail boots – his go-to footwear for surveillance missions. Along with a pair of khaki-colored cargo pants and a loose white shirt from India, they had been what he was wearing when he'd been ambushed hours before.

Rex's mind was working overtime on what he'd do once his arms were free while his hands tied a bowline at each end of the rope he'd created from his shoelaces. He'd learned to tie that knot as a kid out on camping trips with his family, long before the training that reinforced how useful it was. His CRC training taught him to tie it one-handed. He measured the cord around his shoe, and then set the measured end with the closed end of the loop facing away from him. With the short end, he formed another open loop. He held the long or standing end down with his knuckles and used his thumb to hook it and loop it around his hand.

The short end he was still holding in the same hand needed to go under the standing end and come back up and over the loop in the standing end, then back down through the hole. All that he accomplished without even thinking about it. He cinched the knot tight with the loop just large enough to slip over his right shoe and up to a secure position, He slipped the other end of the cord through his wrists and inside the ziptie. He repeated the knot-tying on the left end of the rope and slipped it over his shoe on that side.

Now all he had to do was lean back on his tailbone and pretend to ride a bicycle. Only a few rotations of each foot were enough to snap the zipline, weakened from the friction of the nylon cord against the nylon tie. His hands were free in less than twenty seconds.

With both hands free to pick it up, he drained the bowl of the water, gulping as if he had been about to die of thirst. He looked at the bread and decided it wasn't worth bothering with. Finally, he unzipped his pants and filled the bowl again.

Pissing in my pants. You must be joking.

Before he did anything else, he examined his shoelaces. The covering was a bit frayed, but they were still serviceable. He untied all the knots and threaded them back into his shoes, then put the shoes back on and tied them securely.

Now to unlock that door.

Even if he had a lock-pick it would've been useless. It was an electronic lock. His cell phone had been taken, but they hadn't done more than a cursory search for weapons. He could still feel the slight raised bump in his collar that was the mic for Digger's earbuds, and he had something in his pants pockets. He stuck his hands in them, knowing he'd had nothing, not even a pocketknife, that would help much.

In one pocket, he found a stick of gum, and in the other, a few coins. Not enough to buy his way out of this place. Unless... Something was niggling at his brain. Something from his earlier perusal of the room. What... *Oh!*

He stood and reached for the dangling light socket. He'd remembered right. When he looked at it earlier, he'd noted that the bulb didn't screw into the socket. It was a bayonet-type bulb, which meant there were exposed electrodes in the slots. What were the odds that the lights and the door lock were on the same circuit?

Fifty-fifty, he figured. Either they were, or they weren't. Like John Brandt always said, "the surest way to fail is not to try." He took another look around, in case he'd missed anything in the bare room. Nothing else had magically appeared. His next move would either free him or leave him in the dark until someone came.

He took the stick of gum out of his pocket and began chewing it. When he had it soft and juicy enough, he grasped the coins in his other pocket and came out with a handful of them. He picked one that looked about the right size, small enough to fit into the hole of the bulb socket if he unplugged the bulb and big enough to touch both electrodes.

Then he located the light switch and turned the light out.

He was plunged into darkness with the flip of the switch, but he'd counted the steps from the middle of the room where the light dangled to the wall. He carefully kept the same orientation, stepped back and swept his arm into the darkness in front of and slightly above his head, locating the socket and bulb with the second back-swing. He unplugged the bulb out of the socket and fitted the coin into the bulb socket by feel, holding it in place with his left thumb.

He took the sticky chewing gum out of his mouth and used his right hand to smash the gum onto the socket, securing the coin. Then he sidled back to the wall switch and flipped it again. Sparks flew out of the socket and the telltale electronic *click* sounded nearby.

The door was open!

***

REX HAD NO idea how much time had passed. It had been about three-thirty in the afternoon when he was taken. He'd been unconscious part of the time since then, so his internal clock was almost certainly out of sync with real time.

He'd probably missed the rendezvous with the women, but there were almost certainly guards on them anyway. He'd gathered that one of the seven had betrayed the plan. He also didn't know where Digger was, or if he'd been captured.

Finally, he'd like to have his cell phone and pricey new watch back, and if there was anyone left to rescue, it was probably imperative he get Rehka's scarf back. This whole plan had gone belly up, and there was little doubt she was no longer in the harem. If he was to salvage anything, he and Digger would have to sneak into the harem the back way and from there into the rest of the compound to find the women themselves. No one would be leading them to him. Digger would need the scarf to be of any help to Rex in finding everyone.

So, the first order of business was finding his possessions. In a mansion of this size, it was a crapshoot whether he could find anything before he himself became the object of a hunt and was discovered.

He eased the door open a few inches, careful to keep it from squeaking on its hinges. He looked through the small crack, first with one eye. When he failed to see anyone, he opened it a little further, winced at the squeak it emitted, and stuck out his whole head, ready to fight his way out if necessary.

The hallway was dark, too. Evidently, he'd taken out more than just one room's electricity. But an emergency-lighting strip dimly lit the floor, so he could see where the hallway led, barely. He walked silently, casting his gaze far enough ahead to see any breaks in the dim strip lighting to warn him someone was there. Above about four feet, the space was dark as a moonless night.

He'd gone about twenty feet down the hall and passed cross-halls without detecting anyone. Where was everyone? He'd expected to be guarded. He was also getting an idea of just how big this place was. The halls he'd traveled after dinner with Mutaib hadn't stretched this far before the harem quarters. Maybe he was in another building than the main residence. Another thought intruded.

The lights down here couldn't possibly have been on the same circuit as the ones in my cell. This darkness is for another reason.

His speculation was answered abruptly when he came to an L in the hallway, forcing him to turn left to continue. As soon as he turned, he could see an area with some light up ahead. He slowed, making no noise at all, though he still couldn't see anyone. It was entirely possible the narrow view he had of the lighted area concealed a larger room, with any number of guards out of sight, but just around the corner.

When he eased to the end of the hallway, he could see he'd been right about the larger room. It appeared to be a sort of lobby at the entrance to the building, because he could now make out the source of the light – a security light on a pole outside, shining through glass doors. But the lobby, or whatever it was, was empty. No guards in sight.

As he grew more confident he was alone, Rex straightened from a precautionary crouch. The glass doors were the only vulnerability he'd have while he searched the room, so he kept an eye on them frequently. The room, not a lobby but an office or duty station of some sort, had lockers, a desk with a computer and keyboard, an intercom system and radio, and a set of keys.

Careless of them to let me escape and then provide me with just what I need.

Based on his assessment of the room's function, he'd have bet his quest for his possessions would end here. Somewhere, in the desk drawers, or one of the lockers, he'd find them.

He began with the desk, surmising the lockers probably held the guards' possessions or tools of their trade. Maybe weapons, which could come in handy. But first, his things and hopefully Rehka's scarf – the only thing he couldn't replace.

He seized the keys and examined them, selecting one that should work the locks on the desk drawers. The pencil drawer was of no interest, so he started at the top of the stacked side drawers. There was a set of handcuffs and not much else besides paper. He put the handcuffs in his pocket — they might come in handy at some stage.

The next drawer held detritus of what looked like a month's worth of snacks. It also held a couple of dead cockroaches and one very much alive sucker the size of his pinky finger. Rex slammed the drawer shut with a shudder. Something about those insects aroused a primitive revulsion in most people, and Rex was no different. Logically, he couldn't be harmed by one, only startled.

He opened the bottom drawer with more caution, half-expecting a legion of the disgusting things to swarm out at him. Instead, he found what he'd been looking for. His cell phone, watch, and Rehka's scarf. The only items from his person that Mutaib's guards had bothered to take. He was surprised the watch and cell phone hadn't been appropriated by senior members of the guard detail, but he wouldn't look a gift horse in the mouth. He put the watch on and the cell phone in the pocket that wasn't stuffed with handcuffs. The scarf also went in that pocket.

The next order of business was to get outside, figure out where he was, and find Digger. After that he could see about the women.

Twenty-Three

REX'S IMMEDIATE PROBLEM was to decide whether the glass doors were alarmed, and if so, whether he could find the alarm system to disarm it. Stealth was his friend when it came to rescuing the women. The last thing he needed was a shootout with guards or any other commotion, including blaring alarms. Before he would risk it, though, it would be a good idea to search the bank of lockers for weapons and ammo. The other last thing he needed was being unarmed in a shootout with guards.

He made quick work of the search, and he could not believe his luck when he found an Atchisson Assault Shotgun, known as an AA-12. In close quarters combat assault rifles are well and good, but if you really wanted to cut the enemy to pieces, nothing quite compares to a good shotgun. Especially if it was fully automatic like the AA-12, which fired five 12-gauge shells per second on full automatic from a twenty-round tommy gun-style drum magazine with so little recoil one didn't have to be the Terminator to do it with one hand.

He rejected several of the handguns he found at first, but in another locker, he finally found what he was looking for. His hand weapon of choice. A Sig Sauer P226, with three spare clips fully loaded with fifteen rounds each in a belt that also held the holster for the Sig.

He fitted the belt around his waist and made sure the pistol was easy to draw. The shotgun he'd have to carry in his left hand.

Mutaib's men were in for a nasty surprise. Now he was ready to search for the alarm system. It should be in a closet or small room, along with the telephone system. There were two closed doors beyond the desk, on the other side of the room. He tried the first one, and found it opened into a four-stall restroom with one filthy sink. The stillness in the air had convinced him this building was empty, so he didn't bother to look in the stalls.

The cleaning crew must be on vacation. Surprised there aren't any roaches in here.

Turning, he went out the way he'd come in and tried the next door. Locked. This must be it. He'd left the keys on the desk as he passed it after finding the weapons. Quickly, he retraced his steps.

This was taking too long. Even a lone guard returning to his post would be a problem. Commotion he couldn't afford.

Several of the keys could have fit the door. He made note of the keys surrounding them, so he wouldn't inadvertently keep trying the same one, and started inserting them each into the key slot. The third key turned.

As he'd surmised, the room beyond that door was small, little more than a closet, but bristling with electronics panels and a breaker panel. One breaker was flipped off. Probably his erstwhile cell. He left it off. The others were in proper position, which meant that the darkness in the building was due to all lights being turned off at their switches.

He looked at his watch for the first time. Yes, it was early in the morning of the day when he'd been scheduled to meet the women at two a.m. It was now 3:45, not long before sunrise. He had about an hour to get the women out or the opportunity would be lost for good. Knowing time was shorter than he'd realized kicked him into high gear.

He examined the other electronics panels. One had telephone numbers penned on tape beside pairs of coiled cables. That would be the phone system. The alarm system was a large, shallow, rectangular metal box, locked. Was there a siren somewhere outside the building that would go off if he opened the door, or was it a silent alarm that rang somewhere off premises or in the house? Did it go through the telephone system? Where did the alarm system call – Mutaib's guards, or the police?

Not much to think about. Disable both.

The neat coils of cables, if disconnected from their jacks, might signal an alarm just to alert someone to the problem. But there had to be a power source. He studied the panels.

Best to disable the alarm system first.

He found the key and opened the alarm box. Inside, as he'd expected, there was a battery backup in case the electrical system failed. He disabled it first by tugging one of the wires leading from the system motherboard out of the battery. Next was the electrical cord that descended from the bottom of the box and into the wall. With no time to trace where it went, he yanked the cord out of the bottom of the box and turned his attention to the phone system.

The phone system consisted of another box, this one some kind of hardened plastic. A thick cable ran from it and disappeared into the wall, probably the power cord. From the top of it ran a normal-sized telephone cable upward and several others leading from the system to a cross-connect panel, which, from the number of cross-connects, he surmised the system served the entire compound.

The simple expedient of yanking all the tiny wires in the cross-connect panel disabled the internal part of the system. None of the extensions would work, so cutting the main wire or the power cord wouldn't be necessary. His incursion into the residence would be impossible to report to police unless there were cell phones inside. He'd have to risk that there wouldn't be many.

Once both the alarm and the phone system were disabled, Rex hurried to the doors. It was now or never. If he hadn't done it right, a screeching alarm could sound, and he'd know it. Or a silent alarm might sound somewhere, and he *wouldn't* know it. But he was out of time. In less than an hour, he wouldn't have the cover of darkness anymore. He yanked the door open and scurried in a combat crouch to the nearest place he could see that was deep in a shadow created by the security light.

Resting there only a moment, he scanned the surrounding area for guards. It was almost unbelievable, but Mutaib's security was incredibly unprofessional. If Rex had been in charge, the duty station in the building where he'd been held would have been manned twenty-four-seven, especially if a prisoner were inside. There'd be patrols of this area, too. Instead, these clowns seemed to think the security light was sufficient.

Careful what you wish for, he reminded himself. This was all to his advantage. Rex had never had to rely on luck. His training was superb, he was in top-notch physical condition, and he was always prepared. But lady luck had been smiling upon him tonight, and he was supremely grateful. He hoped he could rely on her goodwill further to complete his self-assigned mission.

Having assured himself that he was alone between buildings, he needed to explore until he found the residence and the courtyard. If Digger was nearby, he'd probably be close to the last place where Rex had given him tactical commands, which was outside the walls, on the street nearest the side of the residence where the women's courtyard was located.

Rex looked up. The stars were no help. Already the heavens were brightening, making the stars fade from view.

Time was short.

He moved to the wall. Unless it attached to any of the outbuildings to impede his progress, following it would eventually lead to the residence.

Five minutes later, Rex spotted a familiar-looking silhouette in a tree above the wall. Digger?

He touched the coms unit in his collar. "Digger. Come."

The tree rustled, and a black shape oozed out of it. Digger was walking along the top of the wall toward him, maybe unable to see him yet. Then a muffled yelp of pain reached Rex's ears through his earbuds. "Shit," he whispered.

Glass on the walls? Why didn't I think of that?

Urgently, he spoke in a low voice again. "Off, boy. Get off the wall."

The silhouette disappeared from the top of the wall, and seconds later, Digger almost bowled him over as he jumped at his chest. Rex didn't have any experience with dogs – just Digger and that long-ago dog that had mauled him. But he was reasonably sure that the frenetic wiggles of the dog's muscular body were a joyful greeting.

He took Digger's big head in his hands and held it while he kissed the top of it. "I'm glad to see you, too, boy! Let's go get Rehka."

Digger's ears went up at Rehka's name. Rex had uttered it often enough that it was a familiar word to him. He'd never met her, but Rex had let him sniff the scarf often enough as he said her name that he was certain Digger would know the woman herself when he detected her scent.

"Find Rehka," he said while he held the scarf out to him.

Digger looked at the wall. Rex realized too late what he'd done by commanding Digger to leave the wall. Digger couldn't get back up. Not from the ground. Not only that, but there was glass at least on part of it. Or was there?

"Digger, give me your paw." Rex didn't know where that had come from. Had he heard Trevor say it? He thought maybe he had. In any case, Digger knew the command. He sat and lifted his right front paw. Rex leaned the AA-12 against the wall, knelt, and gently felt along and between the pads. Nothing. He let go, and Digger immediately lifted the other. Rex repeated the process. There it was. Not glass. A thorn. He plucked it from between Digger's pads and let go of the paw. Digger reached his head forward and licked Rex's cheek. "Aw, you're welcome, buddy."

Rex stood. He looked up at the wall, which was between eight and ten feet high. Hard to judge in the dark. He wondered. Nothing ventured, nothing gained. He stooped and put his arms around Digger's body. "Up, boy."

He didn't know if it was the right command, or if there was such a command, but Digger seemed to know what he wanted. The dog allowed himself to be picked up. Sixty pounds of dog was nothing for Rex. He could have lifted twice as much weight, easily. When he stood with Digger balanced in his arms and lifted him as high as he could over his shoulder, Digger dug his back feet into Rex's chest and leaped for the wall.

Rex staggered from the powerful thrust of the dog's takeoff, but Digger had made it. Not for the first time, Rex marveled at his intelligence. Digger was already threading his way along the top of the wall toward the tree where Rex had first spotted him. When he reached it, he dropped out of Rex's sight.

Now all Rex had to do was figure out a way to reach the courtyard himself, and from there, how to get the women out. But that would involve scaling that wall and he didn't yet know how he was going to accomplish that.

Twenty-Four

REHKA WAS SLEEPING when Digger found her. She'd endured the beating, along with Zoya and Hande. She was sore, but she wasn't badly injured. The three women expected more punishment to come and eventually they'd be sold or killed, but for now they'd been sent back to the harem. Not to their rooms or their beds, though. They slept as comfortably as they could among a few cushions they'd pulled from the furniture. They'd been told they weren't allowed to seek the comfort of the chaise lounges, or even the chairs. It was the floor for them.

They didn't dare disobey, even when their guards left them alone.

The restriction was psychological punishment only. It wasn't even bad, given the number of available cushions. Only the humiliation of being seen by the others in the harem, beaten, dirty, not allowed to bathe or change their torn clothes or use the furniture. It was as if they were mongrel dogs. No one had spoken to them, either. Even the three other women who'd expected to escape with them were silent and avoided them as if they had a contagious disease, fearful that they'd be found out as co-conspirators.

When Digger found Rehka's scent, he entered the room cautiously. He ran straight to Rehka's resting place on the floor and nosed her cheek. She woke, startled, and failed to completely stifle a scream when she saw the big black beast's face inches from hers. Only the thought that she'd be beaten again kept her from crying out.

What's this? Did Mutaib send in this beast to devour us?

Digger immediately sat down and opened his mouth in his friendly grin and let his tongue hang out.

Rehka began shaking in fear. The dog's teeth were enormous!

She inched away from it, squirming toward Zoya, her new friend. The dog followed, wagging its tail. Rehka didn't know any dogs except the feral ones back in India, and they were known to be vicious. She didn't know what a wagging tail meant. When she bumped backwards into Zoya's sleeping form, it almost startled another scream out of her.

Zoya woke in the same state of fear.

"Shh," Rehka warned. "Dog."

Zoya opened her eyes wider and saw Digger. "It is the man's dog."

***

DIGGER SMELLED THEIR fear. He didn't want to hurt them. His alpha, the new one, used to fear him. When he made a sound like barking and showed his teeth, then he was happy, and he didn't fear anymore. Digger decided to make the women show their teeth, bark, and be happy.

He rolled over and showed them his belly, wagging his tail slowly. They watched him, but they still feared. He twisted and snapped at the wagging tail, pretending to try to catch it. The humans weren't showing their teeth or barking. He rolled back onto his feet and sat, then lifted his upper body and folded his forelegs. He always got a treat when he did that.

One human female lifted the corners of her mouth and showed her teeth. He smiled back at her.

When she spoke to the other one, her smell of fear had diminished.

Then the other one lifted her mouth and showed her teeth.

The first female raised to her rear legs and shuffled to a third, who was still sleeping. The third woman woke up and saw him, and she said something he didn't understood and something he understood — his name "Digger."

He grinned wider and went to her.

She stroked his head.

He was so pleased that he rolled over and showed this one his belly. She patted it. He liked this one. The first woman he'd woken stopped fearing. Rehka. That was Rehka. His alpha wanted him to bring her to the wall.

Digger stood and took Rehka's foreleg covering gently in his mouth and tugged. All three females got up. One, the one who'd said his name, left the room, but Rehka and the other one followed him to the place with the tree by the wall.

***

REHKA AND ZOYA followed the dog obediently. Hande had told them he'd take them to the courtyard. She'd said it was later than agreed, but she was sure the dog was there to take them to Rex. She would gather the other women and meet them there.

Hande hurried to the rooms of the others. Two were reluctant to follow, now that they'd seen what happened to Hande, Zoya, and Rehka. One was not in her room. It was the one with the little daughter who reasoned that this would be her only chance to save her child from her own fate. She went with Hande to give the other two one more chance.

By that time, those two had made their final decisions. One had been summoned to the prince's room, a rare but not unheard-of dawn obligation. She wept, but they all knew if she didn't go they'd be discovered. She promised to keep their secret and begged them to come back for her someday.

"You must tell the world what we suffer. Perhaps the rulers of our countries will force the Saudi government to punish the prince and set us free."

Hande promised that if they survived and managed to escape and get back to their countries, they would do everything they could to get her out. She also promised to convey the message to Rex, and quickly left before the escorts came to the room. It was heartbreaking to leave her, but if she didn't go to Mutaib as ordered but was found missing, the escape would be discovered, and she and they would be dead in any case. The only way she would stay alive and would have a chance, remote as it might have been, to be free one day, was for her to go.

The other woman would go with them. Hande, the two women she'd gone to fetch, and the five-year-old girl made their way through the maze of the harem quarters to the courtyard. Fearfully, they peeked outside, to find Rehka and Zoya waiting alone.

Where was the man who would rescue them? Could he really do it?

Rehka and Zoya had doubts of their own. The last time they'd seen the man, he was shackled to a chair in the private prison where Mutaib kept his enemies while extracting all information they had before killing them. The building was the stuff of fearful legend for the pleasure wives. As new women came to the harem, those who'd been there before them whispered of others who'd disappeared and those who had been beaten and told tales of atrocities they'd seen while they were there.

Finding the courtyard empty when they got there immediately raised their hackles. How had the dog known to come to them, if its master was still imprisoned? But if he was not in custody, then why was he not where he was supposed to meet them? How was it even possible that he could have escaped?

As the minutes passed, fear and doubt settled in. Had they'd made a grave mistake by following the dog?

When the others arrived, they communicated the fear, and they were all ready to flee back to the harem and make peace with their lot when the dog did something they would not have believed if they had not seen it.

The courtyard had beautiful gardens around the walls, including stunted trees that no grown person could have climbed without breaking the higher branches. As they whispered their fears to each other, one of the women said, "Look!" She pointed toward the wall.

The dog had climbed into one of the trees and was balanced on its highest sturdy branch. As they watched, he gathered his muscles and leaped to the top of the wall. Once there, he ran along the wall to a tree that grew outside it and overhung it and disappeared into its branches. The women stared after the dog in shock.

Were they supposed to follow the dog's route? Impossible!

Zoya and Rehka turned to Hande, a question on their faces. She shrugged. In answer to their unspoken question, she addressed the entire group.

"I do not know what we should do now. If I had to guess, I'd say the man is commanding the dog in some way. Maybe he has escaped the prison but is unable to join us here. If you are fearful for your safety, return to your rooms. That way you might stay alive. But I am going to stay here. I would rather die than remain in this place."

The others murmured among themselves, arguing the pros and cons of staying here as dawn broke, and being found in the courtyard trying to escape.

Then a whisper from the tree outside the wall reached their ears. "I'm here. Is there any way for you to climb over?"

Hande moved closer. "No, we cannot. How will you reach us?"

"Leave that to me but be ready. We don't have much time."

Rehka said something Rex couldn't hear, and he asked Hande to repeat it.

"She spoke in Hindi."

"Tell her to come closer and tell me. I can speak Hindi."

Hande repeated his words to Rehka, pushing her closer to the wall.

Rex spoke reassuringly to Rehka, who seemed surprised that he spoke in her language. A flood of Hindi poured out of her.

"You saw how they beat us. How could you have come to give us hope and then fail us in that way? Now we will be killed if you do not help us quickly. The sun will rise soon. Your escape will be discovered, or they will find us here. I do not wish to die."

Rex understood her anxiety. "They didn't discover it from me. One of you betrayed the plot. Ask the others who it was if you must, but that isn't important now. Its critical now that you stay calm, and I'll have you out soon."

Rehka turned to Hande. "Who was it? Who betrayed us?"

Hande barely understood her broken Arabic, but for the first time, she took stock of who was there and remembered there were two missing. One had refused to come. She hadn't found the other. "Where is Aliya?"

Zoya said, "Didn't you bring her? Where is Rania?"

"Rania would not come. She was too afraid after we were beaten. Aliya was not in her room."

"Perhaps she was with the prince?"

One of the others heard and spoke up. "No. She is with child. She has been excused from her duties until the child is born. The foolish woman thinks the prince will marry her."

Hande and Zoya stared at each other. "It was Aliya."

Rehka understood the simple statement. "Tell him I will come. He must wait. I will go and kill her." She turned quickly, as if she'd run to do what she'd threatened.

Zoya grabbed her arm. "No! You must not. The child will die. The child is innocent."

Somehow the message crossed the language barrier. "Then she must face her karma in the future," Rehka hissed.

Twenty-Five

REX REALIZED HIS reconnaissance had been interrupted and there was now no time to plan for the women to escape the compound. They couldn't scale the wall, and neither could he. But his capture and subsequent escape had one silver lining. He now had enough weaponry to abandon his original desire to spirit them away by stealth. He could now fulfill his vow to exterminate the vermin who'd beaten and degraded his charges.

He now understood that the original plan would have been problematic if not impossible without a ladder anyway.

As soon as he'd persuaded Rehka to trust him and persuaded them all to calm down and wait for him, he made his way around the walls that surrounded the compound. With Digger at his side, he felt bolstered.

Dawn was rapidly approaching, so he used the techniques to avoid discovery that were second nature to him, crouch-running from cover to cover when the coast was clear, waiting in the shadows if a vehicle passed when he reached the street side, surveying the visibility of his next move carefully before he made it, and always watching for enemy patrols.

One more example of the lax security was that there were clumps of landscaping, leafy bushes and other forms of visual entertainment to soften the line of the walls, every few yards along them. And as far as he could tell, no patrols outside the walls. There hadn't been any inside, either.

If I'd overseen his security, all this would never have been allowed. Aren't there any cat burglars in Dammam?

Mutaib must have thought himself untouchable. He was about to find out how wrong he'd been.

Rex and Digger made it to the front of the compound where he'd been brought as an honored guest, a little more than thirty hours previously. The gates were closed and locked, of course. A small guardhouse near them contained a sleepy guard, whose attention was on the street and gates. Rex observed him for several minutes. The guard had a pattern – he looked through the glass window directly ahead at the street, but never very far to his right, where Rex was concealed behind a large urn holding a palm tree and Digger behind a bush next to it.

The guard never turned his head all the way to his right side to look through that window. Then he'd look to his left and over his shoulder, through the open side of the guardhouse, at the gates. Finally, he'd lower his chin to his chest, apparently taking micro-naps. Every few minutes he'd repeat the pattern.

After watching for about ten minutes, Rex was confident of his approach. The next time the guard lifted his head and looked straight ahead, Rex was standing in front of the guardhouse, the shotgun pointed at him. And Digger started snarling in the doorway to the guard shack. Rex saw him open his eyes and gestured upward with the shotgun in the universal signal for 'hands up'.

The guard's eyes grew round as skeet targets and his hands shot toward the ceiling. He tracked Rex as he walked around to join Digger.

"Unlock the gates. One wrong move, and you disintegrate. That means don't touch the alarm."

Rex thought he'd disabled the entire alarm system, but he couldn't be sure. Before he started World War Three in the compound, which he fully intended to do, he had to gather everyone who would come running at the sound of gunfire or shouts. This guy was the key to the first salvo.

When the gates swung open, Rex told the guard to get out and show him where the others were. As they walked to the gates, the guard still holding his hands in the air, Rex asked him how many men were in the compound.

"Iskandar, maybe six others. There were more, but some were injured in a fight yesterday. They haven't yet been replaced. The prince, of course. The eunuch who oversees the harem."

"Ten, counting you and the eunuch," Rex said. The sound of the final word made his stomach lurch. He didn't think he'd ever had occasion to speak that word aloud.

"He won't present a threat to you," the guard said. His tone indicated contempt, and his arms started to sag. Rex

242

nudged him in the back with the shotgun and the arms quickly shot up again.

They'd reached the front door. Rex shook his head when the guard simply opened it. It hadn't been locked.

What kind of incompetent…

He didn't have time to finish the thought. Someone had been alert. Four men rushed him from two sides. The first burst from the shotgun scattered half the remains of the guard who'd been leading him all over the anteroom and the four attackers. The man's torso and legs fell in opposite directions, his midsection gone.

Rex jerked the shotgun to the left and pulled the trigger, the two attackers on that side were flung back a few yards, with gaping holes decorating their upper bodies and faces. Digger leaped at one of the attackers on the right, which threw him to the ground, and went for his throat. But the second one got through. He was right on top of Rex, so there was no time to swing the shotgun around. Rex dropped the shotgun and moved his upper body to the left, out of the way of his attacker's swinging fist. On his way back to the upright position, he kicked out with his right foot and hit the man in the left knee. As the man tilted to the left when his knee gave way, Rex's right hand shot out and punched him in the throat, crushing his larynx. Game over.

When Rex stepped back, he saw Digger's muzzle was covered in the blood of the man Rex hadn't killed. The body was missing a large chunk of its throat. Rex tallied — five down, five to go. Counting the eunuch.

Do I need to kill the pour soul? I guess it depends on how he behaves himself. I'll cross that bridge when I come to it.

There were two more guards to account for, and they couldn't have failed to hear the shotgun blasts. Rex had to try and keep one of them alive to show him around or he'd have to find his own way to the harem quarters. He didn't know where Mutaib's bedroom was, and he didn't want to take the time to clear the mansion's rooms one by one. The women would have also heard the gun fire and would be getting anxious again.

"Scout," he told Digger. "Find the man. Bring him to me." He wasn't certain Digger had understood the command. He knew Digger understood 'scout', but he hoped enough of the meaning had gotten through that Digger would at least hold any captive he got, rather than killing him. Although, he wouldn't bet on it. Digger seemed to be in the same foul mood he was.

He pointed to his left, and Digger trotted away. Rex went right.

He cleared the rooms as he went, hoping at each doorway that he'd find his targets. He assumed Iskandar would be in Mutaib's presence, a last stand against anyone who would seek to harm his master.

Rex had a special treat in mind for that bastard, actually, for both bastards.

A sound behind him made him whirl, shotgun up. When he saw a man he'd seen before, one of the guards who'd been in the fight when he'd been taken prisoner, walking reluctantly with Digger behind him growling and nipping at his heels, Rex relaxed, but only slightly.

"Where is the other one?" he asked.

The guard spoke guardedly. "The beast… killed him." He swallowed convulsively, and his eyes went blank.

Rex could imagine what he was remembering. The sight of a Digger kill could be disconcerting. Something about the thought of having one's throat ripped out by an animal triggered a primal dread, equaled only by the thought of having one's head lopped off by these barbarians. Rex smiled.

"There were six of you here tonight, plus Iskandar and the prince. Is that right? Speak the truth. The dog knows when someone lies. He likes the smell of lies. It makes him hungry."

The guard swallowed hard again and then stammered. "Y-yes. Six guards, Iskandar, our leader. The Prince."

Like I thought, Iskandar is the leader, then.

"The other guards are all dead. Take me to the prince's rooms. Iskandar is there, am I right?"

The guard quailed. "I cannot! Iskandar would kill me for such a betrayal!"

"Iskandar should be the least of your worries because I am about to kill you if you don't."

Like any human would, the guard opted to stay alive for as long as he could. He hung his head after nodding his assent.

Move it!"

Rex called Digger off and fell into step behind the man as he turned and headed through the door Rex would have checked next, if Digger hadn't found the last two guards. Digger stayed tense at his side.

"It's okay, boy. I've got him," Rex reassured the dog.

Digger's tail did a half-wag, his version of "Okay, but I'll just make sure you don't make a mistake."

As they approached an elaborately-carved set of double doors, the man slowed. When they reached them, he turned.

"This..." he began. His eyes widened.

Rex had drawn the pistol with his right hand. In what looked like one move, he kicked the doors in and shot the guard who was standing to his right through the heart with the pistol. The shotgun in his left hand was trained on the doors.

Before they were all the way open, Digger knocked Rex to the floor just before a blast shattered the one panel. Rex would never be able to relate which had occurred first, or how Digger had known. Later, he'd chastise himself for letting his rage lead to a moment of carelessness. At the moment, he didn't even think about it. He fired the shotgun with his left hand from the ground, the Sig still in his right.

As he fired, Digger leaped through the shattered panel on the right, narrowly avoiding the blast from Rex's shotgun. Screams from the room beyond included a high-pitched one from a woman.

Rex scrambled to his feet, Sig and shotgun both pointed forward as he crashed through the remains of the doors.

Inside, the largest bed Rex had ever seen harbored the screaming woman and Mutaib, who was trying to hide behind her. Digger was standing on Iskandar's chest snarling and biting his defensive arm, which he was trying to protect his throat with.

"Digger, off."

The dog stopped and backed down but didn't move far. Only enough to stand with his front paws on the fallen shotgun at Iskandar's side.

Rex ignored Mutaib and the woman for now. They were no threat. Keeping his eyes and his weapons trained on Iskandar, Rex nudged Digger off the shotgun with his hip and kicked it under the bed and out of Iskandar's reach.

"Get up," he snapped.

Iskandar stood, strangely defiant for his situation.

"I can't tell you how glad I am to see you again, douchebag. We have some unfinished business if my memory serves me correctly. Don't we?"

He laid the shotgun on a nearby table and dug in his pocket for the handcuffs. He held them out to Iskandar. "Cuff your owner," he demanded.

The woman had stopped screaming but cried out in pain when Mutaib thrust her into Iskandar and tried to crawl away.

Rex motioned with the Sig for her to get out of the way and then pointed it at Mutaib before speaking.

"Listen, you royal coward, I can shoot you and Iskandar both before either of you blink an eye. Stop and allow him to cuff you, or I'll shoot you in the stomach to start with."

The woman scrambled off the bed and stood near Digger, who turned his head and licked her hand before returning his baleful stare to the two men.

Mutaib almost eagerly submitted to the handcuffs.

Rex kept the Sig and his eyes trained on Iskandar while he spoke gently to the woman. "I'm taking some of the women, those who want to go, away from here. If you want to go with us, go and find them in the courtyard. Tell them I have everything under control and will be there soon."

She spoke for the first time. "I know of this, and of you and your big dog. I will tell them. Thank you," she sobbed, before running out of the room.

When she'd left, Rex addressed Iskandar. "You'll now show me where the women's passports are kept."

Iskandar told Rex to go and perform an anatomically impossible obscenity and crossed his arms.

Rex almost admired him for his stubbornness. He himself would have refused, in Iskandar's place. He would have liked to torture the information out of him, but Mutaib was right there, and an object lesson would loosen his tongue, no doubt. Rex said, "Have it your way," and shot Iskandar with a double-tap – through the heart and then through the head, right between his eyes.

He turned the pistol toward Mutaib. "Your turn. Where are the passports?"

Mutaib had lost control of his bladder at some point, Rex assumed when he'd shot Iskandar. He stumbled over his words in his eagerness to tell Rex anything he knew. Rex motioned with the gun for him to get off the bed and stand up. Mutaib did so with difficulty. It wasn't a pretty sight. He'd been enjoying the woman who'd fled when Iskandar burst in to report the residence was under attack, and there'd been no opportunity since then to clothe himself.

Rex didn't give him the time now. Mutaib's modesty wouldn't matter to him in a few minutes, and it was now well past dawn.

"Move."

The prince waddled as fast as he could out of the room and down the hallway, his handcuffed hands cupped in front of his privates. Rex followed, his Sig never wavering from the back of Mutaib's head. After a turn or two, they entered Mutaib's study, where his desk resembled the impressive one in the office building – bare of anything related to business.

"Where is it?"

"In the center drawer, there is a remote control," he said nervously. "It opens a panel, behind which is concealed my safe."

Rex told him to sit, and the prince lowered his naked backside to his leather chair with as much dignity as he could gather, folding his hands in his lap. Rex found the remote and opened the panels. Behind them stood a gleaming stainless-steel box, a little shorter than Rex and about four feet wide, with double doors.

"Combination? Don't bother to give me the wrong combination. I've disabled all alarms. If I use the combination you give me, and it does not work, I shoot you in the right knee. Got it?"

Mutaib was utterly defeated. He recited the combination and continued to sit meekly, even when Rex shoved the Sig into its holster and turned his back on him and worked the combination.

The double doors swung open to reveal a stack of shallow pull-out drawers on one side of the safe, and a set of fixed shelves on the other side. If neatness were truly a virtue – the only virtue – then Mutaib would have been a virtuous man. A six-inch by nine-inch card file contained passports, one for each of the women under his dubious protection. Rex took the entire box. He'd leave it in the harem quarters after each woman identified her own passport.

He took an external hard drive from one of the shelves on principle. If he'd been a betting man, he'd have bet it contained all the sensitive information on Mutaib's scummy business, from the weapons suppliers he bought his arms-trade inventory from to the illegal small-time dealers he sold them to throughout the world, to his offshore bank accounts and their passwords. Making sure Mutaib knew he wouldn't leave the hard drive in any case, he asked if his bet would have paid off.

Mutaib nodded. "My entire life's work is backed up there. Please…"

"Don't beg. It doesn't become a man of your royal stature, and it won't help anyway. Are there any passwords or ciphers I need to know about?"

"There's just one to open the drive. A password-protected file contains the rest."

"The password… and quit stalling."

"My oldest son's birthday, in your calendar. July fourth, two thousand. July written out, capitalized, the rest in numbers. For encrypted files, the cypher is the Gettysburg address."

The irony struck Rex hard. This piece of trash loved a son born on Independence Day, and he'd used Abraham

Lincoln's poignant speech about the core belief of America, that all were created equal and by right should enjoy life, *liberty*, and the pursuit of happiness. Though the Founders had said all men, the word men meant humans all of them — *all* men, and *all* women, not just the privileged or those of a certain skin color.

Rex left the ugly, gaudy gold chains and rings in Mutaib's jewelry box. They'd be bulky and difficult to get through customs back in India or anywhere else. He helped himself to the loose diamonds, though, something to add to his collection in his own safety deposit boxes in India.

The collectible gold coins were bulky, too, but he had an idea for those. "How much are these worth?" he asked Mutaib, expecting no answer or a false one.

"About a million and a half," Mutaib said miserably.

"Riyals?" Rex clarified.

"US dollars," Mutaib corrected.

Over two-hundred-thousand apiece for the seven women. They should be able to get a decent new life with that.

Two-hundred-thousand wouldn't go far in the States, but in the countries where the women would likely make their homes, it would set them up for life. He couldn't get the women into the US, anyway.

As his gesture of generosity unfolded in his mind, he knew some of them wouldn't know how to handle money. Rehka had a degree in computing; maybe he could hire her to track down the money in the offshore accounts, set up a system to invest and distribute it, and keep the others financially sound for the rest of their lives. It would give her a job that wouldn't be vulnerable to an unscrupulous boss or coworkers and allow her to live in dignity, free from the worry that someone might take advantage of her again.

The last thing he found in the safe changed his plans for Mutaib's demise. He'd meant to beat him bloody, slice him up slowly, feed him his own genitals, and then shoot him or slice his throat. But that would take time, and time was what Rex didn't have.

The only fate for him that Rex found satisfactory was one that would leave no doubt of his depravity. Rex took the bag of white powder from one of the shelves. He didn't bother to point the pistol at Mutaib – the man would cooperate now without it. He surely understood what was about to happen.

"Get up."

Mutaib rose awkwardly to his feet, still trying to keep his privates hidden, and stood mutely waiting for further instructions.

"Time for you to take a bath I reckon. You at least need to wash the piss off you." The grin Rex turned on the man resembled an evil twin of the Cheshire cat.

Mutaib obediently led the way to his bathroom. He probably had no idea what was going to happen next.

Maybe he thought he was really going to have a bath, put clothes on and go somewhere.

Rex began filling the large tub, and then handcuffed Mutaib to a towel ring while he found the rest of what he needed. He could have forced Mutaib to snort the cocaine, but he wanted to inject it if possible. Injected, a large dose of cocaine would treat Mutaib to unbearable anxiety before it killed him. And the anxiety might be focused on being found in his bathtub, unconscious from an overdose of a forbidden drug – something he'd be executed for if it didn't kill him outright.

Rex found a prescription bottle of testosterone and the syringes and needles he'd need for injecting the cocaine in a tall chest. A heavy crystal glass sat on a tray near the faucets, so he didn't have to go searching for the kitchen. He dissolved about a teaspoonful of the powder into half that amount of water and drew up the dose. Half a gram of the cocaine would be enough to give Mutaib a thrill first, before it killed him. Twice that, as he'd prepared it, should give him an immediate but swiftly fading rush, followed by screaming paranoia.

Just what Dr. Dalton ordered.

Twenty-Six

AS HE FOUND his way through the mansion to the harem quarters, led by Digger's nose, Rex anticipated what he'd find. The noise of breaching the residence, clearing it of guards, and the final screams of terror from the dying prince would have echoed through. He knew there were far more women in the harem than those who had planned to escape with him.

Am I going to have to kill any? I hope not.

He also expected to encounter their *faharmana*, which was how he thought of the eunuch. To consider him an overseer of the women's well-being, a chaperone or companion of sorts, like the older women often in charge of wealthy Spanish girls, was more comfortable for Rex than to consider him a man. He'd already chosen to spare him, if he didn't fight but only tried to protect the women.

A few minutes later, Rex knew where he was, as Digger led him through familiar passages to the ornate doors to the harem quarters. For a moment, he considered whether to knock politely to announce his presence or go in with guns blazing. The possibility of innocent women and children waiting on the other side fearfully made his decision easy.

He knocked.

He had a few seconds to recognize the incongruity from the perspective of the women. They'd no doubt heard what sounded like an attack by people who wished them harm, and now a meek knock on the door. What would they be thinking?

One side of the double doors inched open, and one of the *faharmana's* eyes appeared in the crack. Rex knew who it was from the bald head above the eye.

"Your master is dead. I am here to remove a few of the women who do not wish to stay. I mean you and the others no harm. Step aside."

The eye went round and wide, and the door was slammed shut.

Rex sighed. He tried once more. "Don't make this difficult for yourself. I mean you no harm. There is no one left to punish you for letting me in. Open the door or I will open it for you, and it won't go well for you."

The soft man was no threat to him, unless he had a weapon. Rex didn't think that was likely. He was running out of time, though. The sun was now rising higher in the sky and leading a flock of women through Dammam's streets to the hotel where his gear was would be inadvisable at best.

He was seconds from kicking the doors in when they flew open from both sides. Hande stood behind them, dressed from head to toe in a voluminous black *abaya*, her head covered in a *hijab*. If she'd worn a *niqab* as well, covering the rest of her face except for her eyes, he wouldn't have recognized her.

"Hurry," she said. "The others are frightened. I told them to dress like this and wait."

"You did the right thing, Hande," Rex told her. "What about the wives and children, and the other pleasure wives?"

"They are too frightened to leave. They have made their decisions and will stay. I cannot say how long we have. Someone may have already telephoned for help."

"Maybe not. I disabled the phone panel," he said, realizing even as he said it that it may not mean anything to her. And that it may not have been the only phone panel, though he would have expected to hear sirens by now if any phone in the residence was operative. It was highly unlikely the women or the *faharmana* had a cell phone. Still, haste was not a bad idea.

Hande led him through the harem quarters to the courtyard, where the women had reassembled. Because Hande had told him how they'd be dressed, he wasn't surprised to see his little flock resembled a murder of crows instead of a group of beautiful women. He was surprised that there was an unexpected seventh figure, much smaller than the others but dressed in a diminutive version of their costume, holding the hand of one of the women he hadn't met yet.

"What's this?"

"Her daughter," Hande said. She must have anticipated the question. "She is an obedient child. She will cause no trouble."

Except that she doesn't have a passport, and children belong to the father in Saudi Arabia.

Rex knew the women probably knew the problem as well as he did. But he could not leave the woman behind, nor could he separate the child from the mother. This rescue was taking more twists than he'd ever imagined. Challenging his moral compass all the time. He would just have to make the best of it. The van he'd rented… when? He'd lost track of the days. The van had sufficient room for everyone including the child.

Now his question was how to get them all to the hotel. Which led to the next question. Was his room still being held, or had they removed his things, towed the van, and rendered his key inoperable? If they'd decided he wasn't coming back, it presented a few more problems to deal with.

First things first.

"Is there a vehicle here that will accommodate all of us?" he asked. He assumed the women were sometimes taken as a group to shop or for entertainment. If not, he'd have to go and examine the available vehicles for himself before taking the women out of the courtyard. He might have to take a couple or three trips to ferry them all to the hotel and his rental van. If it was still there.

His relief was palpable when Hande told him there was a modified Lincoln Town Car, like he'd seen used as limousines in the States. Not suitable for a cross-country trip, probably, but adequate to carry the seven women, the toddler, Digger, and himself as well as food and water.

Speaking of Digger… Where'd he go?

The familiar pressure of the dog against his leg was missing. Rex looked down and found Digger sitting calmly next to the little girl. Her eyes and mouth were at odds. The eyes were frightened. The mouth was smiling. And her little hand was hovering over Digger's head, a stretch for her, since he was as tall sitting as she was standing. She held tightly to her mother's hand as she leaned toward the dog.

Digger was also smiling, and he'd ducked his head, so the child could pet him. She wouldn't know that mouth full of sharp teeth with the tongue hanging out meant a smile, but something in the dog's stillness had reassured her enough to want to touch him.

Rex was touched by the innocence. He'd once been as innocent as that child, and the dog he'd wanted to pet then had nearly killed him. Digger could bite that child in two with one snap, but he wouldn't. Rex was sure of it. Just then, the little girl made a fist and punched Digger square in the eye.

But to Rex's surprise and relief, all he did was close the eye and his mouth.

"Digger, come." Rex spoke sharply. If the kid was going to torment the dog, Rex couldn't be sure of his reaction.

But Digger just turned his head and looked at him. As if to say, "don't worry I've got it."

The next moment the child had pulled away from her mother's hand and was hanging around Digger's neck with both arms, babbling in a semblance of Arabic that Rex assumed was baby talk.

Digger smiled while he looked at Rex. *See, I told you I've got it.*

Rex sighed in relief. He was right. The dog knew the little girl was just a baby and would tolerate a little pain from her explorations of this new friend.

The potential crisis averted, Rex told Hande to lead the way to the garage. The women fell into line behind her, some in twos, others walking alone. The woman with the toddler swept her up into her arms and Digger followed them. Rex brought up the rear, but as they passed into the home, he hurried to catch up with Hande, so he could defend if anyone challenged them.

When it happened, Rex didn't even have time to get involved. The *farharmana* stepped in front of Hande from the other side, but she simply swept him aside with one arm. It had been a token effort, not worth Rex's attention.

When they reached the garage, Hande led them straight to the limousine. About a dozen other vehicles were neatly arranged in rows to both sides. Rex expected to have to break into the limousine and hotwire it, but Hande showed him a row of hooks with the keys to each vehicle hanging from it. They were organized in the same order on the hooks that the cars lined up in the row with the limousine. On the other side of the garage, a similar set of hooks and keys lined up with those cars. Rex took a beat to admire the organization, then lifted the Town Car key fob and pushed the button to unlock the doors.

He noticed the women climbed in with the same sense of order that they'd lined up behind Hande.

Pecking order?

The trip through town was uneventful, though Rex had a bad moment in the lobby of the hotel. He knew he looked like a mugging victim, but there was no help for it. He wasn't going to put on Mutaib's clothes, even if they would have fit him. Nor was there time to search the guards' quarters for a suitable set. When he approached the concierge kiosk, intending to pass to the desk to inquire if his room key was still operational, the concierge stepped in front of him in false concern.

"May I help you? Do you need the police?"

"Not at all," Rex replied. "You should see the other guy," he said in English, a slight grin on his face. The grin faded when the concierge switched to English.

"I must insist. We cannot have you disturbing our guests."

"I *am* a guest," Rex said, producing the key from his shirt pocket. "However, I was… detained… and I'm not certain my key still works."

The concierge's frown eased slightly. "I will inquire. Please wait here."

He returned in a few moments. "You are fortunate. The room is scheduled to be cleaned out today. The desk requests that you settle your outstanding bill, since you have not left a credit card. Then you will be permitted to return to your room. We must ask that you make other arrangements if you wish to stay in town."

Rex nodded. "All right. So much for Saudi hospitality. But I'll need to return to my room to settle the bill. Maybe someone could go with me."

The concierge called a security guard to accompany Rex to his room and back to the desk with the cash Rex had left in the room safe. Once he'd settled the bill and had been allowed to return for his things, he'd been away from the limousine for forty-five minutes. He would have appreciated a shower and a change of clothes, but he'd left the Town Car running to keep the women cool, and it would run out of gas before long.

His plan was to take the women to Oman, a more liberal country, if any Muslim-dominated country could be called liberal, but in that sense more liberal than the other countries he could go to. At least from there with their passports returned to them, they could return to the countries of their origin or perhaps stay and find more palatable ways to support themselves.

However, Hande, when hearing his plan, soon had convinced him that crossing the desert as he'd envisaged would be a long and difficult and risky process. The chances that they'd run out of gas and die in the heat were just too high. Then, even if they made it to the border, the crossing wouldn't be easy with all the women. Rex accepted it was not going to be as easy as it had been for him a few weeks ago when he'd fled Afghanistan through Pakistan and into India. And easy wasn't the word he'd use for that trip, either.

He'd been impressed with Hande. She had kept the women calm, shown ingenuity in the broken plans, made just the right move in having the women dress for the escape, and had even known about the limousine, where to find it, and where to locate the keys.

"So, what's the alternative?"

"Mecca," she said simply.

"Mecca... are you..."

She nodded. "Yes. A trip there, if anyone notices us, can be explained as a pious necessity. We are making a pilgrimage to Mecca. There are hundreds of thousands of people, and we can easily blend in with them. From there, it is only a few more miles to Jeddah. We can find passage to anywhere and from Jeddah out of the country."

Rex had to admit it was a great idea. No pursuer would think their escape route would lead back through the heart of Saudi Arabia. They'd be watching the port in Dammam, or the coastal highway into nearby Qatar. There were plenty of small towns where they could take rest stops and get food on the twelve-hour journey to Mecca. And where else would a lone man be taking seven women and a kid?

"Mecca it is."

Twenty-Seven

THE TRIP TO Mecca was long, but uneventful. Rehka and Hande knew how to drive, so Rex was able to catch a few winks now and then. But he slept lightly, concerned about trouble if they were seen at the wheel by police. Digger slept while Rex was driving, but Rex set him to keep watch during the quick naps. In this way, they were able to drive straight through.

Rex had the radio on, listening for news and as expected the news about the carnage at Prince Mutaib bin Faisal bin Saud's compound broke when they were about two hours out of Dammam. By the time the media got the news the police would have known about it for an hour or more. Rex would've liked at least a three-hour head start. He expected the police to be searching close to the city at first but would call in help and widen their search.

Straight through with seven women and a child was a different matter, though, than straight through with only himself and Digger. It seemed they had to stop at every small town for someone to make use of a restroom, and sometimes between towns, the women forming a modesty barrier by encircling each other in turns.

Then there were prayer times. They'd left a little later than midway between *Fajr* (the dawn *Salah*) and *Zhur* (midday). Though they were in the car and nowhere near a *muezzin*, the Muslim women knew when it was time and insisted Rex stop the van, so they could pray.

Rehka refused to pray, however. Being Hindi, she said emphatically that she was tired of being forced to pray to a deity that was a stranger to her. Rex didn't blame her.

Rex made the best of it, choosing to believe that if six women and a little girl were praying for their safety, surely Allah would get his faithful servants, and he could only hope, their driver and his dog to Mecca unharmed.

Fortunately, they didn't have to waste time figuring out which way Mecca was for the prescribed direction in which to pray. They only had to turn their faces in the direction the van was pointing.

Once on their way again, they hadn't gone much farther when the child complained of hunger, and they had to stop in the next town for some lunch. By pushing hard and imploring that they hold their water, Rex persuaded the women he needed to make some progress before *Asr*. They weren't happy, and more strife emerged when two of them, Shia instead of the more common Sunni of Saudi Arabia, disputed what time *Asr* should be offered. Now that they weren't under the thumb of Mutaib's household, they wanted to pray on their definition of the time.

By now Rex had quietly surmised that without a doubt this was one of the most taxing missions he had ever been on, and not because of the danger. He had been in similar or worse danger on CRC missions, but on those missions, he was alone. He went in, got the job done, and got out.

Here, he had to put up with the constant bickering of seven women with conflicting religious views. And then there were the pea-sized bladders which had to be emptied, what felt to him like every half-hour. Instead of progressing at seventy-two miles an hour, the speed limit on the highway, they were averaging around fifty.

As a result of all the stops, Rex was as nervous as he'd ever been, fearful that a pursuit would be mounted in this direction after all. And both *Maghrib* (sunset) and *Isha* (night) prayers had been performed before they arrived in Mecca. Rex had even begun to empathize in some ways with Mutaib and any man with a harem. Keeping seven women and a little girl happy was exhausting, definitely not a one-man job.

He said as much to Digger after seeing to lodging for the women and himself for the rest of the night.

Digger didn't seem to care. He was muttering to himself in dog language about being separated from the new object of his affection, the little girl.

Rex didn't get it. That kid had pulled Digger's tail and tried to pull out tufts of his hair, poked him in the eyes and pushed her little fingers up his nostrils, and used him for a pillow or for kicking practice the entire trip. He'd have thought the dog was relieved not to have to put up with the little terror anymore.

On further thought, Rex was grateful to Digger for keeping the kid entertained. He'd only been about eight when his little sister was this child's age, but he had a vague memory that on long car rides she'd kept up a steady stream of babbling on variations of 'are we there yet?' That would have driven him right over the edge on this trip.

It hadn't been easy to find lodging in the city, which was swollen with tourists. He'd paid a poor man with no family a small fortune to vacate his house and let Rex and Digger stay there for a few days. After the man had left to stay with a daughter and her husband, Rex snuck the women in.

The following day, Rex left the women in Hande's care in the house where they'd stayed the previous night, while he spoke to some dive boat operators, judging their willingness to smuggle women out of the country, though he never asked such a thing. The trouble with doing such a thing was the unavoidable fact that anyone willing to smuggle anything was, by definition, a criminal and therefore untrustworthy. Rex spoke vaguely of other types of smuggling, skirting the issue with phrases like 'transport of sensitive goods'. They probably thought he meant something like antiquities, because who would smuggle drugs or arms *out* of Saudi Arabia? But he never mentioned specifics.

It took several hours for Rex to find a Filipino luxury yacht owner who captained his own vessel and was willing to take on any cargo Rex wanted to transport, leaving that afternoon.

It took the better part of half an hour to persuade the women they'd be safer in Oman than here. The trip would take two days and they would arrive in Salalah, Oman after sunset.

Fortunately, the yacht had Wi-Fi capability. Rex would spend the two days of the journey helping each woman choose where she'd want to go.

***

REX CONSIDERED WHAT he'd use for funds to get the women to their preferred destinations. Some intended to stay here in Oman, but in Muscat, the largest city. A couple of the others, Hande and the woman with the child, were going home. Hande would assert her independence, and the young mother was confident that her family would be elated to have her back. All of them would need transportation and some money to get started, for lodging, food, and clothing. Rex didn't want to tell them about the gold coins and what he had in mind until he had something set up to manage the money and assure everyone got their equal share.

After some thought on the matter, he risked a visit to two of the banks where he had accounts in Indian branches and withdrew sums of cash just short of ten-thousand dollars avoiding the banks' obligation to report the withdrawals. He gave each woman a thousand dollars in cash and used the rest of it to purchase airfare for Hande and the young mother and to pay the yacht owner to take the rest, except for Rehka, to Muscat.

To his gratification, the young man was also willing to help them find lodging together when they arrived.

However, before they set off, he took the young man aside and enlisted Digger to help put the fear of God in him.

"I want to give you some good advice. So, listen very carefully now. If you in any way shape or form, cheat these women, try to take advantage of them, or let harm come to them... my dog and I will find you and you *will* regret the day you were born. Are we clear?"

Something about Rex's demeanor, the look in his eyes and Digger's stare must have convinced him, because the young man, a Catholic, hastily crossed himself before saying, "I swear to God and to you, I will not violate your trust."

Satisfied, Rex gave the man an email address where he could contact Rex if required. "Do this and do it well, and we will do business again." Rex insisted that the man send him an email with his contact details on the spot, from his smartphone, and checked that he received it.

Rex then gave the women each a prepaid cell phone with the number of the one he'd keep with him programmed in.

"Call me with this phone when you are settled. I will make sure someone is always available if you need help, and I want to know where you are living and what you are doing, so I can be sure you're safe."

He didn't expect physical demonstrations of gratitude or farewell but that didn't stop them from showing their emotions and tears. Rex even had to blink a few tears away when the young girl clasped him around the knees and said goodbye. Her mother touched his hand on her daughter's head and whispered a thank you. Hande, always the bold one, actually moved in for an embrace, but stopped and waited for a frowning man to pass before she stepped in again and almost hugged the stuffing out of Rex. He couldn't say he didn't enjoy it.

When Digger saw it was time to say goodbye he took up position next to Rex to make sure he also got his share of hugs and pets and scratches. The little girl was crying while she hugged him, and her mother had a hard time explaining why Digger couldn't come with her.

When everyone but Rex and Rehka had departed, Rex did a search on his smartphone for news out of Saudi Arabia. He learned that the police were still looking for a group of seven women. Police surmised they'd fled the country. It was clear that the media had been ordered to start plastering over the scandal that might soon hit the kingdom of Saudi Arabia, specifically its royal family, if the truth came out. The media speculated about the prince's death but didn't mention anything about the prince's henchmen's deaths. They were wondering if the seven women had some help to get away. If not, it meant they must have conspired to kill the prince and made their escape. If they did have help, then who was it?

It was inevitable, he supposed, that the remaining harem members would help them determine how many had left and who they were. Of course, one of those remaining even knew that a man with a big black dog had helped. Fortunately, no one knew his name but those who'd escaped, and they all, including Rehka, only knew him by the name on the passport he'd had made for this trip.

Rex grinned and looked at Digger. "Buddy, you won't believe this, they didn't even mention that a dog was involved in this. I don't know what we'll have to do to get media attention. We'll detonate a nuclear bomb next time. That'll make them sit up and take note."

Digger must have understood because he didn't smile, he just growled, turned around, and walked to Rehka.

***

REHKA LOOKED LOVELY in modern western-style clothing they'd found in Salalah, though it was as modest as if it had been traditional Middle Eastern costume. She had chosen a tunic in rich purples and reds, long enough to cover her rather tight jeans to the middle of her thighs. A large pair of sunglasses covered more than half her face, so that she might as well have been wearing a niqab.

A scarf of red partially but not completely covered her hair, throat, and shoulders until they arrived safely at the airport, where she took it off and stuffed it in her bag. The jeans were long enough to cover her ankles, but below them she wore canvas flats with no socks. Likewise, the tunic had loose, flowing sleeves that dropped past her wrists to the middle of her hands.

When she took off the scarf and threaded the earpieces of the sunglasses into her hair to hold them on top of her head, she looked like a sophisticated young woman from anywhere in the world besides the Middle East.

Rex had only once in his life taken a woman clothes shopping. His long-lost first love, Jessie. And that was a long time ago. It was once only – he was young and stupid then and had made the mistake of answering honestly when she asked if the dress she liked made her look fat. Now he was older and more mature but still didn't know how to behave, where to look, or what to say when Rehka came out of a dressing room to model what she'd chosen and asked his opinion. Fortunately, she didn't ask if it made her look fat. Not that it did, but he'd learned his lesson – don't ever answer that question. Nevertheless, despite his misgivings it turned out he actually enjoyed most of it.

Now, Rex could hardly take his eyes off her, until she shifted and asked him to stop staring.

"I'm sorry. It's just that you are a beautiful woman, Rehka. And I mean that in the most respectful way," he said. Immediately, he tried to get out of the embarrassing situation. "Have you thought about what you'll do when we get you back to India?"

Since sending off the others with instructions to get him a message when they arrived at their chosen destinations, he and Digger had been alone with Rehka. It was evident that she had gone through a hard time for a long time and that she had sustained emotional damage which would take a very long time to heal. He'd been trying to find a way to tell her that he knew her parents and it had been her rescue he'd come for. He didn't want to make her feel obligated to him in any way. He did it because it was his moral duty to do it. He was trained to help and protect the weak and defenseless. He couldn't just walk away from her grieving parents and leave them to their lot. For the same reason, neither could he leave the other women in the harem who wanted out.

He'd never intended to leave a trail of bodies behind him as he literally stole almost half a Saudi prince's harem. But he had no regrets. Those whom he'd killed were culpable, those he'd saved were innocent victims, and that was all that really mattered.

Rehka interrupted his thoughts. "I think I'd like to see my parents," she answered. "They live in this tiny little town in Northern India. I won't be able to stay there, but they must be worried. I haven't been able to communicate with them since…"

She paused, and her throat worked. Rex could see she didn't want to finish the thought.

Since she was forced into prostitution. But that is the fault of the men who victimized her, not hers.

"Rehka," he started, making his voice gentle. Digger picked up on his emotion and laid his head across Rex's knee, his snout just touching the side of Rehka's leg. "I know your parents," Rex continued. And he began to tell her the story of how they came to be here, waiting to fly home to India. He showed her the photos he took of her mother and their house.

Twenty-Eight

THE FLIGHT TO Mumbai was an emotional one for Rehka. After she'd heard that he went to Saudi Arabia specifically for her, she couldn't stop thanking him between bouts of weeping. At first, he'd tried to comfort her. She'd explained that her tears were for joy. She would stop crying and sleep for a while, and then he'd become aware that she was silently weeping again. He wasn't good with crying women and decided the best was to just give her the space to grieve for her innocence, sob out her anger, and shed the tears she claimed were of joy.

By the time they landed, Rehka seemed to have found some peace, except for the shame she felt at what she would have to tell her parents when they were finally reunited. Rex had some thoughts about how to handle that, but he reckoned the drive from Mumbai to Bilaspur would offer a chance to do that in the privacy of the car.

They went straight from the airport to her former apartment, only to find she'd been gone so long that it had been re-rented, her possessions sold for back rent. Rex thought she seemed more relieved than upset about it, but her secondary concern was having to go home with nothing to help her start over.

"Don't worry about that," Rex told her. "You saw that Digger and I helped the others, and we'll help you as well. In fact, I have an offer to make. But let's get something to eat, and I have an errand to do. After that, we can get on the road to your parents' house and we will have enough time to talk about my proposal."

Rex went to the tobacconist's shop in the building where he'd questioned Kabir Patel. There was a For Lease sign in the window. Rex assumed it meant Patel's money laundering business was no longer in operation, at least not on that premises and that he was no longer in residence above the shop, also.

He called his policeman friend, Aarav Patel. He didn't give his name or any introduction. "You know the gentleman who had that accident, the last time we talked?"

"Let me call you back."

Twenty minutes later, Aarav called again. The caller ID said "Anonymous". Patel had the instincts of a survivor, not surprising for an undercover cop.

"Okay, it's safe now. I'm at a pay phone. What about him?"

"Do you know where I can find him?"

"That accident laid him up severely. He's still in the hospital, and he has company. A few of my colleagues are guarding him day and night. Have you got more business with him?"

"Well kind of... unfinished business. As you know, last time when I went to see him he was... how shall I put it... I found him to be somewhat incapacitated. If he is in better shape now I would to just pay him a brief visit and give him a message. Do you think you could arrange that?"

"Of course. No problem. I'll relieve one of my brothers-in-arms for a few minutes. Shall I meet you there in say half an hour?"

Rex made sure he knew which hospital and drove there immediately. He asked Rehka to stay in the car with Digger, so he could leave it running. Digger wouldn't be allowed into the hospital, and Rex didn't want Rehka to know what was about to happen to her former creditor until he was ready to tell her she'd have no problems from him ever again.

Rex parked the car in a spot of shade and went to meet Aarav in the lobby.

The two men clasped hands and slapped each other on the shoulders. When Rex saw Patel's face light up at the sight of him, he knew he'd made a friend. Until that moment, he didn't know how much he'd missed the periodic camaraderie he'd enjoyed with the CRC team between missions. He'd lost Trevor, Frank, and the other Phoenix members in a more permanent and personal way, and he still missed them. But the feeling of knowing he had made a new friend, a backup when he needed it, came back in that glance at Aarav.

Letting go of Aarav's hand, he said, "I won't need much time with him, but I will need some time to leave afterward, well before anyone else goes into the room. Are you okay with that?"

"I'm okay with anything you think appropriate, my friend. You must remember, I owe you my life. And I owe that pig nothing at all. You made my life easier by taking that scumbag and his cronies off the streets."

Rex grinned. "I've got no idea what you're talking about. I didn't do anything of the sort."

Aarav just laughed, turned, and led the way.

They rode up the elevator together, but Rex turned aside to wait for Aarav's signal that he'd relieved the other cop on duty. When his phone buzzed with a thumbs-up emoticon in a text message, he strolled in the direction Aarav had gone until he saw his friend. With a nod of acknowledgement, he opened the door to Kabir's room and stepped in.

Kabir was asleep, but he woke up quickly when Rex put a big hand over his mouth and nose. Rex had moved the call button far out of Kabir's reach before doing so. As soon as Kabir sputtered awake, Rex put a finger to his mouth to shush the man's weak cries. Kabir went pale and stilled.

Rex took his hand away to let Kabir breathe but showed him a scalpel he'd found on a rolling cart while waiting for Aarav to give him the all-clear. Kabir nodded slightly to show he understood.

"I have one more message for you, you piece of shit. Get out of the indentured service business, or I'll be back. I have a man who will be watching you."

Rex looked at the sharp scalpel, decided Patel wouldn't have the guts to repress a scream if he felt its blade slice all the way through his finger as Rex had planned when he picked it up. Instead, he grabbed a pillow and slammed it over Patel's face.

"This won't kill you. If I have to come back and teach you a lesson, I'll do it the right way and watch you die." He slashed Patel's wrists across the veins, knowing Kabir would receive help before he even lost much blood. The right way would have been deep slashes lengthways down the forearms to open the vein, but Aarav might have to explain how a man under his guard had gotten dead. This way, it would look like a pathetic attempt at suicide.

He took the pillow away, wiped the scalpel on a piece of tissue, and stuck the tissue in his pocket. Then he pressed Patel's fingers around the scalpel, one hand at a time.

"This was a suicide attempt. If my friend doesn't call and let me know that's exactly what you said, the next attempt will succeed. Your death will be slow, and I'll make sure it's excruciatingly painful. Do we have an understanding?"

When Rex let go of Kabir's fingers, he dropped the scalpel somewhere in the sheets and nodded his head frantically, tears streaming down his fat, ugly cheeks. "I will tell them. Please, call for help."

"You'll get help in time."

Rex left the room and spoke to Aarav. "Give me fifteen minutes, and then go and give him the call button. He's going to need some medical attention. Now, just remember, whatever you find in there must have happened before you took this post. You didn't look into the room and no one else was in there while you were on guard."

Aarav smiled and nodded, "Of course, that's exactly how it is."

The whole operation had taken no more than a couple of minutes. Aarav would be fine, and so would his colleague. After meeting with Rehka and seeing the emotional turmoil the young woman was going through, Rex would have preferred to end Kabir right then, but his hospital stay complicated things too much. Leaving him in terror would have to be enough, unless he screwed up. Then he'd better believe the threat would come to pass.

***

"YOU'RE SURE THEY won't turn me away? I have brought shame on the family," Rehka said, not for the first time.

In answer, Rex put a comforting arm around her shoulder. "Rehka, your father is a noble and fair man, and he's very proud of you. Your mother has an idea of what may have befallen you, but she has kept her worries from your father. All you need to tell them is you were taken against your will to another country and treated like a slave. I promise you, they will welcome your return with open arms. Can we agree you won't worry anymore?"

He'd told her this several times before, and each time she seemed to accept it a bit more, but she'd never committed to not worrying. This time she did.

"Okay," she said, pronouncing the Americanism with an adorable accent and then reverting to Hindi. "I will not worry. What is the offer you have?"

"Eat first. I'll tell you on the way."

Rehka was so happy to be back in her country of birth where she could keep her face uncovered that she insisted on having a picnic in a park before they got on the highway. Digger approved. He was happy to be off-leash, and Rex watched for people who might be frightened of him, so he could cavort all he wanted to. The necessities dealt with, they finally set out for Bilaspur late in the evening. With two drivers, they'd make the journey without stopping, but it wouldn't be as hard on Rex as the days-ago trip in the opposite direction had been.

On the way to Bilaspur, Rex told Rehka what he had in mind for her employment.

"I have several hard drives with encrypted files that I haven't had time to decrypt and explore," he began. Glancing to his side where Digger had given up his prized front seat to Rehka, Rex observed her reaction to what he'd said.

She'd turned her head sharply to look at him when he said hard drives, and her eyes had widened in surprise when he said encrypted. But she said nothing.

Rex went on. "I have reason to believe they contain information about a great deal of money hidden in tax havens in numbered secret bank accounts all over the world. I'm wondering where I could find someone to help me sort it all out."

Another sideways glance showed him she'd begun to smile, enjoying his roundabout way of offering her a job.

"I may be able to refer someone," she said, barely suppressing the glee in her voice.

"That would be great. I'm also going to need someone to oversee and manage investment and distribution of a rather large sum of money I expect to come into. There are some beneficiaries I'd like to help out from time to time."

Rehka gasped. "That's why you gave us the phones."

"Yes. But I have things to do, and places to be. I'll need my associate to monitor the requests at times. Also, if this person were able to develop administrative and computer systems to manage all that, it would help me a lot."

Rehka didn't do anything overly demonstrative. She just said, quietly, "Thank you. The person I refer will have all those skills and do everything you ask. But you might have to teach the person where to invest the money. That is not an expertise the person has. And you must give the candidate a few days to think about it."

"We can talk about that and the terms of employment later," he said.

***

IN DUE TIME, he and Digger were gratified to have the privilege of watching the joyful reunion. Gyan wrung his hand over and over again, and Akshara pulled him down for a fierce hug, whispering her undying gratitude. Rex patted her on the back and said it had been no trouble. Her wise old eyes conveyed the information that she knew it was a lie, but she said nothing.

Then she walked over bent down and hugged Digger, who looked as if she had just given him a piece of steak.

Rex was about to take his leave after telling Rehka he'd call her the next day when Gyan stepped forward at his wife's nudging.

"We would be most honored if you will attend a feast of celebration tomorrow evening," he said.

Rex paused. "Will we play a game of Chaturanga?"

"If you wish," Gyan said. With a twinkle in his eye, he added, "You think you have improved any since our last time?"

Rex winked at him. "You'll find out tomorrow night."

Gyan giggled. "We shall see. This time, my whole family will be there to observe your humiliation."

"I accept your gracious invitation," Rex said, laughing so hard he could barely make the words intelligible.

The following day, Rex and Digger presented themselves at Gyan's door, and Rehka answered. They were both invited in. The intervening hours had worked a miracle. Her eyes were clear and without doubt, her lips smiling. She was lovelier than ever, Rex noted. And then he chastised himself. His life had no room for a romance. He wondered if she expected one and hoped he wouldn't have to break her heart. But then it struck him that she would not be remotely ready for a relationship with any man. She had practically been raped on a continuous basis by various men for months. How could she even trust any man ever again? Let alone allow a man to touch her.

The ensuing feast topped the first one by a country mile. He'd never seen so many tasty dishes in one place before, not even at this very house when he'd been invited before. This time tables were set up outside, the family being too large to fit inside the house at one time. The women scurried about, helping Akshara or herding children, as the men ate.

Afterward, the men gathered around to watch the Chaturanga game. Always a quick study, Rex came close to winning, but Gyan rallied at the last minute and won. His cackle was the signal for Rehka to come over and chide her father for inhospitality. He should have let their guest win.

Rex was smiling broadly.

In English, he said quietly, "Don't. Let him have his fun. But Rehka, I know this celebration will have taxed their pocket. May I give you something to help them? I know it would insult them if I tried to give it to them directly."

"Do not worry about them. I have just come into some money a few days ago and I also had an excellent job offer, which I've decided to accept. I will send money for their keep. I will take good care of them."

Rex had a wide smile on his face as he shook her hand to seal the deal.

Twenty-Nine

MARISSA AND JOSH eventually caught up with the Phoenix team member who'd stayed in Afghanistan. After following lead after lead, they'd finally come back to Kabul and discovered him hiding in plain sight – at the former Phoenix headquarters. There was a new name on the discreet sign at the gate. They gave their cover story and the man at the gate called for permission to let them enter.

Inside, they found their target, a youngish, maybe mid-thirties, American man, former Army Rangers according to his file, surrounded by half a dozen cell phones, a fat cigar gripped in his teeth, his feet on the desk.

"Help you?" he asked, grinning around the cigar.

Marissa deferred to Josh, who asked if they could talk to him about his former employment with Phoenix Unlimited. The grin faded, and he took his feet off the desk, sitting up abruptly.

"Who sent you?" he asked. "And cut this journalist bullshit. If you're journalists, then I'm the Easter Bunny."

Josh looked at Marissa, who nodded.

"We're here to get more information about your former team and a man who used your outfit for logistics support."

"Rex Dalton," the former Phoenix operative stated.

"Exactly."

"What do you want to know?"

"Obviously, you were not part of the team who went out on the ill-fated mission. By the way, are you taking over the Phoenix contract?"

"Nah," he said. "Too dangerous. Import export." He took the cigar out of his mouth and waved it around. "Can I offer you a fine Cuban?"

Marissa wrinkled her nose, but Josh accepted. He put the unlit cigar in his shirt pocket 'to smoke later' and leaned forward.

"We're interested in ascertaining that everyone on that mission, including Dalton was killed in the explosion. Have you heard anything that leads you to doubt it?"

The guy leaned forward and offered his hand to Josh to shake. "Jerry Blake, by the way. And as for doubt, that depends. I'll tell you a story, and you can decide if it answers your question."

Josh shook the proffered hand, and then Jerry offered it to Marissa, who also shook it. He pointed to the empty chairs in front of the desk and invited them to take a seat. Then he leaned back in his chair and heaved his feet back onto the desk.

"It seems that explosion wasn't the only thing that destroyed a house around those parts that week," he said.

"Rumor had it that the top dog drug dealer in the whole country was attacked and killed in his own house, along with several guards and three other high-level dealers. That happened a day or two after the explosion."

"Is that so?" Josh interjected. Marissa frowned at him. They already knew that. But she remained quiet.

Jerry continued. "Yep. Whoever did it used an antique sword to make their heads part company with their necks. Then set the place on fire. When cops and fire trucks arrived, there wasn't much left. Funny thing, though. Safe was open but empty."

He paused, waiting for another expression of interest. This time, it was Marissa who spoke.

"Go on. Did they ever find who did it?"

"Nope, not that they've said. All I hear every now and then is that it's an ongoing investigation," Jerry answered. "But I hear tell that the cops think there was a fortune in cut diamonds in that safe, along with quite a bit of cash, and the backup drives for the top guy's computers."

"Interesting," she murmured.

"I'd say so. They're still running around like headless chickens, squawking about some mysterious ninja type assassination team. Don't know what they know for sure, but they think the culprits lit out for a neighboring country."

"Which direction?" Marissa asked.

"Police ain't saying. But in my mind, quickest way across the border is to Pakistan. Relations aren't too friendly between here and there."

"I don't know. That's unfriendly territory, like you pointed out. Not a clever move I'd say," Josh objected.

"Maybe, but depending on which route you take, it isn't far into India. And with a handful of diamonds and cash, they could disappear there, no *problemo*. Those Indians are giving the Chinese a run for their money when it comes to population numbers. With one point three billion of them you could disappear like the proverbial needle in the haystack. Don't you think?"

Marissa nodded thoughtfully. "It's worth a shot," she said to Josh.

After a bit more back and forth and some pleasantries, they thanked Jerry for his help and left. Before contacting Brandt, they decided to make some discreet inquiries at the local CIA office to find out if they'd heard more from Kabul police than Blake had heard.

It turned out the police had hedged their information with disclaimers that they couldn't guarantee it was accurate. All they had to go on was former employees' intelligence that there were diamonds and cash in the safes. The drives from all the computers were missing, and if the drug dealer, whose name was Usama, had a laptop, it too was missing. The former employees insisted he'd had one.

When they finally reported to Brandt and asked for new instructions, he agreed with Marissa's assessment. It was worth a shot. The MO sounded like Rex, Brandt told them that incident was his main reason for believing Rex was still alive. If there was a man who could do that much damage and killing on his own, it was Rex Dalton. And if it was him, he now had enough money to hole up forever if he decided to do so. Even so, Brandt suggested, Rex wouldn't be splashing money around. He'd conserve it, go to ground, and stay hidden for as long as he needed to cover his trail.

What Brandt didn't tell them was his fear that Rex was going to turn up out of the shadows one day, in America and then there would be hell to pay. Usama and his friends' killings were going to look like a Sunday school picnic.

Marissa and Josh returned to their hotel, packed, and took the next flight out of Kabul to New Delhi, the nearest city where Rex could have found help with new identities, exchanging the diamonds for cash, and possibly plastic surgery. They assumed if it was him, he wouldn't want people who knew him to be able to spot him on sight.

Thirty

WHEN THE KING of Saudi Arabia heard about his distant relative's death, he made a show of piety, expressing his belief that his dear fourth cousin twice removed would be waiting to greet his family at the day of judgment, and would be found worthy of Paradise. Privately, he asked, "Who?"

While pretending sadness over a relative of whose existence he barely knew, he was genuinely shocked at the carnage that was privately reported to him and outraged at the ramification it suggested, which was that there could be rebellion in the ranks of a harem. Even more so when the king was told that there was a possibility of outside help.

Several headaches would no doubt emanate from the situation. First, as the head of the House of Saud, it was his job to sort out the protection of the three wives and dozen or so other women in the harem, along with their children. They would either be sent back to their families, or if that proved impossible taken under his wing or another family member's. Nothing about the process was simple, and as a head of state, it was beneath the importance of his attention, and yet he must do it. Maddening.

Next was controlling the publicity. He gave orders immediately to the state-controlled media and to the law enforcement agencies involved, from the local police to the border control agency, that no word of the deaths of anyone but the princeling himself was to be leaked. The henchmen were unimportant, he decreed. They were to spin the whole thing as an untimely but unremarkable death for Mutaib from a heart attack or stroke, coinciding with an escape by a few women who were inexplicably unhappy with so much luxury and preferential treatment. The hue and cry for the escapees was to be contained as well. News outlets must not report it, not even that the women had escaped, much less that they were suspects in the death of their lord and master.

This, he reasoned, would prevent copycat crimes, which could not be allowed to occur. The very idea of uprisings and murders by harem residents in other households could lead to social unrest across the kingdom.

At the same time, he had to worry about publicity. What if these women fled to their families and reported inhumane conditions in his relative's harem? Why else would they have fled? He ordered a well-trusted advisor to oversee the media response to any such allegations. They were to treat it as unreliable propaganda of western troublemakers. Women living in harems had a life of privilege and extravagance which very few women in the kingdom would ever have.

And finally, though it was imperative he keep his own hands clean of such dealings, his advisors made him aware of at least two terrorist organizations and several criminal bosses who were clamoring for delivery of unfulfilled orders from Mutaib's arms business. They were also demanding to be given new suppliers. Until all such unrest was settled, his empire was at risk. He handed that chore off to another trusted advisor as well.

The whole thing was a damned inconvenience. Despite a public showing of prayer with the extended family during the mourning period, but once he'd sorted out who the misborn son of a diseased camel had been, he cursed the name Mutaib in private.

***

ON THE OTHER side of the coin, quite a few security agencies across the globe were elated with the news of Mutaib's death and the chaos it had caused among his customers. Among them were MI6, the Mossad, and the CIA.

Mutaib had also been on the CRC's database of scumbags. Through the CIA, news of his death came to the attention of The Old Man, John Brandt. A sixth sense made him wonder about the details that weren't being given. He requested more information about the circumstances of the death from the CIA, and he wanted it warts and all – not the media version.

The CIA in turn tapped their assets in Saudi Arabia to get the real story, not the media version, which everyone knew had been sanitized. Only Brandt, who was still looking for Rex Dalton, gave a care about the details. The other agencies only cared to know Mutaib was gone and were watching for who would take his place. In the meantime, they were all grateful to whoever it was for clearing a bit of trash off the international lawn.

Brandt didn't know and couldn't tell from the dry report he got back from the CIA whether the information had shocked the messengers. He didn't even hear whether they had any theories of their own or anticipated any action in response. For all he knew, it *could* have been a Mossad or MI6 operation. Definitely not CIA — it wasn't their style. They would have outsourced something like that to CRC or some other black ops outfit.

Reading through the report, which included the statements of witnesses, some eyewitnesses, others hearsay, it first struck him that they mentioned only one man doing all of this.

Rex Dalton, if he was alive could've done this. If he's alive he's on the run, though. He wouldn't engage in this type of activities. Or would he? But why?

He kept on reading and then came across the mention of a big black dog accompanying this man. It was unclear to whoever had interviewed the women whether the dog was a djinn or a real dog. The women were too agitated to be clear on the subject, and only one claimed to have seen it. The others were repeating her assertions.

Nah, not Rex Dalton. He has no dog-handler skills and as far as I know he does not work with djinns or any other evil spirits. He prefers to work alone. A dog or djinn would have cramped his style.

Nevertheless, Brandt couldn't help but think that if Rex were alive, this was a mission he would have been assigned. An audacious stunt like this would have been exactly his style, and he had the skills to get the job done.

In the end, Brandt decided to inform Josh and Marissa and let them decide whether it was worth investigating or not.

Rex Dalton, the Ghost aka El Gato, the cat, in Spanish, aka Alshaytan, the Devil, in Arabic...

He shivered.

***

REX WAS UNAWARE of any of the speculation. He watched the news but reports of a manhunt had dropped from Saudi Arabia's media, and as usually happens when anything of only local interest was in world news, global media followed suit. If the Saudis weren't interested, why should anyone else be? He could find nothing even in the back pages of online news outlets. Saudi newspapers of course were not available in Bilaspur.

By the sounds of it he'd gotten away clean, along with the other women and his new charge, Rehka. That didn't mean that the king had not ordered a secret mission of assassins to find and eliminate them. After all, the word assassin had its origin in the Arabic language.

To Rex's relief, one by one, the phone calls from the women came in and he started a file with their addresses, employment situations or prospects, and in the case of the four who'd elected to stay in Oman, which ones had chosen to live together for the time being.

Two of the four were still tentative about being responsible for themselves, having been taken from or sold by their families or someone else when they were just children. Rex was happy to hear that each of the older women, who had some idea of how to live as independent adults, had taken one of the younger ones under their wings. Nevertheless, he considered it of top priority to get their lifeline of funds in place.

Hande had elected not to return to her village, but to remain in Ankara as an independent woman. She had confided to Rex that she knew it would be difficult, but she was going to find a school with female American or European teachers who would support her 'modern' views.

Rex found it poignant that Hande believed she could only be befriended by women, and that those 'modern' views were nearly a century old in some parts of the world. Nevertheless, he didn't express those thoughts. To do so would have taken the wind out of her sails, and he had no intention of ever doing that. She was heading in the right direction and would find those things out along the way.

The woman with the little girl reported that her family had accepted her return without recrimination. Her mother was especially happy to have a grandchild, even though the child had no father. She went on to explain that her mother's opinion didn't mean that the father was dead, but that, since she was not married, the child was a bastard and literally had no father. It would be difficult to find a husband for her now, but she didn't care if she never had to share another man's bed. A husband was not one of the thoughts that occupied her mind at all.

Rex believed that the woman might eventually heal and change her mind about that. The money that would be coming to her might make a marriage more palatable to the man her parents chose. He hoped, though, that she would come to understand that she didn't need to be dependent on her father or any other man. She only had to make her way to a country where she could be her own woman, whatever that entailed for her.

To facilitate that transformation, he gave her Hande's cell phone number and encouraged her to stay in touch. Then he called Hande back and confessed what he'd done. Hande didn't mind. She thanked him and said she would do her best for her 'sister'.

***

THAT LEFT ONLY Rehka's employment and personal situation to settle. They'd been in Bilaspur for a few days and Rex had visited once or twice. He wanted to give Rehka a chance to reconnect with her family and process her new freedom before taking her back to Mumbai. They'd discussed setting her up in Bilaspur instead, but Rehka had demurred.

"I'd rather go back to Mumbai. There is more opportunity there for me to normalize my life."

Rex had agreed but had urged her to take a few days for herself, and then let him know when she was ready. He was in no particular hurry and hadn't yet decided where he'd go next. For now, being in Bilaspur where there was a lot to see in the surrounding areas, was as good a place as any to be.

A couple more games of Chaturanga and a few more opportunities for Digger to play with the Gyan grandchildren occupied Rex's time between seeing to his own needs. As he'd always done after a mission, he used the down time to rest and recuperate physically, emotionally, and mentally. However, only so much rest was required before the itchy-feet syndrome set in and he had to move on.

He had resumed his physical training regimen, and residents of the town grew used to seeing the man running miles before dawn and practicing a strange form of martial arts with very slow and weird movements, which none of them had ever seen but were told was tai chi, from China. He always had a big black dog at his side.

Rex also visited a school where the Indian martial art known as Kalaripayattu was taught. He was fascinated by the history and philosophy of the art form, said to be three-thousand years old. One of its early masters, the Buddhist monk Bodhi Dharma, may have introduced its principles to the Shaolin Temple that popularized kung fu. Originally practiced in South India, Kalaripayattu was enjoying a modern revival as a source of inspiration for self-expression in dance forms, fitness, and the theater and movie entertainment industries. Like many of the cultural expressions in India, it drew its own inspiration from the power and graceful movements of wild animals.

About ten days after their arrival in Bilaspur, Rehka met him at the door when he visited for a game of Chaturanga with her father.

"I'm ready," she said.

"Now?"

"No. Father is looking forward to this game. I have told my mother we will leave in the morning. She asked me to invite you to dinner tonight."

"Tell her thank you. I'll be here. Now, where's that rascal Gyan? It's time I beat him at this game."

***

THE NEXT MORNING, Rex was at the door again just after dawn. He'd been stuffed as usual with Northern Indian delicacies the previous night and had slept only about six hours in the meanwhile. But he was alert and looking forward to the drive. He had all sorts of details to discuss with Rehka.

On the way, they talked again about what he wanted her to do first, which was to bank the cash he'd get for the gold coins taken from Mutaib and develop the systems to track down his money in other places, to invest it, manage it, and distribute it to the seven women, including herself.

Rehka protested. She told him he had offered her a generous salary and she didn't need to share in the money as well.

"Nevertheless, you will do as I ask?" Rex smiled. "We have become friends, do you agree?"

"Yes, Ruan, we are friends, and you have my eternal gratitude for my rescue."

"I treasure that friendship, Rehka. But as your employer, I expect adherence to *my* terms." Immediately after saying that and realizing what it might sound like to her, he held up a hand in apology. "I don't mean in the ways you've experienced before."

"I know you would never do that, Ruan." Rehka didn't spell out what she understood. Both were thinking about the demands her last employer had placed on her body. "You're saying I must include myself in the systems I create for distribution."

"Yes."

"Then I will do so. As long as you note that I do so under protest."

Rex figured that was the best he was going to get. She'd see later what it would mean for her. Her share could help provide for her in her old age or send her children or grandchildren to school, she had her parents to support, and there were many family members she could help if she felt so inclined. Never again would a member of her family be put in the position she'd been put in and forced to indenture herself to an unscrupulous moneylender.

He didn't say all that. The matter was settled. She would learn for herself in due time. Instead, he began to discuss her preferences for living and work locations.

Once again, they drove straight through, sharing the driving duties, not because Rex was in a hurry, but this time because Rehka was. The closer they got to Mumbai, the more excited she became. Rex enjoyed every minute of the drive.

Digger, of course, insisted on frequent stops as usual. He and Rehka had become good friends, it was as if he sensed and pre-empted her bouts of sadness and would snug up close and comfort her at those times.

Rex knew that there would be an extended retraining session needed to break the bad habits he'd let the dog fall into. Human food, for example, was now all he'd eat. He stood a chance of developing lifestyle diseases if Rex didn't put a stop to that. Although he had read and was going to check it with a vet at the soonest opportunity that dogs can eat some human food. What he read all came down to the fact that most of what is healthy for humans is also healthy for dogs, with a few exceptions.

He'd been quite surprised to learn that dogs thrived on vegetables and that it was actually good to give them a carrot every day, which helped to keep their teeth clean and of course had all the other healthy stuff in it. So, healthy eating was in the cards for both of them, which, he decided, was probably not such a bad idea after all.

Rex also thought he might stick around Mumbai for a few weeks and get his buddy some obedience training. Or rather get *himself* better trained in handling Digger. He just didn't know how to maintain discipline with the dog like his late friend Trevor did. The obedience school would be as much for his benefit as Digger's.

Rex, Digger and Rehka arrived in Mumbai in the afternoon of the second day after leaving Bilaspur. Rehka had submitted to Rex's plea that they stop for a decent night's sleep, a shower, and food other than that found in convenience stores, on the second night, just a few hours short of Mumbai.

Rex got hotel rooms in the same place he'd stayed with Digger before and asked Rehka to inquire about apartments for her new home while he did a few errands. They had decided she would work from her apartment rather than getting her an office, which was an unnecessary expense on the funds he was about to turn over to her.

Meanwhile, he called Aarav Patel.

"Can you take a short break? I need a little advice. There's a coffee or tea and some cake or sweets, whatever you prefer, in it for you."

"What I wouldn't give for a great cup of coffee," Aarav joked. He named a place where he'd meet Rex in half an hour.

Sitting at an outside table under an umbrella that riffled in the breeze, Rex asked where he could exchange 'a few' gold collector coins for a fair price, and what establishments in the diamond trade were the most reputable.

Aarav considered his answers carefully and then answered with caution. "Can I assume you won't be able to prove the, ah, provenance of the items you mention?"

"I could, if I am asked for it, but I prefer not to be asked. I'd like a quick transaction, but I don't want to be robbed."

Aarav suppressed a grin. "I don't suppose anyone *wants* to be robbed," he remarked, "although I can imagine that some people deserve to be."

"Just so," Rex agreed. He didn't bother to suppress his own grin.

"And these... *items*... were not um, *acquired*... in my jurisdiction?"

"Not even in your country," Rex assured him.

"In that case, I can give you some names. However, I would still recommend caution in approaching the establishments. Wait for my all clear."

Rex nodded his understanding. Aarav was going to refer him to people who might be under observation by law enforcement, but who would treat him fairly.

"Should I mention your name? As a reference?" Rex asked.

"No, I suggest you don't. It might make them nervous."

"You've got it."

Aarav gave him the names and they chatted for a few minutes as they enjoyed their coffee. Rex brought up another favor he'd like to ask.

"I have an interest in a young woman who's had a difficult time over the past few months. Strictly business," he added. "Would you mind checking on her now and then? I'd like to introduce you if you're willing."

"Please don't tell me…" Aarav began. He stopped when Rex violently shook his head.

"Nothing like that. Wrong choice of words. I assure you, it is quite the opposite. Her plight came to my attention through her parents. I investigated and was led to our mutual friend who divulged where I would find her. I went and removed her from that situation and brought her back. I have since learned that she is very well qualified and hired her to manage some financial business for me."

Aarav's face betrayed confusion, and then he said, "Oh, that friend. The one who I have the misfortune of sharing a surname with? I see. A wise decision on your part. The young woman's business would not be in the entertainment industry?"

Rex was getting tired of the oblique references. "Can I trust you, my friend?"

"With your life. You forget I owe you mine." Aarav leaned forward.

Rex leaned in to meet him. "You may have seen some news, about two weeks ago, maybe less, about an international search for seven women from the harem of a deceased Saudi prince?"

"Indeed. Our department received a request for information. Are you telling me…?"

"I'm not telling you anything. I'm just asking if you read the news."

Aarav grinned and nodded. "Then this young woman will not become a problem for us on the streets."

"Absolutely not. That would be the last thing she'd do."

"Okay, so what is it that I can do to help you?"

"She is going to live here in Mumbai. She needs someone trustworthy, like yourself, to make sure she is safe. She has enough money and I'll pay her well for the work she does for me. It's personal safety you can provide."

"That will be my pleasure. Please, bring her to dinner tonight at my home. I will tell my wife to expect an honored guest."

It was more, and more personal, than Rex had expected. He wasn't certain Rehka would be happy about the invitation. He hadn't thought through the implications of an older male visiting Rehka at her home, either for how it would look to her neighbors, or how it might complicate Aarav's life with his wife. Introducing her to his family would solve both issues. He accepted the invitation on Rehka's behalf and hoped he wouldn't regret it.

When he returned to the hotel, he rang Rehka's room and discovered she'd found a few apartments she'd like to consider.

"Make appointments for tomorrow. We have a social engagement tonight."

To his relief, Rehka welcomed the idea of meeting a family in Mumbai. She hadn't made many friends in Mumbai before her life took a turn for the worse, and those she had made had turned against her because of the "scandal" they chose to believe without checking the facts.

The dinner was a roaring success. Rehka impressed her older hostess with her respect and her facile ways with the two children, two girls of ten and twelve. It was a different experience for Rex, who had only been entertained for a meal by Rehka's much older and more traditional parents. In Aarav's home, his wife served everyone together – her husband, Rex, Rehka, the children, and herself at the same time, family style at a large table.

A lively conversation about everything except anything that would've intruded on her recent life drew Rehka in and made the evening seem short. After dinner, the children went reluctantly to bed and the adults talked a bit more. Aarav told the story of Rex's intervention that saved his life, making Rehka's eyes light up with appreciation. When Rex and Rehka rose to take their leave, Aarav rose with them, glanced questioningly at his wife, and upon her nod, addressed Rehka.

"We are so happy to know you, Rehka. Any friend of Ruan's will always be dear to us. You are my wife's young sister now, or if you prefer, the older sister to our children. You are always welcome in our home, and if you need anything, you have only to call and I or my wife will be there to help you."

Aarav's wife stepped forward and embraced Rehka, who seemed overwhelmed by the show of affection from people she had only met a few hours before.

"I can't thank you enough." For the first time that evening, she alluded to what she owed Rex. "He saved my life, too, Aarav. I gladly accept your friendship. And if you ever want to take your lovely wife out without the children, I'm a decent babysitter. I have about two dozen nieces and nephews."

Aarav and his wife both smiled.

***

THE FOLLOWING DAY, Rex helped Rehka choose an apartment and then went shopping for furniture and appliances for it. She was like a kid on Christmas morning, he reflected. Rex correctly anticipated that Rehka was going to be frugal and did some research before. So, at the first indication that she was hesitant to buy an item because it was too expensive he told her what the budget was and that he expected her to use it, all of it.

"Look at it as revenge shopping. It's Mutaib's money, and you more than deserve it."

Once the furnishings and appliances were complete, he took her to buy linen and kitchenware. Then they went computer shopping, getting all the equipment she would need, including a desktop computer and nice office desk for her home office, as well as a tablet and a laptop for when she wanted to be mobile.

Then he took her clothes shopping again. Rex sat back in a chair, relaxed, and enjoyed the views as she paraded the garments for him. She was now free to purchase clothing that appealed to her without considering whether wearing it would get her arrested. However, when he saw her starting to look at underwear, he hastily made himself scarce and found a coffee shop.

Finally, they went car shopping and bought her a car. On Rehka's insistence they chose a small model that would be nimble in the city and fuel efficient for trips home to see her parents. The gift of the car so overwhelmed her that she asked to go back to the hotel to process how her life had changed so dramatically.

Rex left Digger with her to provide his unique brand of comfort after he got the all-clear from Aarav, while he visited the diamond establishments Aarav had recommended.

One of Rehka's first tasks would be to deposit the enormous sums of cash in small increments to his various bank accounts, including a new one he would establish with her for the women with the proceeds from the gold.

The next few weeks would be busy ones for them, as she worked on the systems he'd requested, and he trained her in how to handle covert money transactions.

***

Rex was already feeling the call of his original plan to wander. He'd taken on an anchor of sorts that he never anticipated, but in a much deeper way than he'd thought possible, he was content with it. It seemed he was not cut out for a life of nothing but leisure and travel.

As soon as Rehka was comfortable in her new life, he and Digger would set out for new adventure. He was not going to hunt trouble, but if trouble found him along the way, he and Digger would be glad to sort it out.

~The End~

Rex Dalton's Next Adventure

Sideswiped

Rex and Digger are visiting the Taj Mahal when he almost bumped right into someone from his past. Josh Farley. A CRC agent, and with him was a woman Rex didn't know.

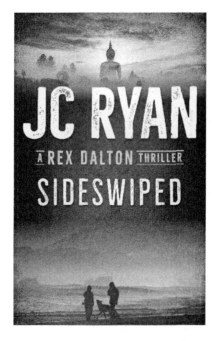

Were they looking for him, or were they on some other mission? Or were they on holiday?

He didn't have a good feeling about it. Cops, spooks, soldiers, military analysts, and many others don't believe in coincidence, and neither did Rex.

Coincidence is the word we use when we can't see the levers and pulleys. Emma Bull

Get it here getbook.at/sideswiped

MORE REX DALTON

No Doubt – A Free Short Story - http://dl.bookfunnel.com/9frvkrovn5

The Fulcrum – Book 1 – http://getbook.at/thefulcrum

The Power of Three – Book 2 – http://getbook.at/thepowerofthree

Unchained - Book 3 – http://getbook.at/unchained

Sideswiped - Book 4 – http://getbook.at/sideswiped

The Inca Con - Book 5

The French Girl – Book 6

ALSO BY JC RYAN

The Rossler Foundation Mysteries
http://myBook.to/RosslerFoundation

Here's what readers are saying about the series:

"All in all, a brilliant series by a master of the techno thrillers turning old much debated mysteries into overwhelming modern engrossing sagas of adventure, heroism and a sense of awe for the many mysteries still unexplained in our universe. Enjoy!"

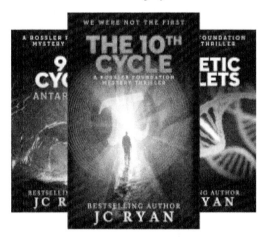

"I LOVED this series! It's readily apparent that the author drew from a large body of knowledge in writing this series. It's just believable enough to think it could happen someday, and in fact, aligns quite well with some of the current relationships that exist between present day countries and the USA."

The Carter Devereux Mystery Thrillers

myBook.to/CarterDevereux

Here's what readers are saying about the series:

"Omg this series is awesome. Full off adventure, action, romance, and suspense. I've you start reading you are hooked. Carter and all characters are awesome, you will fall in love with all of them they become like family. I love the way J C weaves the human and animals together in the story. Try it you will love it."

"The best! What a joy to read these four books about Carter and Mackenzie Devereux bad their adventures. A very good read. I will look for more of JC Ryan's books."

"Suspenseful! Fabulous just fabulous! I enjoyed reading these books immensely. I highly recommend these books. Bravo to the author! You won't regret it."

"What a wonderful and intriguing book. Kept me glued to what was going to happen next. Not a normal read for me. But a very enjoyable series that I would recommend to everyone who likes adventure and thrills."

The Exonerated
http://myBook.to/ExoneratedTrilogy

Here's what readers are saying about the series:

"J.C. Ryan is an author that writes tomes. The great thing about that is that you get great character development and the plots are all intricate, plausible, suspenseful stories that seems to draw you in from the first scenario right up to the end.

The Exonerated series is no exception. Regan St. Clair is a judge. Together with Jake she has her own way in pursuing justice in ensuring that the legal system is applied ...well, justly."

"What if you had the power to make a difference? Would you? Could you? What if in order to do so you had to join a super-secret organization that might not always play by the rules? What if you stumbled across this mysterious organization only to find out it had been polluted? What if you were a judge that has been worn out and disillusioned by the very justice system you thought you loved?"

"What a great series of books. It seemed like one book instead of three books. The story flowed seamlessly through the three books."

Your Free Gift

Rex Dalton and his dog, Digger, visited the island of Olib in Croatia.

A girl was murdered.

The police said it was her boyfriend who stabbed her to death, but Rex and Digger had no doubt they were making a big mistake.

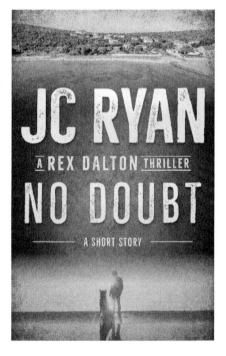

Dalton decided to conduct his own investigation and bring the real killer to justice.

A thriller with a quirks and twists that will keep you guessing until the end.

Get your free eBook here
http://dl.bookfunnel.com/9frvkrovn5

ABOUT JC RYAN

An interview with the author by the editor of Books 'N Pieces Magazine, http://www.altpublish.com/jc-ryan/

JC Ryan

Editor's note: "JC Ryan and I enjoyed an extensive two-hour Skype session where we spoke of all manner of things, especially his ranking as an author. The visibility of an author is often at the hands of readers. If you look at JC's ratings, each book enjoys several hundred or more four and five-star reviews, enough to make him notable, and on par with mainstream novelists. I encourage you to read one of his books, or listen to his audiobooks, now in production. You'll be hooked."

Printed in Great Britain
by Amazon